William Cochrane

Memoirs and Remains of the Rev. Walter Inglis

African missionary and Canadian pastor

William Cochrane

Memoirs and Remains of the Rev. Walter Inglis
African missionary and Canadian pastor

ISBN/EAN: 9783337394554

Printed in Europe, USA, Canada, Australia, Japan

Cover: Foto ©Raphael Reischuk / pixelio.de

More available books at **www.hansebooks.com**

MEMOIRS AND REMAINS

REVEREND WALTER INGLIS,

AFRICAN MISSIONARY AND CANADIAN PASTOR.

BY THE

REV. WILLIAM COCHRANE, D.D.,

BRANTFORD, ONTARIO.

———————

TORONTO:
C. BLACKETT ROBINSON; WILLIAMSON & CO.
EDINBURGH: JAMES THIN.
1887.

PREFACE.

NEARLY a year ago I was asked by the office-bearers of Stanley Street Church, Ayr, on behalf of the congregation and other friends, to prepare a Memoir of their late beloved pastor. I hesitated to undertake the task for many reasons. There were other brethren associated with Mr. Inglis for a longer period, who knew him more intimately —although they could not love him more than the compiler of this volume—and were better fitted for the work. The materials also for a Memoir were comparatively scanty. Mr. Inglis kept no written record of his life, either in Africa or Canada, and at first sight it seemed almost hopeless to present anything like a complete and worthy portrait of the man.

At the same time, I felt that if ever the life of a Canadian pastor should be written, it was that of Walter Inglis. He stood, in many respects, alone. Commanding in outward appearance, the inner man was far above the average of his age. Under a somewhat abrupt manner, and associated with an original mode of speech, his nature was most tender and gentle and lovable. To see the man in public and in Church courts was one thing; to know him as a friend, and hear him at the family altar, was quite another.

In the preparation of this volume I have been assisted by many kind friends, to whom my thanks are due. The chapters giving an account of Mr. Inglis' early apprentice and college days, as well as some portions in other parts of the Memoir, have been supplied by his brother, the Rev. William Inglis, of Toronto. The widow and family of our departed father have also assisted me to the utmost of their ability. Principal Cairns, of Edinburgh, has given many reminiscences of his old and much-loved friend; while the Rev. John Thomson, with all the admiration and affection of a son, has prepared an entire chapter, covering the whole period of their joint-pastorate in Ayr. The larger number also of the "Outlines of Sermons" are from Mr. Thomson's shorthand notes. I have also to express my indebtedness to the Rev. J. A. R. Dickson, B.D., of Galt; Rev. Wm. Robertson, M.A., of Chesterfield; Rev. James Pringle, of Brampton; Rev. Robert Hamilton, of Motherwell; Rev. Peter Wright, B.D., of Stratford; Rev. Dr. Waters, of Newark, N. J.; Rev. J. S. Hardie, of Ayr; Rev. Robert Pettigrew, of Glenmorris, and others, for contributions and suggestions. Several editorial notices also that appeared at the time of Mr. Inglis' death have been exceedingly helpful.

It would be very unfair were the readers of this volume to regard the "Outlines of Sermons," contained in the Appendix, as any indication whatever of Mr. Inglis' pulpit powers. Almost nothing has been preserved of his earlier preparations, and in later years his notes were of the briefest kind. Some men in the pulpit fall far below their pulpit preparations; others rise immeasurably above them. Mr. Inglis belonged to the latter class. Unexpected outbursts of true eloquence, more or less frequent, occurred in every sermon; while his impassioned, though rugged, manner of delivery indicated the deep feeling and thorough sincerity of the man of God.

That these pages may stimulate the present and coming generation of ministers in Canada and in foreign lands to similar acts of self-denial for Christ's sake, is my earnest prayer.

> Armoured in honest thought and speech,
> He saw, and said, and wrought his best.

Brantford, March, 1887.   W. C.

CONTENTS.

CHAPTER VI.—AFRICAN LIFE—THE VOYAGE AND ARRIVAL.

CHAPTER VII.—MISSION LIFE IN SOUTH AFRICA.

CHAPTER VIII.—RETURN FROM AFRICA, AND APPOINTMENT TO CANADA.

CHAPTER IX.—THE VILLAGE OF AYR.

CHAPTER X.—ESTIMATE OF MR. INGLIS—HIS CHARACTER AND WORK.

MEMOIRS AND REMAINS

OF

REV. WALTER INGLIS.

CHAPTER I.

BIRTH, BOYHOOD, AND EARLY SCHOOL DAYS.

Brothershiels—Fala—The Lammermoors of Scotland—The French War
—High Rents — Hard Work and Lenten Fare — Parentage—A
Mother's Piety and Influence—The Burghers and Anti-Burghers
—Sectarian Feeling—Youthful Wantonness—Parish Schools and
Schoolmasters—Rudimentary Scholarship—The Minister's Opinion
of the Boy.

WALTER INGLIS was born on the 22nd November,
1815, in the Parish of Fala, at Brothershiels, a
pastoral farm among the Lammermoors of Scotland,
and about sixteen miles distant from Edinburgh.   His
forefathers had lived for generations as farmers, in the
neighbouring Parish of Heriot, and now sleep quietly
in its little romantically-situated God's acre, on the
banks of the head waters of the Gala.   A few years
before Walter was born, his father removed to Brothershiels, where the family has ever since resided.   The
region is still somewhat bleak and uninviting, but in
those early days there was scarcely a tree or a house
within sight.   The nearest church and school were
about four miles distant, and the road, or rather bridle-
path, to the village lay over a dreary, desolate moorland.
The farm was taken at a time when, on account of the

French War, all agricultural products were very dear, and the rent was correspondingly high. Before, however, the subject of these memoirs was born, the war was at an end, and war prices soon disappeared, though war rents continued. The result need not be described. There was a continued struggle with a high rent, ungenial seasons, loss of stock, and low prices. That struggle was severe, and all the family became familiar with hard work and Lenten fare. It was, however, carried through successfully, though the old father farmer used to say, in somewhat regretful tones, that "had he gone to America when he came to Brothershiels, it would have been greatly to the advantage both of himself and his family."

The subject of these memoirs owed a great deal to both parents. They were a devout, God-fearing pair, who sought to command their children and their household after them, that they should keep the ways of the Lord. His father was, for his position, a remarkable man. With few early educational advantages, and with but a scant allowance of books, he kept his mind alertly active, and to the very end was eager and earnest in his pursuit of knowledge. Under a somewhat stern aspect, and with a rather passionate temper, he was really genial and friendly, nay, even affectionate. He belonged originally to the Established Church at Heriot, where he and his wife now lie buried, and of which church his father had been an elder. After his marriage, however, somewhere about 1813, he went with his wife to the Fala Burgher or Associate Church, of which both were members, and which after 1820 was known as the United Secession.

His mother was of a meek and gentle spirit. Her whole being had come under the influence of the truth, and she ever spoke and acted as in presence of the Great Master. Her husband's heart entirely trusted her. Her children rose up and called her blessed. She ruled by gentleness, though she was firm, and, when necessary, could be severe. It was among her children's earliest memories to have them taken separately to her room, where they knelt beside her and heard themselves commended, in language they might at the time but vaguely comprehend, to the care and guidance of the Good Shepherd. This humble farmer's wife moved among her household with all the quiet composure of a saint, and yet with all the earnestness and despatch of a true house-mother. How much Walter Inglis and all her children owed to her can never be told. She had none of the world's wisdom, and her range of knowledge was but limited. But she had known the Scriptures from her youth. Matthew Henry and Poole were her familiar guides. Boston and Flavell, Bunyan and Brown, Brookes, and Hugh Binning, with other kindred writers, afforded her never-failing pleasure and profit. She had, of course, her cares and troubles; but these only brought her and kept her nearer her God.

Mrs. Inglis was of the good old Anti-Burgher stock. She was, in her younger days, a great favourite with her minister, Mr. McEwen of Howgate, at whose church she was a regular attender. Howgate is a small village about five miles from Penicuik. The Howgate congregation was Anti-Burgher or General Associate; while that in Penicuik was Burgher or

Associate. The former denomination was specially strict, and did not scruple to exercise discipline upon any member who might ever worship elsewhere. Mrs. Inglis used to tell how that on one occasion she was threatened with the Session, because, being about seven or eight miles from Howgate, she was one day absent from the church, and therefore did not know that next Sabbath there was to be no service. She and one of her brothers on arriving at the church found the door shut, and accordingly went on to Penicuik, where the Sacrament was being dispensed and an out-door service was going on. The two young Anti-Burghers leaned over the dyke and listened to the sermon for about a quarter of an hour. That was the whole offence ; but a *dour* old elder, whose conscience was sorely vexed by such a misdemeanour, insisted that the two sinners should be "sessioned," and "sessioned" they would doubtless have been but for the minister, who resisted the excessive zeal of his elder by a common sense not always found in those bygone days. The story is also told of the son of this Howgate minister (the late Dr. McEwen of Glasgow), that when his mother was dying and apparently cut off from all intercourse with the outer world, he remarked : "There is just one thing that will rouse my mother—if that won't do it she is gone." He accordingly went up to the bed, and said in a loud voice : "Mother, d'ye ken the Duke o' Wellington's turned a Burgher !" She opened her eyes and said, with a look of righteous disgust at the idea of admitting such a man to membership : "They were aye a lax set." Indeed, with all her gentleness, Mrs. I.

herself somewhat shared the sternly strict ideas of her Church, and had even a slight element of incipient persecution in her nature. A poor old weaver in the neighbourhood had wandered so far from the current orthodoxy as to be the one solitary Socinian of the district. Sometimes he brought his doubts and difficulties to Brothershiels, and once in a while possibly rather puzzled the house-mother in spite of the help of Poole and Matthew Henry. On these occasions she would warningly shake her finger in his face, and say : "Ah, ma man, if I had the pooer I wad mak your feet fast." All this indicates the atmosphere in which Walter Inglis and the youth of his day were trained.

Walter, the second son and third child of this humble couple, grew up amid such surroundings a stirring, energetic, impulsive, and somewhat thoughtless boy. He was fond of fun, full of tricks, frequently involved in juvenile scrapes, and not seldom made practically acquainted with parental discipline. The education to be had at parish schools in those days was but scant in quantity, and often not to boast of in the way of quality. It so happened that some of the pedagogues, under whose care young Walter Inglis' ideas were expected to shoot, were physically weak and educationally contemptible. The results were not encouraging. Rebellion broke out again and again, when it is to be feared the young hopeful from the hills was generally a ringleader. Tradition has it that once at least he challenged the teacher to single combat, and for years the roof of the schoolhouse bore marks of his mischievous ways, in inky ornaments which he had made with a pocket syringe. His mother's minister was at last tempted to interfere, little to his own satisfaction and greatly to the disgust of the boy's mother, whose gentle nature was moved to indignation by her spiritual adviser assuring her that her son was on the fair way to the gallows !

All his teachers, however, were not of this description, and so by the time he had reached the age of fourteen, young Walter was fairly well acquainted with the three R's, the Shorter Catechism, the vaguest suspicion of grammar, and the merest smattering of geography.

CHAPTER II.

Chooses the Trade of a Currier—Poor Wages—Leaving Home—Mother
and Son on the Lonely Moor—Her Prayer and Parting Words—
Impressions Left—Character of his Shopmates—Monthly Visits to
Brothershiels—Physical Strength and Mental Activity—Moral and
Political Questions of the Day.

FROM a brief sojourn in Edinburgh, when very
young, he had taken a fancy to the trade of a
currier, and so, at the age above mentioned, he quitted
school, and was bound for seven long years as an apprentice to the business of his choice. The scene of
his first start in life was Dalkeith, then a small but
pleasantly situated town, about six miles from Edinburgh and ten from his parental home. The wages
paid him were ridiculously small. The strong, young,
country lad was to receive for the first year the munifi-
cent sum of thirty-seven and a half cents per week—
about eighteen pence—and board himself! The rate
of subsequent increase was very moderate, as in his
seventh year he received only $1.75 per week—about
seven shillings sterling—though by that time a young
man of twenty-one. His parting from home and final
leave-taking with his mother were often afterwards
referred to with the deepest emotion. Mother and
son went so far over the lonely moor alone. The time
for parting came at last. It was in all the hushed
quietness of a summer's day. Scarcely a breath of
wind stirred the heath. The lark was at its daily

song ; the peewits, or lapwings, hovered around, and
the weird sound of the curlew could be heard in the
distance. Mother and son kneeled down on the heath,
and the boy that was going out into the world was
tenderly commended to the care of his father's and
his mother's God. As the last good-bye was afterwards spoken, while hand clasped hand, he had to
take with him these final words : "Now, my dear
bairn, if you go astray you will bring down your old
mother's gray hairs with sorrow to the grave." No
word of threatening. No reference to hell, though
hell to her, who dwelt daily under the shadow of the
Almighty, was a terribly significant and unmistakable
reality. Simply and pathetically she had but to say:
"My son, go wrong, and you will break my heart."
And so they parted—the boy to what to him was the
great world of life ; the mother to her humble· yet not
unimportant duties on the moorland farm, with her
heart full of loving trust that the God of her fathers
would be her children's God as well.

His mother's parting words, with all the surrounding circumstances in which they were uttered, took
possession of the boy's imagination and heart. They
haunted him not only for days, but for years. They
made him brave and strong, and, until a mightier
spiritual force came to transform and regulate his
whole being, they were so far the watchword of his
life. The possibility of his ever bringing his mother's
gray hairs with sorrow to the grave followed him with
such anxiety and alarm that frequently he cried himself to sleep over the bare idea of such a thing taking
place. Such tears, however, did not make him weak

and dreamy. Of him it could be said, as of Mrs. Hemans' Indian—

> Oh, scorn him not; the strength whereby
> The patriot girds himself to die,
> The unconquerable power that fills
> The free man battling on his hills—
> These have one fountain deep and clear,
> The same whence gushed that childlike tear.

He had need of all his own resolution and all his mother's prayers, for the workshop to which he was sent, and in which he was destined to spend seven of his most susceptible years, was morally a very Gehenna, though this fact was not known when the indentures were duly signed. Drunkenness, profanity, licentiousness, and ostentatious infidelity of the coarse, vulgar type, often met with in such places, ran riot. There were exceptions among his fellow-workmen, but these were few. The majority were vile, the journeymen apparently taking pleasure in making the apprentices, if possible, ten times viler than themselves. It was a dreadful risk for a raw country boy of fourteen to be thrown into such a seething cauldron of iniquity. Many would have become moral wrecks, but Walter Inglis, through the blessing of God, came out of it, strong and resolute for the right, with his whole moral fibre hardened as if into steel against all that was immoral, licentious, and unbelieving. The story of this, his first great struggle against temptation, need not be told at length. The monthly home-coming helped him wonderfully. He had to walk ten miles on Saturday afternoon, and back on Sabbath evening, but very seldom indeed did he miss his tryst, which was not only strength to himself, but also afforded pleasure to the household among the hills. His month's doings and experiences were all gone over on such occasions. His difficulties and dangers were discussed. The books he had read were mentioned; how he had managed with this workman, and been threatened by another; how he had been sent to Coventry, or refused, by ill-natured and brutal over-seers, all directions about his trade; how he had not only himself declined to go for the journeymen's drink, but had gained such influence over the other apprentices that they also refused, and resisted all invitations to join in debauchery; how this one was drunk, and another swore, and how, in spite of the high wages which many of the journeymen received, their wives and children were miserable, and their homes the most wretched abodes of poverty. The Rev. James Pringle, of Brampton, speaking of Mr. Inglis' apprenticeship in Dalkeith, mentions a fact that shows his determination and decision of char-acter. There was at that time, he says, a great deal of whiskey and beer drunk in the workshops of Great Britain, and in the shop where Walter Inglis served his apprenticeship, it was the custom for the youngest apprentice to go for the liquor. Walter refused to do so, and, when one of the men took hold of him and threatened to throw him into one of the tan-pits if he would not go for the drink, he turned upon his assailant and threw him into the pit, which he was well able to do. After this the young currier had no more trouble in that way.

While these personal annoyances might seem more

than enough to engross the attention of the young apprentice lad, he was far from silent regarding the great questions of the day. The Anti-Slavery agitation was then in full swing. Garrison's voice was already being heard, even in Scotland, and the boy's soul was stirred to its very depths by all the incidents associated with that struggle. Political questions also ran high. Reform was in the air, and the sturdy young currier held very decided views regarding this and other matters, which were all discussed around the family fireside.

His apprenticeship in Dalkeith was no doubt a trying and dangerous ordeal, but it was a bracing one, and the result was one not to be regretted. The tears which were often shed, over the possibility of breaking a mother's heart, gave him a mighty amount of strength. His mind also became eager for knowledge of a more practical kind than he had imbibed at the parish school. He begged or borrowed books which might help him in his daily controversies. Two and three o'clock in the morning often found him reading and studying, although he had to be at work by six. The Christian evidences were gone over, and infidel objections met as he best could. His hard manual labour developed a powerful physical frame, and gradually the resolute and somewhat defiant look gave intimation that any attempt at personal chastisement would, to say the least, be awkward. The younger apprentice boys finally came to regard him as their leader. They all became abstainers and refused to become brethren of the craft, or pay their fees and drink money. They were cautioned by the older workmen against such

nonsense, and even threatened if they persisted. But
the " big apprentice " was becoming decidedly "ugly,"
as far as physical contests were concerned, and he had
to be reckoned with. The boys accordingly stood firm
against defilement, for Walter Inglis was regarded as
the champion of all the reforming young rebels, and
would not see them wronged.

A visit to Edinburgh, during the crisis of the Reform
Bill, when black flags and cross-bones figured in the
procession, and when the air rang with—" The Bill,
the whole Bill, and nothing but the Bill," gave a
mighty impetus to Walter's political education and
enthusiasm. He had, as most young men have, his
heroes, and he worshipped them with all his heart.
The disenchantment of course came, as it comes to
almost every one, and he, by and bye, wondered that
he could ever have become so excited over the inflated
harangues of the political leaders of that day. The men
disappeared from their positions of honour in his estimate, but the principles they advocated but grew with
his growth and strengthened with his strength.

CHAPTER III.

EDINBURGH UNIVERSITY.

Spiritual Awakening—Melancholy—Church Membership—Reading
  The Anti-Slavery Agitation—Sympathy with the Downtrodden—
  Determination to Become a Missionary—Begins Latin—Edinburgh
  University in His Day—Neglect of Classification—Examinations
  and Graduation—Sir William Hamilton—Professor Wilson—Essay
  Writing—Testimony to his Diligence by Principal Cairns.

MEANWHILE the great spiritual change, which made all things new in Walter Inglis, had taken place. Of the particulars of that change he spoke but little. Its history, as given in answer to certain questions put at his ordination as missionary to Africa, will be found in a subsequent chapter. His quickened religious life brought him more than ever into sympathy with his aged mother, and made her heart to sing for joy. He had, like many strong characters, his spiritual troubles, his Doubting Castles and his Valleys of the Shadow of Death. With all his buoyancy and whole-hearted elasticity of spirit, there was an undertone of sadness, which sometimes sank to positive melancholy. Indeed, it was some years before he came to enjoy the full freedom and peace of believing. In the meantime life went on neither unhealthily nor unhappily. He had made the acquaintance of some wise and pleasant friends, had joined the Presbyterian Church, read as he could, and was ever ready for discussion with all comers. He was now face to face with life, and his reading, if not very systematic, was upon the whole edifying and invigor-

ating. His commonplace book, begun when but a boy,
showed his favourite passages carefully copied out, and
often thoroughly committed to memory. "Watts on
the Improvement of the Mind," "Foster's Essays,"
"Combe's Constitution of Man," and other works of a
similar character, afforded material for thought and
talk at every turn. Stray copies of Garrison's *Liberator*
put him into a ferment, and the account of the Boston
riot made his eyes flash fire, and his heart beat quick.
The debates on Negro slavery, between George Thompson and Peter Borthwick, added fuel to the flame. His
whole soul was stirred with the wrongs of the black
man, and he desired to go as a missionary to that down-
trodden race. Gradually his wishes took shape, and
matters were definitely arranged, that when his term
of apprenticeship expired, he should study for the
ministry with a view to missionary work in Africa.
To this end he started at once on the study of Latin.
Mr. Pringle says of that period: " When I went to Dalkeith, in the fall of the year 1835, as assistant teacher
in ' Dalkeith Academy,' I became acquainted with
Mr. Inglis. He was then serving his apprenticeship in
a currier's shop. We were both members of the Rev.
Joseph Brown's congregation, and also teachers in his
Sabbath school. As I was at that time a student of
divinity, in connection with the United Secession
Church, he was led to tell me of his strong desire to
study for the ministry, and to begin the study of Latin
without delay. Believing him to be decidedly pious
and of good mental powers, I encouraged him, and
helped him for a time, in the study of Latin. But as
my time was very much taken up with my own studies,

I got the junior assistant, Mr. William Steele, to super-intend his studies." In view of his determination to enter the ministry, it was thought advisable that the last year should be taken from his apprenticeship, but as this could only be done by the payment of £80 stg., the rated value of his work above his wages, and as the hill farm could not afford the outlay, his release was not obtained. A few months, however, were thrown off, and in 1836 he was free, leaving the scenes of his many conflicts for more agreeable, though not less arduous toil.

His previous training had been, of necessity, very imperfect, and he was not in a condition to take full advantage of his opportunities when he entered Edinburgh University in November of that year. He resolutely, however, did his best, and his profiting appeared to all. At that time matters were managed in Edinburgh University in a way as absurd and inde-fensible as could well be imagined. There was no entrance examination to any of the classes. Every one could matriculate without question asked or inquiry made. Not the slightest care was taken that some small amount of antecedent fitness for the work of the college should be secured. No subsequent examina-tions were thought of, in order to test the fitness of individual students for passing from one grade to another. In most of the classes there was not even the pretence of any instruction, except what could be derived from lectures somewhat perfunctorily delivered, and unchanged from year to year. Graduation had fallen almost entirely into desuetude. As Sir William Hamilton phrased it, the honour was affected chiefly

by country schoolmasters and Highland ministers.
The result of all this was as deplorable as well could
be.   Students came of all ages from twelve years up
to thirty or forty, with all degrees of cultivation except
the highest and best, and with every diversity of intention as to their future.   The country schoolmaster
in his stupid conceit sent his half-taught, or rather
wholly untaught, pupils in order to his having local
credit for preparing scholars for the University.   The
ambitious lad thought that he could not spare time for
preliminary training, and accordingly rushed *in medias
res*.   The best boys of the city classical schools were
also there, and all took whatever classes they pleased.
There was not even an attempt at classification.   No
advice, on the part of the authorities, was thought of.
Boys who had spent six and seven years at steady
grind on Greek and Latin took their places on the
same benches with whiskered countrymen who had
not been so many months, perhaps not so many weeks
at such work.   In such circumstances what could be
expected ? only what too often occurred—disappointment and life-long injury—a pitiful smattering, and a
most inadequate idea of what education really was.

In the junior Latin class the most elementary
matters were begun with, while at the same time there
was no possibility of anything like drill being carried
out.   The very rudiments of Latin Grammar, with
the first part of "Mair's Introduction," were taken up,
and these university students maundered over " *bonus
puer discit ; mali pueri ludunt.*"   Of course the other
extreme had to be attended to, and at the very same
time.   Unfortunate mortals who had scarcely mastered

the mysteries of "*Amo*" had to wrestle with a book of the "Æneid," and had to try to relish the society of the jovial, though not very moral, poet who claimed Mæcenas for his patron.

In Greek, matters were still worse. The Professor at that time was a dull, uncultivated peasant, who had never risen in spirit above his original condition. The work of the session in this man's first class began with the Greek alphabet. The grammar used was in Latin, and many, who could scarcely translate an easy Latin sentence to save their lives, were expected to get all their knowledge of the Greek parts of speech and of their construction, from a directory in the classic tongue of Rome. The least shadow of order was not maintained in the class-room. System there was none; drill there was none. For the great body of the students it was simply loss of time, money and brains. At the end of the season there was no examination, written or oral, to test the progress or the retrogression of any or all. The Professor had a form of certificate, with blanks, which he filled in according to his own will and pleasure, and no one called him to account for the waste of money and ruin of lives. If possible, the lectures this man gave were funnier and more preposterous still. To these poor, raw, uncultured lads, this unutterably dull, though slightly learned Theban, lectured on the "Greek Drama"—"Why do scenes of distress, chiefly fictitious, etc.?" and so on. Some, from native force of character and resolute determination to go forward, profited considerably, but with the majority the whole thing was a farce, and a very sad one. They were sent forth with the thinnest possible veneer of classical learning, which very soon, and absolutely, disappeared in the rough work of after years. What the University magnates did would have puzzled a conjuror to make out ; for, let it be repeated, they had no matriculation examination, no progressive examinations, and no curriculum, which students were even recommended to follow. Every one could do as he pleased ; pay his fees and take his chance—sink or swim !

Into such a burlesque of an institution for the cultivation of higher literature and science, Walter Inglis found his way in November, 1836. Nobody asked him what he had learned. Nobody tested his fitness for the work he proposed to take. Nobody dreamed of giving him advice. He paid his money, got his ticket, learned what books were used, and— *voila tout.* The trifling pedant, whom Byron has immortalized as " paltry," strummed and talked on the " Humanities "; told stories as in former days ; lectured on General Grammar ; maundered about his visits to Rome, and repeated his worn-out classical witticisms *ad nauseam.* It was evident that the young Hercules, fresh from the workshop, and in a perfect ferment of intellectual activity and evangelistic zeal, was but poorly equipped for appreciating fully the mysteries of irregular verbs, the woes of Æneas and the loves of Dido, especially as he was one of a hundred and twenty as miscellaneous individuals as could well be picked up in a summer's day. Why talk of the five months' effort ? The best possible in the circumstances was attempted and accomplished. A good school would have benefited him more, and yet he came out far ahead of many of his associates ! He also made friends, many of them valuable, and almost all of them life-long ones. He attended prayer meetings and religious conferences, studied his Bible, and managed to have his hungry heart fed, though his intellect had to be satisfied with Lenten fare, which was meagre at the best, and cooked and served in a marvellously confused and somewhat repulsive fashion.

His second college session brought him under the influence of Sir William Hamilton. That great man was then just beginning his work as Professor of Logic and Metaphysics. The more thoughtful of his students were raised to a high pitch of enthusiasm by his prelections and personal magnetism. But to the great mass of the ill-trained and somewhat commonplace individuals, who, for professional reasons, had to pass through his classes, his discussions, it must be acknowledged, were "leather and prunella." Essays were written by a comparatively small number, and read aloud in the class. Some of these were of great excellence, and gave intimation of what their writers have since achieved. But the great majority were as immature and trifling as could well be imagined. For the great mass of his students the great man spoke as if in an unknown tongue.

Walter Inglis, who had never, so far, received one hint from any human being as to the aids and mysteries of English composition, did his manful best in essay writing, and not without success. His sentences were somewhat rugged and incondite, and his modes of thought were emphatically his own. But he had something to say, and he said it as he best could. His essays were not models of graceful composition, and, doubtless, some of the writers of smooth, flowing commonplaces around him fancied themselves greatly his superiors. On that point, however, they were greatly mistaken. The Rev. Dr. Cairns, of Edinburgh, referring to this stage in Mr. Inglis' student-life, says : "Mr. Inglis and I had been in the same classes in the University of Edinburgh from about 1838, but we began to know each other familiarly only about 1840. Hence I cannot recall anything of his appearances in the classes of Sir William Hamilton or Professor Wilson (Christopher North). I only remember his own statements as to how much he had been impressed by both, and his vigorous comments on some of their speculations. He had little of the regular metaphysician about him, but his native sturdiness of mind enabled him to grapple with any kind of thought, whether in the field of mental study or of morals ; and he was, doubtless, one of those powerful spirits whom the lectures of Wilson, and still more of Hamilton, with the awakening around them, roused into action. I do not remember anything definite about his other classes, save that he had taken more than usual pains with Greek, and in particular had attended an extra-academical course by a modern Greek scholar of the name of Negris, from whom he had learned the system of reading Greek according to the accents and other peculiarities of the modern Greek pronunciation." With these and other kindred preliminary studies in classics and philosophy, Walter Inglis was thus at length prepared—though, doubtless, in his own estimation very poorly—to enter upon the higher problems of theology, in order that he might eventually go hence as an ambassador of Christ to the heathen world.

CHAPTER IV.

THEOLOGICAL STUDIES AND ORDINATION.

Accepted by London Missionary Society—Spiritual Depression—Return to Brothershiels — The Independent College — Drs. Wardlaw and Ewing — Friendship Between Mr. Inglis and Mr. Russell — His Father's Death — Impressions Made—Illness and Restoration to Health—Choice of South Africa—Missionary Spirit of the Period—Studies in Secession Hall under Drs. Brown and Balmer—Marriage —Ordination.

IN the early months of the year 1838, while attending college, Mr. Inglis offered his services as a missionary to the directors of the London Missionary Society, and in due course was accepted. He left for London, in the early summer, and was sent to Ongar, near London, to study under a gentleman of the name of Cecil, who then took charge of the education of some of the society's students. Of his experience there we know but little. It is to be feared that the somewhat flat aspect of the district, and the not very congenial character of his instructor, exercised a rather depressing influence upon his mind and heart. Be that as it may, certain it is that he fell after a while into a state of deep spiritual depression, and that at last he was told that unless this could be shaken off his engagement with the society would have to be cancelled. The doctors recommended change, and he returned to the old moorland farm, as he thought, a broken down and disappointed man. Outdoor exercise, active work on the farm, and better perhaps than all, his old mother's sympathies and counsels, had a

restoring influence upon his whole being. The cloud
passed, and to a great extent he enjoyed—if not perfect peace—at least a very large amount of spiritual
gladness and settled trust. His engagement with
the society was held good, and he was directed to put
himself under the tuition of Drs. Wardlaw and Ewing,
of Glasgow, who were at that time the professors in
the Theological Institute of the Independents, or
Scotch Congregationalists. Upon his work there he
entered with characteristic ardour and the most gratifying success. Combined with his studies he was
required to do more or less missionary work in the
city, and in carrying out this he began to preach in
the streets, not without personal profit, but at first
with some sacrifice of feeling.

"My knowledge of Walter Inglis at this time, says
Dr. Cairns, "was greatly helped by his intimacy with
a common friend, Mr. James M. Russell, who was one
of the most gifted men of his college period, but who
died in the spring of 1844. Mr. Russell was the son
of the parish minister of Muthil, Perthshire, whose
father again was the well-known Russell of Kilmar-
nock, introduced by Burns into his 'Holy Fair.' The
Russell family, after the death of their father and
mother, had lived in Edinburgh with an uncle and
aunt, the parents of Dr. Daniel Wilson, of Toronto,
and his brother, the lamented George Wilson. Here
everything had tended to call out the genius of James
Russell, who became dux of the high school, and then
went through the university, leaving a deep mark in
classics and philosophy, enhanced by the singular
modesty and sensitiveness of his spirit, which revealed

an original humour, a poetical fancy, and a highly mystic but deeply earnest religious feeling. He had passed through great spiritual conflicts, but only to strengthen his faith in the essential points of the Gospel, while his Presbyterian training had yielded to Independency, and he had become a student of the Independent Church, under Dr. Wardlaw. A younger brother moved in the opposite direction, and after a distinguished career, has just died amidst universal regrets, as Archdeacon of Adelaide, in South Australia. Had James Russell lived he would certainly have been a light in his generation, and his verses, published with those of George Wilson, sufficiently attest his poetic gifts, though his classical enthusiasm and fine speculative faculty have left no memorial. There could not be a greater contrast than between him and Walter Inglis as they met for the first time at the Independent College in Glasgow : the one scholarly, refined, almost fastidious in the play of enthusiasm over his dark and finely-chiselled countenance ; the other a block of Nature's purest granite, fresh from the quarry, and only brightened by the vague sense of power. These two young men, however, became fast friends, on the strength of a deep human insight which was in both, and still more of a central Christian fervour which was soon to light the one to death, and to burn in the other through a hard mission career and somewhat rough colonial experience. The friendship of James Russell brought Walter Inglis within the range of George Wilson, also of the delightful family circle, in which a strong, unconventional missionary was always a person of interest. This period of his

life was one of the happiest, and gradually his power
of expression began to do more justice to the great
thoughts that struggled within him."

While busily engaged with his studies at Glasgow,
sickness and death came to the lone farm-house among
the hills. The old father, possessed of a vigorous constitution, had enjoyed all but unbroken health for
many years. He had toiled with unwearied energy,
and, upon the whole, with sustained hopefulness and
good humour. His toil, however, had been of a very
Sisyphean character. The stone which he had, for
so many years, been slowly rolling up the hill had
often escaped from his grasp, and had tumbled back
again to the bottom. The never-ending, still beginning, process had gone on, and it had gradually, but
surely, told upon this strong, and withal, hopeful tiller
of the ground. The firmly-knit frame gradually gave
way. The buoyant energy of other years became a
thing of the past. The clear, strong eye almost insen-
sibly grew dim, and a chronic tiredness took the place
of the jubilant elasticity of past times. The worker
had, perforce, to become a mere onlooker. But the
end was not thought very near, perhaps not thought
much of at all, as if it were looked upon as incongru-
ous to associate the idea of death with one so full of
vitality and power.

A full family gathering took place in the old home
at New Year, 1840, and there was no specially apparent
reason for fearing that it might be the last. The two
student brothers, Walter and William, in due time went
their several ways—one to Glasgow, the other to Edinburgh, and as it so happened, in a few days thereafter,

to the Isle of Man. The call, however, came speedily, for on the 29th of February in the same year the strong man bowed and gave up the ghost. Walter only managed to get home to see the close, and a mighty and permanent effect that close had upon his thoughts and feelings in the coming years.

The death of the old father was peaceful and full of hope. The old rugged sternness had disappeared, and the inherent tenderness of character, which had all along been too rigidly kept in the background, asserted its rightful place. The intellect continued strong and clear to the very last. Farewell words were spoken to each, with the deepest feeling, but with Spartan-like calmness. As the end approached, the Twenty-third Psalm was sung. The voice of the dying patriarch, strong and clear, though somewhat cracked, could be heard throughout, till, as one after another dropped out in silence and tears, it held on firm and alone with : " Yea, though I walk through death's dark vale," on to the close. The old couple, who had been so much to each other, had now to separate. This too was done with a quietude and peacefulness not destitute of dignity. " Are ye no comin' wi' me ? " queried the dying one, as he gave his last strange look ; and the touching, but composed, reply came, with equal significance : " No yet, by and by—by and by ! " And so they parted, the one into something more and better than the " divine silences," the other quietly and firmly to take up her burden and resume her humble, yet not unworthy, toil, till twenty-three years after the Master said : " It is enough," and the separated met once more to go no more out.

The young missionary student, as may well be believed, was deeply moved by all this. His professional and spiritual education was greatly promoted by this closing and convincing evidence of how Christians could part and how Christians could die. The old house-mother knelt beside her dead, and felt she could add a new petition to her family prayer, for the widow and the fatherless were there. When the Sabbath came there were tears, but there was no bitterness :

> The sun of hope shone through them,
> She would see his face again.

The worn-out, weary frame at last had found rest, and was in due time in sorrow, but yet with unfaltering hope, laid with the kindred dust of many generations in the "Auld Kirk Yaird," among the heather hills. The old widowed one fitly, and with a stroke of unconscious pathos, if not even of poetry, told the whole story as far as she was concerned, when some time afterward, in writing to her other and absent son, she in her own quiet way remarked : " On Saturday nights I sorrow for a dead husband ; but the Sabbath soon dawns, and I can then rejoice in a living Lord."

Referring to the death of his father, Mr. Inglis wrote to his eldest sister, under date 11th April, 1840, as follows :

DEAR SISTER,—The spirit which your letter breathed pleased me very much. My absent father comes often to my mind more vividly of late than in the weeks immediately after his dissolution. Last night I was dreaming that he and I were in Dalkeith together. He was old and frail, yet he had such a heavenly mildness about him ; I was never thinking that he was or had been dead. Yes! he is gone; but is he not now raising a sweeter strain, by far, than ever he did on earth? A strain on that new harp he has received, which shall never be laid aside, but shall ever swell out in higher and higher tones as eternity rolls on. May it be our blessed portion to enter these bright realms and join the innumerable throngs that surround the throne, ever to be filled with that joy which is unspeakable and full of glory. Imagination often pictures out many fantastic and delusive fancies concerning time's things. It stretches, often, far beyond and over realities. But it cannot take too bold a wing concerning that immortality of happiness or misery beyond the grave. My dear sister, seeing that the glories of the Lamb are the chief attractions of heaven, may it be your sweet experience, as it has been mine, to have the eye of the mind raised from off changeful self—wicked self—and have it placed on a risen Lord. What a happy change this has wrought in me! This last year, I have had a serenity of mind I never enjoyed before. Evidently, God had been with me on that wonderful day at Ongar, both with me and with beloved Fairbrother. Then the storm was hushed. That morning I shall never forget. I was sitting in deep despair. I took up Russell's letters. I had not read a page when a ray of light entered, which raised my downcast soul. The Lord has led me in strange paths, yet He breaks up my way.

To the same sister he writes under date of 19th July, 1840, from Bridge of Allan. After referring at length to the sudden death of a friend, a missionary in the South Seas, he adds :

If I could but shake myself free from the many clogs that press down my mind to the dust: if I could keep the eye of faith upraised to the Eternal God, to my Blessed Redeemer, to the Spirit of all grace, and

continuously implore that all the promises of the word
of truth might be fulfilled in my pilgrimage journey,
how unspeakably precious would my thoughts be ! If
I were but emptied of self, those stupid imaginings
all blasted, and God to be all in all ! Pray that I may
be enabled both to anticipate and enter upon the
functions of the missionary with an apostolic spirit.
There is far too much of a professional cast of soul
among our ministers, I fear. I dread such a fatal rock.

I rejoice to think that you are seeing religion to
be of greater importance than you have ever done
before. All that I have to say to you on this matter is
—think of God, look to Him. Have nothing to do with
self. This, this alone, is Christianity. All else is
blackness and despair. May it be your blessed experience, as well as my own, ever to glory in the cross of
Christ. May we ever say with Paul : " God forbid
that I should glory, save in the cross of our Lord Jesus
Christ."

On the 29th January, 1841, he writes to the same
sister :

DEAR SISTER,—The great truth that supports my
own mind is Christ crucified. Upraise your eye to
Him. Think of Him. This act is the beginning of
religion, the middle, and the ending. What a glorious
object to contemplate ! If we are unhappy it is because we are away from Him, and there is nothing for
it but to find our way back to Him—Christ crucified
the hope of glory.

In the summer of 1841 he went to London to
acquire some knowledge of medicine. On the 1st of
July of that year, writing still to the same sister, and
referring to the turmoil of a general election then
going on, he says :

These matters don't affect me as they once did.
Not that I would have others to be uninterested, or

that politics are of little moment, or that civil liberty and good government are of small importance. No ; but I do feel that I have consecrated myself to a higher object, and to it I would bend all my energies. What is the use of me troubling my mind about the wranglings of party-spirited men ? What I anticipate is to be a legislator myself, and hence the propriety of having my mind balanced with those great principles, upon which all governments rest ; and chiefly to have my mind thoroughly indoctrinated with the mysteries of the kingdom of God—to have my soul nerved with those modes of thought and feeling regarding the scheme of redemption as shall make me endure all things, even death itself, with that cool fortitude becoming one who feels that there is in store for him an eternity of bliss, after the toils and pains of this shifting scene have all completely closed.

Deeply sensible I am that I have before me an arduous course, and nothing but the infusion of the spirit of holy, heavenly principles can make me say, "None of these things move me."

During the latter part of 1839, the whole of 1840, and a considerable part of 1841, Mr. Inglis continued to prosecute his theological studies. At one time the iron frame, which no physical toil could exhaust, threatened to break down entirely under the pressure of study. After a severe and trying illness, however, through which he was tenderly and skilfully cared for by friends in Glasgow, he was permitted to see the object of his intense and sacred ambition within reach, and was definitely appointed to accompany the Rev. Robert Moffat, on the return of that well-known missionary, to his evangelistic work among the Bechuanas of South Africa. His choice of South Africa was doubtless largely due, first, to his intense hatred of slavery and sympathy with the oppressed, and next to the influence of Robert Moffat. As Dr. Cairns remarks, "no one who has not experienced something of it can have any idea of the sensation produced by 'Williams' Missionary Enterprises in the South Seas,' or 'Moffat's Missionary Labours in South Africa,' more than forty years ago." The whole bent of Mr. Inglis' nature drew him to the latter field. There was something in the solitude of the desert, in the energy and freedom of the Caffre and Bechuana races, and in the great success which Mr. Moffat's book unfolded, strengthened by his commanding personality, which was peculiarly fitted to take hold of a youth of ardent and generous character. Mr. Inglis was filled with enthusiasm, and often his missionary ideas and anticipations found vent in the circle, where now they were most appreciated. The idea of self-denial in connection with missions filled him only with disdain. It would have been much greater self-denial to have been chained down to the routine of a minister's life at home. But there was no affectation in his resolve. It was only the impulse of Divine grace working upon a robust and adventurous nature.

On the 1st of August, 1842, Mr. Inglis was united in marriage to Margaret, third daughter of the late Rev. John Dickson, who for many years had been a missionary in Russia under the liberal policy of Alexander I., but had been obliged, with the other Scotch missionaries, to withdraw when that policy was reversed after the accession of Nicholas.

After having been for upwards of forty-two years the faithful and beloved companion in all her husband's

South African and Canadian journeyings and experiences, Mrs. Inglis is still spared to her friends and family, and spends the evening of her life amid the affectionate sympathy and respect of the people among whom and for whose benefit her husband laboured so assiduously during his closing years. Three daughters and a son were born in Africa of this marriage. The son died in 1873. All the daughters are still alive.

The ordination of Mr. Inglis was quite an event in the history of Scottish missions. It stirred the religious community of Edinburgh to its very depths, and created an interest in down-trodden Africa that has been followed up by churches of every denomination, and doubtless prepared the way for the exploring expeditions of such men as Stanley, who have, in late years, revealed to an astonished people the sad condition of the Dark Continent of Africa. The ordination took place in Broughton Place Church, Edinburgh, under the presidency of the venerable Dr. John Brown. A very large number of Mr. Inglis' personal friends were present, among whom may specially be mentioned Dr. George Wilson, the eminent Christian scientist, who had hardly recovered from the severe surgical operation which left him lame for life. The chief attractions of the meeting were, as might be expected, the young missionary, Mr. Inglis, and the older missionary, Mr. Moffat. Mr. Inglis gave a manly, unaffected statement of his religious history (which will be found in the following chapter), while Mr. Moffat, in his ordination charge, referred to the peculiar trials of missionary life in Africa, and narrated a good many anecdotes gathered from personal observation. One of them was the story of an old Dutch missionary, who, when asked by a newly-arrived brother how he was to qualify himself for his work, met him with the one word, "patience," and on being asked for something more, only repeated the same word.

From many different accounts furnished us of that most interesting service we select that of the Rev. John Mitchell, an uncle of Mrs. Inglis, which was sent to another niece the day after the ordination:

7 Calton Hill, Edinburgh, 26th Oct., 1842.

MY DEAR NIECE,—I ought to have acknowledged before now your kind letter of the 17th inst., but I purposely put it off till Mr. Inglis' ordination should take place, that I might give you a short account of it. It took place last night, in Dr. Brown's chapel, Broughton Place. It commenced exactly at half-past six, and did not dismiss till twenty minutes to ten. Mr. Cooper of Fala gave out a few verses of Psalm lxxii., then read the same Psalm, and prayed. Again, a few verses were sung, when Dr. Paterson and Mr. Inglis went both up into the pulpit. The Doctor, after a few words of address, put the usual questions to Mr. Inglis, which he answered in firm tone of voice, and in a fine style of language. The account which he gave of his doctrinal sentiments, the manner he was brought to the knowledge of the truth, and how he had been led to devote himself to the missionary work, was most interesting, and was listened to by the audience with almost breathless attention, and, I have no doubt, endeared him to every serious Christian who heard it. After he had replied to the questions, the Doctor and he came down from the pulpit to a large space before the precentor's desk, which was literally crowded with ministers of different denominations. He sat down at a small table, leaning his head upon his hands on the table, when Dr. Brown offered up the ordination prayer in a most fervent and energetic manner. When they came to the laying-on of hands so many ministers pressed forward that the one-half of them could not reach his head, but they stood all the time with their hands stretched out the same as if they had been resting on his head. This being over, a part of Psalm lxviii. was sung, and Mr. Moffat went up to the pulpit, and in a very affectionate strain, addressed him for a full hour, pointing out the nature of the field of labour upon which he was about to enter, and giving him a solemn charge to be faithful in the discharge of the duties that will devolve upon him when he reaches the scene of his labours. In this he included Margaret, and pointed out to her what she would likely have to do. His words seemed full of love and brotherly affection, and seemed to produce a deep effect on the audience, which he also addressed for more than half an hour. Having spoken for more than an hour and a half, part of another Psalm was sung, and Mr. Swan concluded by prayer. Every corner of the chapel was crowded to almost suffocation, all the passages were densely filled to the very doors, and the pulpit stairs were filled so that the ministers who had to go up and down could scarcely work their way. I have never seen such a crowded audience since the days of Rowland Hill, when he used to preach in the Circus, now called the Adelphi Theatre. And, what is remarkable, they all kept their places till the very close—not one did I observe going out before the blessing was pronounced, and, I think, they took fully half an hour to dismiss. Old Mrs. Inglis was present, and, I am sure, must have been highly gratified. Her three sons and three daughters were also present. I am sure it was a most gratifying occasion to dear Margaret, and also to Elizabeth and Isabella, for I am fully persuaded that such a respectable and interesting ordination has not been witnessed in Edinburgh for many years, and, indeed, I very much doubt that such an one has ever been wit-

nessed here. To me it was of the highest possible
interest, not only on Margaret's account, but also on
account of the solemn manner in which it was conducted, and the deep interest which the unprece-
dentedly large audience evidently took in the whole
service. Your aunt was very much disappointed in
not being able to attend, in consequence of a sore leg,
which confines her to the house; but I hope that,
through the Divine blessing, she will soon be able to
go about. On Monday evening Mr. Moffat addressed
the children of the Sabbath-schools in Dr. Peddie's
Chapel, and, although only a certain number of children from each school was selected to attend, the
chapel was so crowded that about a thousand of the
children could not get admittance. I, of course, could
not get in, and therefore cannot give you an account
of this very interesting meeting. But perhaps Mrs.
W. Inglis will give you an account of it, for I am told
that she laid hold on Mr. Moffat's *coat-tails*, and in
this way got herself conveyed through the crowd that
surrounded the door. I believe Mr. Moffat is going to
Glasgow this week, but will return here in the beginning of next week, and the week following there is to be
a public meeting of his friends to present him with a
copy of the "Encyclopædia Britannica." I believe he
then intends to visit Liverpool for the purpose of assisting at the ordination of another missionary who is to
accompany them to Africa, but, I understand, they will
not embark for that country till the month of January.

We have had a very early beginning of winter here.
Yesterday and to-day we had heavy falls of snow, with
hard frost, but this afternoon it turned into a thaw,
and now we have rain. Your Aunt joins in kindest
love to you, and was much cheered by your kind letter.
Most likely you will get all the accounts I have given
you above from your sisters, but a good tale is not the
worse of being twice told. Let us hear from you when
you have time.—I remain, your ever affectionate uncle,

JOHN MITCHELL.

CHAPTER V

Doctrinal Views—Experimental Religion—Motives and Events Leading to Missionary Consecration—Proposed Plans of Working—Certificate of Ordination.

THE answers given by Mr. Inglis to the several questions put to him by the council, who were delegated to ordain him, are as follows :

You are desired to state, briefly, what you believe to be the distinguishing and peculiar doctrines of the Holy Scriptures.

In returning a brief answer to the proposed question, it seems to be taken for granted that I believe the Holy Scriptures to contain a revelation of God's will—that the holy men who wrote these books spake as they were moved by the Holy Ghost—that they are truth most pure ; but on account of the various opinions believed and widely circulated among men, who professedly acknowledge the Bible as their rule of faith and manners, the question seems to suggest an answer such as shall show what I believe to be the grand, ancient, revealed truth which tends to and is the reason of the godly life.

Your time won't permit me, nor does the question require a statement of the long list of very important truths or doctrines, yet of a secondary or consequential order, regarding which there has been much dispute. All I intend to lay before you are central, essential truths, or what may appropriately be termeds tartingpoints, and that without any amplification or illustration. It may be observed that all present who are acquainted with the constitution of the " London Missionary Society" will be prepared to hear from me a firm declaration of what are called Evangelical doctrines. The four following statements may be given as my most solemn belief, which I conceive to be essential for a right apprehension of the grand design which God intends to accomplish by the Scriptures. All who hold these statements I shall esteem as brethren, though we may differ widely on other points. I shall feel it my duty to exercise towards them that charity which beareth all things, hopeth all things. All who do not hold these statements I believe to have completely erred from the faith once delivered to the Saints, and to be both deceived themselves and deceiving others :

I. The Holy Scriptures teach and enforce, in the most emphatic manner, that all men, in all ages and in all countries, are by nature completely depraved ; that they are guilty in the sight of a Holy God and Righteous Moral Governor, through and by our first parents, who were originally created holy in the image of their Creator, but who continued not in their first estate, by breaking a special commandment that God saw fit to give as a test of their obedience. Men are not only guilty, but under the wrath and curse of God, and most justly exposed to eternal punishment on account of breaking God's holy law.—" All have sinned and come short of the glory of God." " The imagination of man's heart is evil from his youth."

II. We have brought before us in the Scriptures a

great remedial scheme which had been conceived and determined upon by God from all eternity; by the provisions of which scheme an offer of salvation is given to all men. In order that this great plan of salvation may be accomplished in the fulness of time, we have the one only living and true God most distinctly revealed to us in the mysterious relationship of three persons equal in power and glory—" God the Father, God the Son, God the Holy Ghost." God the Father is represented as sustaining the dignity of law-giver and law-dispenser. God the Son is represented as sustaining the character of mediator between God and man. In executing this office he became man, the man Christ Jesus, and after living a life of activity, sorrow, and suffering, he offered up himself a sacrifice for sin, that through his atonement the law and justice of God might not only be satisfied, but a new and living way opened up to "immortality and bliss." " God the Holy Ghost" is represented as the efficient though unseen agent in dispensing among men the blessings obtained through the death of Christ. It is the work of the Spirit to change and quicken the souls of men who are dead in trespasses and sins. He renews them to faith and repentance towards God and love towards Jesus Christ. He carries on the work of sanctification, and shall at last present God's chosen people spotless and unblamable.

III. On the ground of the finished work of Christ, both salvation from the power and consequences of sin, and also eternal life in the heavens above, are fully, freely, earnestly and particularly offered to the whole human race, and whosoever from among men shall believe with the heart and confess with the mouth the Lord Jesus Christ to the glory of God the Father shall be saved. The Scriptures declare that "we are justified freely by his grace," that we are justified by Faith. "Not of works, lest any man should boast."

IV. While the Scriptures declare that works or merit on the part of man are altogether discarded as the procuring cause of salvation and eternal life, they at the same time tell us that works, good works, viz., righteousness and love, both towards God and all men, necessarily flow from a real belief in the finished work of Christ as the only sure ground of hope to obtain eternal life and glory, and that works, good works, viz., righteousness and love, are the only evidence of a living faith both to ourselves and our fellow-men. "Show me your faith by your works" is the spirit of the Apostle James.

As it is indispensably necessary that he who undertakes to teach Christianity to the heathen should not only know what the Bible teaches, but be a Christian himself, you are desired to state what are the grounds on which you are led to conclude you are such, with any memorable circumstances connected with your first religious impressions, and the period of their commencement.

Am I a Christian ? What are the grounds I have for coming to the conclusion that I am a Christian ? are questions of grave and overwhelming importance to a sincere and earnest being, convinced of the truth of Scripture. To such an individual nothing appears so necessary and reasonable as a humble, prayerful, and conclusive investigation of his actual position towards God, and his prospects for the eternal world. Sincerely can I say that no questions have I been more solicitous to put to myself. Through all the changes of a somewhat thoughtful yet chequered life, there has existed in my mind a deep-settled consciousness that I was an immortal being, responsible to a heart-searching and rein-trying Jehovah. It has seemed to me when alone with this great eternal being, and all thoughts of men had given place in the solemn interview, that my hopes and prospects for eternity were such as not to make me ashamed. Yet in standing before so many of my fellow mortals, and giving you a reason for the hope that is in me, I cannot divest myself of feelings of a hesitating and painful nature. _ There is something so relieving and satisfactory when alone with God, to utter even amidst the stirrings of conscience, " Thou God seest me. Thou knowest all things. Thou knowest that I love thee." It is altogether different with men completely ignorant of all that you are and have been. Every thought and feeling is interesting to an infinitely wise and gracious God, who appears to delight in hiding from the observation of his creatures the first formation of their own characters. The history of men is narrated, and you mark the most trivial events, giving such a powerful influence as changes the whole current of their thoughts and course of action. Who does not reflect upon such events with a hallowed satisfaction ? and yet they cannot be repeated so as to give interest to others. While I thus think and feel in regard to the question proposed, I have, at the same time, never been able to view it as a thing altogether out of taste

to give a public declaration of what God has wrought
for you by his powerful and outstretched arm, by his
life-giving Spirit. To use the language of the excellent Howe: " A design for an immortal state is not so
mean and inglorious, or so irrational and void of a
solid ground, that we have any cause either to decline
or conceal, either to retain or be ashamed of our hope,
though all the while we are not so solicitous to have
our end and purpose known as to obtain it." I see no
necessity for supposing that right thoughts, or even
enquiries after God, are of such a nature, that mature
retrospective reasoning invariably induces men to
hide all the struggles and revolutions that may have
transpired when passing from darkness and doubt to
the light and peace of the kingdom of God. There
have been, and still are, thousands of redeemed men
whose moral history is of such a striking, tangible, and
twofold order that no person can hear or read without
exclaiming: " Behold what God hath wrought ! "
" There is something hallowed to the individual himself whose religion can be traced back to the ebbings
and flowings of youth, when the ear listened to the
prayers and earnest instructions of devout parents ;
but in the great majority of such individuals there is
little that can bear to be repeated—a mother's prayers
and tears, instructions and admonitions, no doubt were
heard and blest." From her lips I learned " that the
fear of God was the beginning of wisdom "—from her
instructions I was led to wonder what could be the
nature of the " peace of God that passeth all understanding." I well remember when these two ideas
were told me, and what an influence they have exerted

upon my whole future character. Amidst the ardent and impetuous buoyancy of schoolboy days, when life's gay morn was gilded with streaks of exquisite joy, arising from the dreams of an ever-active fancy, the speaker often had his foolishness crushed under powerful impressions of an ever-present God, who noted all thoughts, words, and actions in a book of remembrance, to be preserved until the day of judgment, at which all men are to give an account for themselves.

My native home being among the wild and sterile solitudes of Nature, where nothing was heard to break the deep silence, save a solitary note from the passing wild bird, and the bleat of straggling sheep, habits of reflection upon religion were forced upon me as I travelled the long, dreary moor, year after year, to school. Often, I was astonished and grieved in observing that I had an inclination to encourage wicked thoughts. I had a strong conviction that all these wicked thoughts were suggested by the tempter. My religious impressions during these years were chiefly of a fearful foreboding nature. I saw and felt that I was guilty in the sight of God, but had no perception of the love of Christ. The first time that I have a distinct remembrance of being deeply affected by the love of Christ was one evening when about eleven or twelve years old. Being greatly delighted with a little book containing Bible stories, I continued to read with the light of the fire after my brothers had retired to rest. I came, at last, to the story which gave an account of Jesus Christ. His sufferings, his death, melted me to tears. I felt myself drawn to the Redeemer with tender affection. His love for sinners seemed to me beyond thought. My brothers were asleep, and I continued to weep and pray. If you had a full account narrated of what I have thought and felt from my youthful years up to the present time, I am sorry to say that you would have little else than the description of a hard-fought combat between the elements of right and wrong, truth and error. For several years I was greatly perplexed with sceptical speculations; doubts and difficulties beset me on all sides, in enquiries after the evidences and nature of the Christian religion. These have long since been chased away. The combat still goes on between the old and new man, but the scheme of redemption appears now to me admirably adapted for my poor, perishing soul. I have long encouraged sentiments of a joyful nature in anticipating the time when I shall be separated from all sin and sorrow, through Jesus Christ, my Lord. He is all my boast; his finished work, all my hope. To look upon him as exhibiting the glory of the Father, human nature in a state of perfection, I find to be my chief delight. Conscious, as I am, of much imperfection, of finding it still necessary to reason with myself, to contemplate the great and glorious perfections of God, as seen both in his works and word, still I cannot evade the conclusion that my spirit is withdrawing itself from the dark shades of sin, around which it has hovered with a weary wing. Year after year, to my sweet experience there seems to be a concentration of my thoughts and affections around the infinitely holy and ever blessed God, whom I have found most fitted to give me consolation when encompassed with weakness and depressed with sorrow. Blessed be God! the hope

which gladdened David's heart is possessed not only
by the speaker, but by hundreds within these walls,
who daily indulge in calm anticipations of regions
bright with eternal day, where we shall have our souls
elevated to a continuous thrilling ecstasy of holy joy
in beholding the glories of the Lamb.

*State briefly the motives and course of events that
induced you to think of being a missionary to the heathen.*

While I have traced my first impressions, both of
the fear and love of God, back to the years of childhood, there seems, however, to have been a powerful
impulse given both to the strength and activity of my
mind when about fifteen years old. My thirst for
knowledge of an historical, political, geographical, and
religious nature was so great, that I occupied all the
time I could command in reading books and magazines
bearing upon these topics. Several definite causes
might be mentioned which proved at this time a powerful stimulus both to my thoughts and feelings upon
religion, which cannot be noticed, as they do not bear
directly in answer to the question. Having left home
to learn a business, I was in the habit of spending a
Sabbath every month with my parents. On one of
these occasions my mother was absent at a neighbouring farm, for the purpose of waiting upon her own
aged mother during the closing months of her earthly
pilgrimage. I went over the hill, and spent the Sabbath afternoon beside my mother and grandmother.
No person was in the room save ourselves. The scene,
though full of peace, was solemn to one that had
never been in the sick chamber. I well recollect the

subdued calmness of my mind. The conversation was chiefly on the extent, duration, and glory of the Church of Christ. My mother told me that the one thousand years mentioned in the Revelation were interpreted by some expositors in the sense of prophetical language—viz., a day for a year; consequently they thought the millennium would continue for three hundred and sixty-five thousand years. She mentioned that the late Culbertson of Leith gave this as his opinion in his lectures. The idea was completely new to me. The period was so vast that it awakened the little breadth of understanding and force of imagination I possessed. My mother thought that it was more becoming to think of the full development of the scheme of redemption, as extending throughout a very long course of years; but whether it would be exactly three hundred and sixty-five thousand years she could not determine. As she continued to talk, her heart was warmed by the grandeur and beauty of the theme : All tribes and tongues doing homage to the Prince of Peace ; the teeming populations that would fill all lands; thousands of generations passing into glory. She thought there was no doubt that when time had run its ample round, the company of the redeemed would be much more numerous than the company of the lost, that Christ would see of the travail of his soul, and be satisfied. To this conversation I most distinctly trace the formation of my desires to be a missionary.

The current of my thoughts received a permanent bend. It was as the grain of mustard seed sown upon prepared soil. I left, bidding farewell to my venerable relative, having no hope of seeing her in this world, but the subject of conversation followed me to the busy scenes of life. The idea of the three hundred and sixty-five thousand years lived and grew day after day, till my desire to read Culbertson's lectures became painful in the extreme. I entered a library which had the work, for the express purpose of reading the lectures about the millennium. More knowledge gave a fresh impulse for a still more extended enquiry. All my investigations and musings ended in a fixed and hallowed impression of the lovely aspect the world would necessarily present during the millennium, and consequently the desirableness of having the Gospel preached among all nations. There were several missionary magazines in the library that I had joined. In strict truth, I may say that I read them often with exquisite delight. No preacher ever affected me half so much as the simple confessions and accounts of the poor negroes in the West Indies. There was something in their statements that was clearly and firmly grasped by my understanding. The operation of divine truth upon their dark, polluted minds astonished me, and though not formed by nature to weep much, or easily made to weep, the whole circumstances of the groaning Christian slave wrung from me many tears. While the flash of indignation swept over my naturally free and independent spirit, as I figured before me the heartless grinding tyrants their masters, my sympathies for the oppressed ran so strong that I was times without number compelled to implore God in his wise and good providence to break up my way, that I might be borne to the dwellings of the negro, and there to spend my days in teaching them the gospel. It appeared to me not only duty, but the highest privilege, to send the gospel to the heathen, and still more so to be the actual agent in saying to poor ignorant mortals, " Behold thy God." From all the magazines that I was in the habit of reading, the continual cry was : " More money, more men." What, then, was more natural to the mind of a mere youth than the thought, " Money I have very little to give, but I am willing to offer myself if my services were required." I did not see my way clearly how it was possible for me to be a missionary, the strong probability that I had not talents suitable for a preacher oftener than anything else. Indeed, I may say that was the prominent hindrance to my having an undisturbed possession of a fixed intention to be a missionary.

Amidst all my doubts and fears I stepped back and consoled myself with the thought that I certainly would be able to act either as a catechist or a teacher. and, as a last desperate resource, I thought of all my former purposes to go to distant lands and amass riches; and why cannot I go still, and consecrate all my talents and bodily energies as a man in business. The lowest position appeared to me then, as it does still, most honourable. I was careless of a mere office. I wanted to be in a position where I should have full scope for all my capacities, but—in a situation I was not competent to fill — such ambition seemed to me unworthy of a holy and good cause. Often I have adopted as my own the language of the excellent Milne, when told by some of the committee of the London Missionary Society that they feared he would have to occupy some subordinate office on the mission field, he calmly answered: "I am willing to be anything, a hewer of wood and a drawer of water, to assist in building the house of my God." Such is a mere glance at the circumstances and motives that induced me to devote my whole energies to the missionary cause. For two or three years the idea, though progressive, was floating and unformed in my mind. When about seventeen I came to the fixed resolve to go as a missionary. During these years I never thought of mentioning my intentions to a single individual. My joys, my fears, and sorrows were all my own. As the idea lay brooding in my own bosom, the current flowed on, and, in spite of all my indomitable tendency to keep my intentions a secret amidst conflicting difficulties, I at last ventured to ask an advice from my esteemed friend who commenced the services this evening. I sent him a letter, and, after a long conversation, he said: "Go and qualify for nothing else and nothing less than a missionary to the heathen." He told my parents; they said: "Go, and we will render you all the assistance that lies in our power;" and you, my venerable and faithful friend, have given me every encouragement, and said to me "Go," and many others, whose friendship and advice I highly prize, have said to me "Go." Had it not been for these encouragements, and the strong inherent compelling principle of missionary exertion (ever lovely to me, both in strength and in weakness), neither the paltry motive of human distinction and future ease, nor the absurd expectation that haunts some youth with a spectral force that probably men shall write upon their gravestone: "Here lies learned dust;" I say, neither of these motives would have induced me to continue the life of a student, when once and again my constitution seemed to be much weakened through close confinement. Whatever some men may think of a studious life, it has not been to me as a bed of roses. Through all these necessary preparative labours I have been sustained, and at present I am in the enjoyment of good health, without which it would be rashness to think of going to the wilds of Africa.

I have been appointed to a sphere full of difficulty and danger, but, tragic as the story may seem of one who knows Africa well, I feel no inclination to draw back, and cast a lingering look towards Afric's sons, who are fast rising to the station of perfect men, amidst the verdant groves of the fair isles of the West. It is true my first love was formed in the land of groaning slaves. Yet I rejoice to follow, as a son in the Gospel, the much-honoured and beloved individual who is among us this evening, and whose words I soon expect to feel sinking deep into my inner man; follow him, I say, and mingle among the fierce, free men of Africa upon their native wastes. Unbroken is my first love to the dark, untutored sons of Africa. Who knows but I may be privileged to hear the savage talk in such a manner of the love of Jesus Christ as shall waft back my thoughts to those years when the struggling emotions of hope and fear alternately swayed; and, as I gaze upon him, "clothed and in his right mind," I shall be cheered and fully compensated for all the difficulties I have had to encounter, all the sacrifices and sufferings I have had and may still be called upon to endure. Though I am knit to friends dear and beloved, I am ready this evening to snap the ties that bind me to the home of my fathers and those rugged wilds so full of fresh, tender, and spirit-stirring associations, and, in obedience to the injunctions of a risen and ascended Lord, go far hence to preach the gospel.

State briefly the way in which you intend to prosecute your labours if allowed to enter the field of labour.

As to how I shall act upon the field of labour I do not feel inclined to say much. Plans are often formed that ultimately won't work, or through your own imbecility cannot be put into execution. There can be no doubt that the great laws of conduct are the same in every country. It seems to me that the missionary who takes a comprehensive view of his purpose and situation among savage tribes will exert himself to introduce, along with the saving truths of the gospel, all the elements of civilization; and there can be no doubt the mode of teaching savages divine truth should be of the simplest order.

If God's blessing shall render my labours effectual to the converting a number of the natives, I shall unite them in the fellowship of the Gospel, and observe publicly all the appointed ordinances of God's worship. I shall by all means endeavour to call into exercise the self-sustaining power of the Gospel, that the people amongst whom I labour may have faithful and able men among themselves to whom the oracles of God may be committed, in order that coming generations may be blest with the knowledge, fear, and love of God. I shall not be very solicitous to make the "Africans follow very closely the customs and modes of government among the various sects that comprise" European Christians, as it has never struck me that we have exhibited among us a perfect system of church government; and in addition to this I can easily conceive many customs and a mode of government exactly fitted for Scotland which would do anything but work well in Africa. The law of diversity in human nature, I am afraid, is often overlooked by men who desire to fashion all nations after one rigid uniformity.

While endeavouring to act upon the spirit of two or three centre essential laws for all Christians in all countries, I shall also endeavour to discriminate the individuality of my circumstances, and so shape my course, in the exercise of humble prayer, that God's glory may be most effectually promoted.

As the London Missionary Society was thoroughly non-sectarian, organized upon the broadest principles, and supported by different denominations, it was eminently fitting that in the ordination of Mr. Inglis clergymen of all denominations should take part. The following certificate granted him shows the catholicity of the meeting, and the many noble men who cheered the heart of the young missionary by their presence. Of the eighteen who signed the paper only three survive, namely, Drs. Andrew Thomson and Wm. Peddie, of Edinburgh, and Dr. Joseph Brown, of Glasgow.

At Edinburgh, on the twenty-fifth day of October, eighteen hundred and forty-two years, we, the undersigned, ministers of the Gospel, being assembled in Broughton Place Church, did, by solemn prayer and laying on of hands, ordain to the ministry of the Gospel, Mr. Walter Inglis, having been satisfied of his fitness to perform its functions, and of his call to discharge these as a missionary among the heathen.

JOHN BROWN, D.D., Senior Minister of the United Associate Congregation, Broughton Place.

GEORGE JOHNSTON, Minister, Nicolson Street.

JOHN PATERSON, D.D.

JAMES ROBERTSON, Minister, Musselburgh.

W. LINDSAY ALEXANDER, M.A., Minister of Argyle Square Chapel.

JOSEPH BROWN, Minister, Dalkeith.

JAMES HARPER, Minister, North Leith.

PETER DAVIDSON, Minister, Dean Street, Edinburgh.

WILLIAM PEDDIE, Minister, Bristo Street, Edinburgh.

WILLIAM BRUCE, Minister, Cowgate Church, Edinburgh.

ANDREW ELLIOT, Minister, Ford.

ANDREW THOMSON, Junior Minister of the United Associate Congregation, Broughton Place.

GEORGE BLYTH, Minister of Hampden, Jamaica.

JAMES ROBERTSON, Minister, late of Beith, Ayrshire.

WILLIAM INNES, Baptist Minister, Elder Street, Edinburgh.

G. D. CULLEN, Minister, Congregational Chapel, Leith.

WILLIAM SWAN, Missionary, late of Siberia

JOHN COOPER, Minister of the Gospel, Fala.

CHAPTER VI

Farewell to Scotland—Last days at Brothershiels--Embarkation—Incidents of the Voyage—Letter to his Sister—Opinions of his Brother Missionaries—Journey into the Interior—Baharutse Land—Creed of the Bechuanas—Impromptu Verses to the " Manaloe."

MR. INGLIS' preparation for the active work of the ministry may now be said to close. Before sailing for his distant field he made short visits to his home at Brothershiels, and to other friends. On one of these occasions Dr. Cairns accompanied him. They remained over Sabbath, and heard the Rev. John Cooper of Fala, under whom Mr. Inglis had been brought up, and whose apostolic spirit, with his well-remembered labours in the service of the Scottish Missionary Society in India, had done much to awaken kindred longings and aspirations. This visit was also brightened by the presence of Mr. Inglis' newly-married wife. These autumn days included much roaming and talk amid the wild and beautiful solitudes of that upland region. " I well remember," says Dr. Cairns, " how that he suddenly bound me in a plaid, on which I happened to be seated, and with the help of others dragged me from the top to the bottom of a green slope near the old farm-house."

In the month of January, 1843, the young missionary and his wife embarked in the good ship *Fortitude*, for Cape Town. The dear old home-mother, on the moorland farm of Brothershiels, kept all those things, and pondered them in her heart. She rejoiced greatly that the Lord had spared her to see a son devote himself to service among the heathen; while, at the same time, the parting, though bravely borne, was tender and touching. The most cordial good wishes and fervent prayers of a wide circle of friends followed the young couple to their far-off field of labour and trial, and many cordially endorsed the remark of a life-long friend, as he waved his last farewell to the receding voyagers: "Two truer hearts ne'er left the shore."

The voyage out was somewhat tedious and stormy. In the recently published memoirs of Robert and Mary Moffat the following account is given of it: "Though the embarkation of the passengers took place at Gravesend on the 30th of January, the ship was still wind-bound in the Downs on the fourth of the following month, by which time something like a hundred sail had assembled at the same anchorage. That morning the wind changed round to the north, and in a heavy snowstorm all got under way, and stood down the Channel. The crowd of outward-bound ships spread away each on her own course, the white cliffs receded from view, and next day the company on board the *Fortitude* found themselves on the wide rolling sea. The ship was stout and well manned. The captain was an old and God-fearing man, from whom the missionaries enjoyed every facility for the observance of the Lord's day and for public services, as was befitting so large a proportion of missionary passengers. All were safely landed in Cape Town on the 10th of April, the passage being considered an average one." Mr. Inglis' letters contain little about the voyage. It was

characterized by the usual incidents of pleasant intercourse, and also by busy and more or less disagreeable
gossip, with incipient jealousies and premonitory hints
of possibly serious disagreements.   In a letter written
to his sister, dated Bethelsdorp, South Africa, May 9,
1843, he makes reference to long, journalistic letters,
which cannot now be found, and speaks of certain
troubles that began soon after sailing : "We have," he
says, " seen things great and marvellous, things small
and mean, things absurd and ridiculous, and that from
persons the least to be expected."   Speaking of a brother missionary, named Ashton, who was evidently not
of a kindred spirit, he says : "We agree very well, but
it is the agreement of nothing.   I have not been able
to get a single conversation of a mental or religious
character out of him.   He is not one of my kind at all;
yet a nice, kind fellow, in his way, but has little in-
formation, and has read nothing.   Moffat is a good
soul, and yet, in many respects, just like other people."
During his short sojourn in the capital, at Cape Town,
Mr. Inglis made some pleasant acquaintances, one or
two of which developed into life-long and genuine
friendships.   The journey into the interior of the
country need not be described.   South African modes
of travel were then as they still are, somewhat slow
and monotonous.   Time, apparently, was no object,
and bullock waggons tired the patience of even the
most deliberate.   The Kuruman was at last reached,
and some little time spent at that well-known missionary settlement, in order to have future plans fully
matured, and the different stations assigned to the
new missionaries.   The wild region of Baharutse to

the north was the district assigned to Livingstone and
Inglis. Dr. Philip, the Superintendent of the London
Missionary Society at the Cape, gave it as his opinion
that the sending of these young missionaries to Baharutse was wrong, and subsequent events proved that
he was right. Dr. Moffat, however, thought otherwise,
and so, after a good deal of rough journeying, and not
a few trying and unexpected experiences, the subject
of our sketch was established as a missionary among
the Bechuanas, in the country beyond the Vaal River,
then overrun and claimed by the emigrant Dutch
Boers, whose doings have, in more recent times,
brought them very prominently before the British
public. From among the very few of his African letters which have been preserved, the following one,
written evidently not long after his arrival, to his
sister, will show how deeply interested and hopeful the
young missionary was in his work :

BAHARUTSE, South Africa.

MY DEAR SISTER,—It has fallen to me to add my
supplement, though my views are not many nor important. As you have already heard, we are at last
in Baharutse Land. I have lately had a rugged life.
The Lord has blessed me with good health amidst all
my fatigues. I have been very little with my family
all winter, between building a house, having a garden
made, and on a visit to the Baharutsis, Baralongs, and
Boers. Such things must be so, or we shall stand
still. We have met with another disappointment, from
the Baharutsi not coming on. The account of the
murder of three men by a chief two months ago filled
the whole country with the fear of threatened war.
The Baharutsi had just cause for fear. These rumours
are now completely hushed, and peace is once more

amongst us. The two parties of Baharutsi are at peace for the last three months. Mahura has at last sent cordial greetings to Moiloe. Ten days ago a party went from this quarter to Mahurás with some of his people, and again the Corannas that attacked the Baharutsi have had a rod administered to them for their good. The Spirit of the Lord has breathed upon them. In a letter from Mr. Ross two months ago, he mentions that forty had given evidence of conversion —Godita, the leader of the Commando, included. This man was wicked when I saw him. These things are of the Lord, and wondrous in our eyes; for the tribe have been gospel-despisers for many years. We have built on the junction of one of the largest tributaries of the Mainaloe, and I intend soon to lead out the water, though it will be a serious undertaking. It is a beautiful region where we are. My iron soul felt the strivings of poetry the other day when visiting friends. I dedicated an impromptu, rough and ready, to brother William. It is the second time I ever tried such flights. I first sang to my wife the beauties of the Mainaloe. Since then I gravely attempted to correct one or two verses, which were out of measure. I began, never dreaming of what and where I was going. I shall send the corrected version to brother William. Of course the poetry is a joke, but it will show you that I am in good spirits. The rain-making months have again returned, for which we are thankful. Last week one of their doctors was so fortunate as to destroy the lightning, which they think prevents the rain. The other chiefs came to him with goats and other presents. The notorious doctor that blamed us missionaries last year at the Bakhatla is quite out of repute this year. I went to the village where he resides, three hours' drive down the Mainaloe, but found that he had hidden himself. His people are very friendly to us now. 1 asked them, " Who made the rain yesterday ?" They answered in true native style, " Was it not you ?" The poor things think that we claim the rain in answer to our prayers. I took one of their more sensible men, and explained to him our views—that while " we pray, and believe that God answers prayer, at the same time we do not ascribe the rain to man's prayer, for it would have rained, though not a single praying person was in the country, just as it has rained out at the Molopo River, and up at Mosega, where there is not a soul." We have settled in the midst of the scattered villages on the Mainaloe River. Three villages are close beside us. They attend to hear the Word of God. The chief of one has already mastered the letters, and is a kind, sensible, and amiable man. There are seven villages on the Mainaloe, and four under the Kurreachane Mountains, and four large towns over the Marikna. The largest is about twelve miles distant from us. They are dark souls! They will call you God, and anything for a bit of tobacco. The man who helped me to build the walls of the house was called " Father of God," and his town is called " God " !*

Yours affectionately,
WALTER INGLIS.

*The belief of the Bechuanas regarding the existence of a God, as given by Mr. Inglis, is as follows : " They believe in one god, 'Morimo,' the creator, preserver, and destroyer of men. When any one leaves a house, the inmates say : 'Go in peace ; Morimo be with you.' If you are sick, they will say : 'Morimo will help you.' If their friend dies, the women pour out their bitter wail, charging Morimo that he has not heard. They have no idols. Fetichism prevails very much among them. It is regarded simply as a powerful means for the attainment of the ends they have in view. It is a kind of mystical medicine for the cure of disease. They have no belief in angels or devils, or other spirits, save the spirits of men, who have their abode in the ground, or under-world. They believe, however, in possession, saying, 'Oa-tsemoa'—'He is mad' —that is, entered into or possessed. That there were contradictions in their beliefs Mr. Inglis admitted, but, as he said, it is needless to attempt to reconcile the contradictions of heathendom! He indignantly refuted the common idea that the Bechuanas had no religion, and no belief in a spirit world, and was accustomed to give the following, as an example of

Mr. Inglis' impromptu verses to the "Mainaloe," referred to in this letter, are as follows:

High on the banks of the fair "Mainaloe,"
  My strong homely cottage I raised with clay :
Its fast rushing waters, so clear and refreshing,
  Brought joys to remembrance of youth's early day.

Poets, aroused by the beauties of nature,
  Have charmed the dull swain with the liveliest song ;
Oh ! where is the tongue all pleasant and powerful
  To paint in true colours the Machukubyane !

Thy banks they are lined with the dark weeping willow,
  And other fair trees of a cedar-like form ;
Thy far stretching pools are full of the finny tribes,
  And the dark scaly crocodile there finds a home.

Around thy high mountains no snow tempests bellow,
  For Nature assumes a more tropical form ;
Hailstones, with rain and the loud rolling thunder,
  Compel men and beasts to fly from the storm.

Thy valleys and uplands to me are so charming,
  I place them on par with the proud laird's domain ;
No cutting and carving, and long hedges planting,
  Confine thy wild beasts as they roam o'er the plain.

---

the belief of the Caffres in the world of spirits : ' The old chief, Mokatla, after an exciting public meeting, when it appeared that the town was in imminent danger of being broken, in consequence of his having taken his deceased nephew's wife, instead of giving her to the next brother, after the manner of the Jewish law, retired to the back part of his house, a loose and open building, where he was overheard by one of the pupils of the mission school. The old man, in great distress, stretched himself with his face earthward, and pulling his kaross over his head, bewailed his condition with loud lamentation, and at last, in an agony of soul, he cried to his departed elder brothers in the spirit land, as if there was but a thin partition between them : "Thou, Lebehuri ! Thou, Leuklileng ! don't be angry with me when the hour comes that I shall be with you where you are. I am not destroying the town. I have done everything to prevent it." He rose from the ground with a long and bitter wail that things were in such sad condition in his old days.' "

Long have thy beauties in gloom been enshrouded,
  The rough hand of Violence pressed hard on thy sons ;
Affrighted they fled to the land of the Cora,
  Their all left behind, save the spear and the shield.

Time after time the humble evangelist
  Has fled like the deer from the grim wolf and bear ;
Leaving the dust of his thin worn sandals,
  As witness for truth in the great judgment day.

Time, like a master in driving his chariot,
  Gives many a turn to the long rolling years ;
Now spans with fond hope the rainbow of promise,
  And tells the Morantsi to wipe off his tears.

Roll on, Mainaloe, thy smooth waters blending
  With the varied strains of the birds, beasts, and men ;
Yes, music thou hast, though to poets unknown,
  Thou hast lulled me and freed me from solitude's pain.

Why should my harp be so silent and drooping,
  As one bound with chains in a far foreign land ;
No ! let me strike a note far more in keeping
  With freedom of soul and peace in my mind.

Spirit of life, all gracious and faithful.
  Grant me thine aid while serving the Lord ;
Pour out thy blessing upon these dark nations.
  Till tongues are all vocal, eyes all heavenward.

CHAPTER VII.

MISSION LIFE IN SOUTH AFRICA.

The Cape Dutch—Spoliation of the Natives—Abolition of Slavery in 1834—Disgust of African Slaveholders—The "S' Mouses," or Travelling Merchants—Emigration of Boers from British Territory—Independence of the Boers recognized—The Dutch Republic—Hankering after Slavery—Mr. Inglis and the Dutch Boers—Presence of the Missionaries not relished—Remonstrance of Messrs. Edwards and Inglis against Child Enslavement—Summoned before the Valksraad, or Parliament—Trial for Treason—Official Correspondence—Expulsion of the Missionaries—Strange Conduct of the London Missionary Society—Supplementary Notes.

AS the conduct and policy of these redoubtable Dutchmen had a very important and permanent influence on the whole of Mr. Inglis' subsequent life, it may not be out of place to explain briefly how these Boers came to be where they were, and how they came to assume so hostile an attitude to missionaries and missionary work in those regions. The Cape Dutch, it is well known, though good colonists and profoundly zealous and devout Christians, were, from their first settlement in South Africa, possessed with the idea that, as the earth was the Lord's and the fulness thereof, and, as the Lord had given the inheritance of it to the saints, it was clear that they were entitled by Divine right and promise to enter into possession, seeing that it was a fact not to be seriously questioned that they were "saints." The result of this had been the oppression, enslavement, and spoliation of the natives, and the establishment of the superior and privileged race as lords paramount in the country.

The comparatively feeble races of the Cape region had been either destroyed or enslaved before the British took possession of the country, and the same process went on without let or hindrance during the arbitrary, irresponsible British *régime* of coming years. The conscience of the British people, however, was gradually being awakened on the whole subject of slavery, and, even in South Africa, the quickening throb of a better life was being more and more felt. The Rev. Dr. Philip bore the heat and burden of the day as the champion of the oppressed, and manfully and against formidable odds he battled for the right. The slave-holding feeling was strong. The Dutch farmer, who laughed at Moffat for suggesting the idea of calling together his Hottentots to hear the gospel, and shouted: "Preach to Hottentots! Call in my dogs, and preach to them! Go to the mountains, and preach to the baboons!" was but a type of his whole class. The Lord meant them, they thought, to be a ruling race, patriarchal and slave-holding, like Abraham, Isaac, and Jacob, and as such they would remain. The tide, however, was too strong for them, and the 1st of August, 1834, came in due time and set all their slaves free. The South African slaveholders were disgusted beyond all thought. They did not wish their share of the twenty millions compensation money. They wanted to retain their slaves. This they could not. The compensation money was in due time distributed in bills payable in London. This was done in kindness, for such bills were of more value than if payable in Cape Town. But the ignorant Dutch Boers did not know this, nor would they believe it. They were suspicious and gul-

lible. A class of travelling merchants, usually called
S'Mouses, who made a living by doing a business in
barter, completed the mischief. Cunning, selfish, and
false, these unscrupulous hucksters easily persuaded
the Boers that their bills were "no good," and would
never be cashed. The consequences could easily be
foreseen. The Boers were glad to sell these bills to
their friends, the pedlars, for ten per cent. of their
face value, and to take even that pay in goods, which
were not valued at too low a price. Of course the
S' Mouses got the cash in full; but, instead of feeling
that they had been cheated by their 'cute friends, the
Boers said that the pedlars were paid· because they
were English, but that they themselves would never
have got a farthing.

This embittered matters the more, and led to the
emigration of a large number of the Boers out of
British territory. It was thought that there they
might possess their slaves and their soil in peace.
The English, however, said: "No. You are our subjects, and must remain such, and wherever you go we
shall follow you." This resulted in the early Boer
wars, and the annexation of the country now known
as the Orange Sovereignty, with the regions beyond.

At last, in one of those turns of feeling, to which
the British are occasionally subject, the Boers were
treated with, and their independence recognized. A
promise was given to allow no trade with the natives
in powder and firearms, and almost the only condition
laid down was that the Boers should never enslave the
natives under any pretence whatever.

Things were in this state when Mr. Inglis settled

on the banks of the Mainaloe among the Baharutsi, and David Livingstone began work at Kolobeng. The Boers hankered after their old state of slave-holding, and paid little attention to their treaty obligations. They studied the Old Testament in their own way, and were especially interested in the Book of Joshua and his wars with the Canaanites. It was not difficult for them to transfer these things in a figure to themselves, and to believe that their special work was to follow up that of Joshua as the modern representatives of the Canaanites, whom they took to be the native tribes of Southern Africa.

For a good while Mr. Inglis was on very friendly terms with these Dutch magnates. They came and drank tea at his house, and passed many pleasant hours in social intercourse. They talked with him, discussed the prophecies, speculated on the Revelation, and were strong about Joshua and his feats of conquest. But upon the whole, the missionaries were rather an eye-sore to them. They had not all the freedom they desired so long as such persons were in the country. It was inconvenient to the Boers that there should be so near, men who were able to give testimony to the civilized world of what was going on in these remote regions—men who could be neither cajoled nor intimidated into silence. They could not well plunder and slaughter the natives as they wished. And yet they did a good deal of that sort of work. When one of their cattle happened to be stolen, it mattered not by whom, a raid was forthwith organized into the native country, with this result, that those who resisted were slaughtered, their oxen and cows

swept off, and the wives and children of those whom
they had killed, enslaved. Many instances of such
brutal conduct on the part of the Boers might be
given, gathered from the notes used in the preparation
of this volume. Had the natives been allowed to supply themselves with firearms, they would have made
short work with the Boers, good marksmen though the
latter were. But bound as they were, hand and foot,
they found that the tender mercies of these Dutchmen
were cruel.

It was into such a country, and amongst such a
people, that Mr. Inglis, in the providence of God, was
brought. None could appreciate the good qualities of
those sturdy farmers more fully than did our missionary, and they, on the other hand, were attached to the
frank and genial Scotchman, missionary and anti-
slavery man though he was. On one occasion, indeed, a
deputation of the Dutch Boers arrived to ask him to be
their minister, but prudently added that he would have
to be examined first, as they feared he was not sound
in the faith ! The Rev. Andrew Murray, son of one of
their own ministers, and spoken of as " The African
McCheyne," after such an examination, was pronounced " a limb of Antichrist." It should, however,
be said that many of the efforts of the missionaries
towards the conversion of the natives were not *per se*
looked upon by these Dutchmen with an evil eye. But
the Boers were before all and above all possessed with
the idea that they were a ruling race, and that the
natives, if suffered to live at all, were to be hewers of
wood and drawers of water to their lords and masters.
In pursuance of such a policy outrages every now and

then took place. The children of the Bechuanas were enslaved, under the euphonious title of "apprentices," and the grasp of the Burghers became ever firmer and more oppressive. The missionaries could not but raise their voices against such wrong-doing and such flagrant violations of treaties. Livingstone made himself especially obnoxious, and, as is well known, his house, which had stood safely and unmolested during his first travels, was at last sacked and destroyed by the indignant Dutchmen; his chemical apparatus broken, his dictionaries and other books burned, and intimation made that had he himself been present he would have been summarily lynched !

Messrs. Edwards and Inglis seem to have been more moderate in their opposition, and did not at first incur so much of the Dutchmen's hostility. Their work went on successfully. Mr. Inglis had at last secured what promised to be a permanent settlement, and the prospects of effecting the great ends of his mission were good. He had built a house, had laid out a considerable garden, and planted different kinds of fruit trees; and, in spite of all that the Boers were doing, had settled down energetically to his work. The natives were docile and interested. He had mastered the language, and could also use so much of the Dutch as to make himself understood by the Boers. His family was increasing, and he was coming to know something of the quiet and peace of a Christian home. In short, while there had been other difficulties and trials of a very unexpected kind, and from quarters that could never have been anticipated, these seemed to be passing away, and a career of great usefulness to

be opening up before him in the land of his choice.
The clouds, however, returned after the rain. The
Dutch Republic was by this time firmly established.
There was a President and Parliament or Volksraad,
and all the requisite appliances of law. The subjuga-
tion of the natives went steadily forward, with the
usual spoliation of their lands in the name of God, so
often witnessed when a weaker and stronger race have
come into contact. At last things came to such a pass
that Messrs. Edwards and Inglis felt it their duty to
interfere, so far as to send a humble petition and
remonstrance to the Volksraad, setting forth in very
mild and measured language the child-enslavement
that was going on, and reminding the Assembly that
such doings were quite contrary to the treaty with
Britain. This very mild and civil document was
received with the greatest indignation. The missionaries were called to account for their unwarrantable
proceedings, and for their offensive language. · In due
time they were summoned to Moui River that the
Volksraad might hear what statement they had to
make. The trial was an outrage on both law and
justice. The charge brought against them was high
treason against the might and majesty of the Republic,
and had they not been British subjects, in all likelihood
they would have been summarily shot or hanged.
When the missionaries arrived, Mr. Inglis was ordered
to walk outside, as they had decided to hear Mr.
Edwards first. They told him that hanging was too
good for him, and that he must leave with all haste
and never again be seen in their land. Mr. Inglis was
then called in, and asked if he was of the same mind

as his brother missionary. He replied : " Yes, I hate slavery." The same sentence of expulsion from the territory was then passed upon him, with the imposition of a heavy fine. It was also strictly provided that they should not be allowed to have any communication with the natives before going. Accordingly a Burgher guard was detailed to see them across the borders. Mr. Inglis was not allowed to touch a stick of his house, and he had the mortification of seeing a Boer preparing to take possession, as he was arranging to go away with his family and goods and chattels. The journey was a very exhausting one for many reasons. The Boer riflemen were exasperating in their insults, the heat was intense, and the water they had to drink muddy and filthy. As they travelled on, their anxiety and fear were increased by seeing the tops of a great many waggons in the distance. There was no alternative, however, but to go on and meet this commando, which was on its way to attack Moffat's Mission at Kuruman. Mr. Inglis' waggon was sent on in advance, and as the Boers approached, he said in Dutch, "Good day." The Boer did the same, and at the same time said : " Who are you ? " " I am a Scotchman," was the reply. "Where are you going ? " " Just to Moui River." In this same fashion the entire commando were saluted, until all had passed. The waggons were all loaded with guns and powder, so that the escape of the missionaries and their families was almost miraculous. The journey was then continued to the Moui River, where another examination of the two mission- aries was to take place; but before they arrived at the place of meeting, a black man met them with the

cheering news that the Governor at the Cape had sent
a letter to the Republic, ordering all further hostilities
against the missionaries to cease, and that if any more
of them were driven from their fields of labour he
would order up the English soldiers. This action,
however, was too late to be of any use to the expelled
missionaries, who were accompanied by the Boers to
the borders, treated as criminals, and then assured,
that if they ever attempted to set foot within the
territory of the Republic, a worse fate was in store for
them. Finally the missionaries arrived at Philippolis,
an old mission station, and after a short stay at the
Cape Mr. Inglis and his family sailed for London.

The following official correspondence, published
in the South African papers in Dutch and English,
when Messrs. Inglis and Edwards were expelled, will
enable the reader better to understand the temper of
the ruling powers, and the sufferings borne by the
missionaries :

CORRESPONDENCE OF COMDT. P. E. SCHOLTZ AND THE
MISSIONARIES EDWARDS AND INGLIS.

The missionaries had the testimony of numerous
eye-witnesses, that hundreds of Bakhatla and Bahu-
rutsi children, and many women, were captured ; and
while the commando remained at Mabotsa, even there
children were separated from their mothers — the
former " placed with keepers, and driven to the water
like goats to drink." Viewing these proceedings as
cruel and but slavery, they addressed the following
letter to the commandant, for the reason therein
given ; in doing which, they may or may not, as a
matter of opinion, have acted with sound judgment,
but were certainly not actuated by any hostile feelings

to the emigrant Boers, though strongly disapproving of their measures; but, at the same time, feeling keenly for parents and children thus separated, and most of them, if not all, for ever.

[TRANSLATION.]

Matebe, August 11, 1852.

To Mr. P. E. Scholtz, Commandant:

SIR,—Regarding the present war and the depriving the Kaffirs of guns and cattle, we do not presume to offer an opinion; and indeed we desire to abstain from touching on political matters. But there is one subject which causes us much pain, and regarding which we feel constrained by duty not to conceal our opinion; and this is, the capture of so many Kaffir children in war.

Of this we have nowhere else an example, except on the Western Coast of Africa, where children are caught for slaves. And even though such children as are caught by the commando will not be sent to foreign lands, we would beg to be permitted to remark without offence, as in honesty we are constrained to do, that the separation of children from their parents, and, above all, from their mothers, is unchristian, and contrary to God's law, which teaches us to do to others as we desire to be treated.

In our opinion, the treaty between the emigrants and the British Government has been violated by the capture of children in war, which will be regarded through Cape Colony, England, and Europe as nothing else than slavery. Many of said captive children will probably be taken away, and sold to other parties in distant places, where their parents may never see them more.

We are very well aware that the Kaffirs have as much affection for their children as the whites, and will much sooner part with their land, guns, cattle, or corn, than with their children.

These remarks, sir, are not prompted by ill will, or the smallest desire to give offence to any one, but by humane feeling. Being ourselves parents, we have taken the liberty to utter our feelings, in common with the emigrant clergymen, and hope you will not view the matter in an unfavourable light.

We beg to remain with respect,

Your obedient servants,

R. EDWARDS,
W. INGLIS.

In order to explain to the reader the first part of the commandant's letter, it may be remarked that Mr. Edwards had written to him respecting some of his cattle taken by the commando, and for the release of his herder's boy, and for Mrs. Edwards' two servant women, one of whom, he subsequently learnt, was not taken ; the other is still forcibly detained in the service of some Boer unknown to him.

Kliplager, 13th September, 1852.

To Messrs. W. Inglis and R. Edwards :

GENTLEMEN,—I have received your letters. Much trouble and occupation has hindered me from answering them. First of all, I perceive that Mr. Inglis makes a sort of complaint to our Government, as if he did not acknowledge me. We shall settle this point in due time. The second letter is from Mr. Edwards, regarding his cattle. I do not know that gentleman's cattle. Besides, he has had plenty of time to send for them. The third letter is from the same gentleman, about a little Kaffir. I have caused the ——* to look after said Kaffir, and have not been able to find him. The fourth is one signed by you both, regarding the little Kaffirs. The fifth, a letter from Mr. Edwards, in a newspaper of 19th May, 1852, which calls on another

---

* The translator has been unable to decipher this word.

Power,—a highly unbecoming thing. I therefore hereby summon you (to appear) before the Volksraad, on the first day of October, at Rustenburg, in Magaliesberg; to answer for the contents of your two, or more properly, three letters. I will receive nothing whatever, but shall contend with you before the Great Council.

P. E. Scholtz, Commandant.

Kliplager, 20th September, 1852.

To Messrs. W. Inglis and R. Edwards:

Gentlemen,—I beg herewith to inform you that I have requested Mr. A. W. J. Pretorius, Commandant General, to come hither as speedily as possible to take into consideration the state of the country; therefore you need not now appear at Rustenburg. I therefore desire that you will remain where you are for the present. When Mr. Pretorius arrives I shall apprise you of it; and then you will have an opportunity of appearing before him.

I remain with respect, etc.,

P. E. Scholtz, Commandant.

Kliplager, 18th October, 1852.

To Messrs. R. Edwards and W. Inglis, Missionaries:

Gentlemen,—You are hereby informed that I have been ordered by A. W. J. Pretorius, Esq., Commandant General, to signify to you in writing that you will be put on your defence for two letters written by you; the first a letter of Mr. Edwards' in the newspaper, and the second a letter signed by both of you. You are therefore both commanded by me, in pursuance of the order of General Pretorius, to appear at Rustenburg on the first Wednesday in November next, before the Court of Landdrost and Heemraden, to defend yourselves regarding the writings bearing your signatures. Be pleased to send a written answer, stating whether you are willing to appear.

I am yours, etc.,

P. E. SCHOLTZ, Commandant.

The missionaries arrived at Rustenburg on the 2nd of November; appeared at the Landdrost's office on the 3rd; but were not called up that day. Next morning they received the following note.

Landdrost's Office,

Rustenburg, 4th November, 1852.

GENTLEMEN,—You are hereby required not to quit the village before I shall have received a despatch from the Commandant-General.

I have the honour to be, gentlemen,

Your obedient, humble servant,

P. J. VAN STADEN, Landdrost.

The Rev. Messrs. Inglis and R. Edwards,

Rustenburg.

Early on the 8th, a verbal message from the Landdrost informed the missionaries that differences had arisen among the Boers in a certain quarter of the district, and that A. W. J. Pretorius would leave on the 10th to settle these disputes; consequently, the said missionaries were to remain at Rustenburg until the 20th. Immediately after this verbal communication the following paper, without date or signature, was put into their hands:

Order and Despatch of the Commandant-General to P. J. Van Staden, Esq., Landdrost, to detain the missionaries at the village of Rustenburg till the 20th inst., when they will have a hearing.

Landdrost's Office, November 20, 1852.

The missionaries Inglis and Edwards are hereby required to appear this day, as per above date, at one o'clock, precisely, to defend themselves for having written certain documents detrimental to the Free Republic; and Mr. Inglis to answer for the writing of a certain letter, conjointly subscribed by him and Mr. Edwards.

P. J. Van Staden, Landdrost.

Kliplager, November 25, 1852.

To Messrs. W. Inglis and R. Edwards.

I have to apprise you herewith of my arrival. I have been informed that you are offering your doors and windows for sale, but you will not be permitted to do so. Everything secured with wood and nail (fixtures) must remain undisturbed, according to all prevailing law. I therefore warn you to leave them. The copies of your sentences I have obtained and brought with me, which you can have on paying the charges, to which the Honourable Court have sentenced you—of which you have the bill—which you will have to pay next Monday, at Mr. Inglis'. You are likewise required to use all expedition in taking your departure within fourteen days, along the great highroad, by way of Moui River.

You are most distinctly charged to conduct yourselves inoffensively, and in no respect whatever to interfere with the coloured people.

I am, etc.,

P. E. Scholtz, Commandant.

Matebe, November 28, 1852.

Sir,—I have to inform you that I have considered your case. I told you to stay, but, on reconsideration, I now permit your departure, if you be ready.

I shall report the matter to General Pretorius, and his answer will find you at Moui River.

But let the doors and windows remain in the house; I have appointed a guard over them.

P. E. Scholtz, Commandant.

Mr. Edwards had the following sentence read to him :

The Honourable Court of Landdrost and Heemraden having taken the case of the missionary Edwards into mature consideration, and viewed it in all its bearings, has found R. Edwards guilty of high treason, according to the 9th Article of the existing law of the Territory, and has decided on condemning him to quit the Territory of this Republic within fourteen days from his arrival at his house ; and that as long as he continues within the limits of the Republic he must conduct himself orderly and peaceably. The above-mentioned Edwards is further, at the same time, sentenced to pay all expenses incurred in the case.

The sentence of the Court would, unquestionably, have been more severe, but, inasmuch as he committed the high treason before the negotiation with Her Majesty's Government was concluded, the Court has made this sentence as light as possible. R. Edwards is ordered, on his departure from hence, to travel by way of Moui River.

P. J. Van Staden, Landdrost.

J. S. Potgieter,
J. H. Robbertse,
G. J. B. Robbertse, ⎫
G. Van Rooyen,   ⎬ Heemraden.
C. Grobier,   ⎭
H. J. Stroh,

A true copy.

A. J. Wagner, Secretary,
    Rustenburg, 20th Nov., 1852.

Note.—Mr. E. will hereafter show, as he believes, that all he had stated in his letter respecting the Boers was more than confirmed by what he saw and heard at Rustenburg.

The expenses of the case, which Mr. E. was compelled to pay, amounted to ninety-five Rix Dollars, for which they gave a written receipt.

In the newspaper containing the foregoing correspondence there also appears this "Postscript":

THURSDAY (noon), 20th January, 1853.

Referring to our leading remarks on the narrative of Mr. Inglis, as to what took place on the occasion of his trial, we beg to remark that the treaty betwixt the Transvaal Boers and Assistant Commissioners expressly provided against slavery. Mr. Pretorius, according to Mr. Inglis' narrative, would seem to insinuate that verbally the Assistant Commissioners had given their sanction to this system, by approving of making the natives useful. We must repudiate such an idea. We should be glad to see the natives made useful to themselves. We do not, however, apprehend that slavery would accomplish this object. The habits which natives have acquired of squatting in the neighbourhood of villages, and in the midst of white men, refusing to work, is a subject deserving of attention and remedy.

Thus, apparently, were all Mr. Inglis' prospects overcast, and all his plans for usefulness at an end. He had come to Africa with the single simple desire of benefiting, to the best of his ability, the dark-skinned children of that benighted and long-cursed continent, and now the door was rudely and abruptly closed against him. He had wished to live and die there, but this, his most ardent and disinterested heart's wish, was not to be gratified. He had to wait and see what the future would bring forth. Sad to say, it brought nothing, in the way of justice being rendered,

or compensation given for the losses and indignities
which he and his companion, Mr. Edwards, had sustained. The policy of the directors of the London
Missionary Society was in the circumstances, it is to
be feared, anything but vigorous and decided. There
ought to have been plenty of work in the colony for
the expelled missionaries; or spheres of usefulness in
other heathen lands might surely have been found for
them. Nothing of the kind, however, was proposed,
and so Mr. Inglis returned to Britain. He was em-
ployed by the society for some time in addressing
missionary meetings in different parts of England,
and then his connection with the London Missionary
Society ceased, with no charge made against him, but
on the contrary, a cordial certificate at parting. The
other expelled missionary, Mr. Edwards, was also
allowed to seek a new sphere of labour, and spent his
declining years ministering to a small congregation at
Port Elizabeth, near Algoa Bay.

In closing this account of Mr. Inglis' missionary
experiences in Africa, the question will naturally arise
in the minds of many readers: Why did not the
London Missionary Society, in some way, exert its
influence on behalf of such able and self-denying
missionaries, as it was conceded on all hands Messrs.
Inglis and Edwards were? No missionary society at
the present day, we are safe in asserting, would suffer
their representatives to be so treated. The Christian
world, irrespective of denominational differences, would
manifest such righteous indignation, that reparation
would be made, and effective measures taken to crush
such high-handed and brutal measures as were used

towards these men. If beyond the direct reach of the London Missionary Society, the Government of Great Britain, on being appealed to, could and would most effectively have taught the Dutch Boers a lesson of tolerance never to be forgotten. A nation that had paid such a price to ransom men and women from thraldom could not afford to keep silent if approached on behalf of the enslaved, and, at the same time, would have demanded for its missionaries the rights of free men—not to speak of Christian missionaries. Why, then, did the London Missionary Society pursue a policy that at this date seems cowardly and unfair to those noble men, who had risked their lives and their all in her service ?

The principal actors in African missions embraced in that period, Moffat, Livingstone, Inglis, and Edwards, have all gone to their reward. Robert Moffat and David Livingstone have had their labours eulogized, and their memory perpetuated. The friends and admirers of Walter Inglis, who knew him before his African experience, and the many more who loved him after his return in Canada, do not begrudge the honours paid those veterans. But surely, none the less ought the Christian world to hold in grateful remembrance men who were driven from the field, but who, had they been permitted to continue, would, in so far as man can judge, have equalled in zeal and daring their more illustrious compeers.

It ought no longer to be a secret that Walter Inglis did not receive fair treatment at the hands of the London Missionary Society. Before that he was finally compelled to leave his much-loved Africa, difficulties and disputations had arisen in connection with a scandal within the missionary circle, which Mr. Inglis and Mr. Edwards insisted upon having thoroughly investigated. Other influences, however, prevailed, so that the investigation demanded was never entered upon, although the Directors of the London Missionary Society assured Mr. Inglis that they had the fullest confidence in the representations which he and his co-missionary had made. They feared, however, that the investigation demanded might do more harm than good! This fact, probably, may have made these Directors less sorry to take advantage of the expulsion of Messrs. Inglis and Edwards by the Boers, as these missionaries had insisted that all connected in any way with African missions should be above suspicion, and have their guilt or innocence made conspicuously manifest to all concerned.

In the appendix will be found a lecture, or rather part of a lecture, by Mr. Inglis on "David Livingstone." Accompanying the MS. (sent for perusal to the Rev. Peter Wright of Ingersoll) was the following letter, which, in justice to the subject of these memoirs, we print just as it was written; the date is November 28, 1883:

I never have had the gift of dates; but you may take two or three as approximately correct. Livingstone joined the London Missionary Society in 1838. He and I went to study under the inspection of the Rev. Mr. Cecil at Ongar. My health gave way early in 1839. Livingstone went on with his studies there, and also prosecuted medical studies in London. Moffat came home, and became mightily popular. Livingstone went to Africa in 1840. I parted with him in

Glasgow, where I was studying. Our last words were, as I parted with him a mile out of Glasgow, on his way home to Blantyre: "Now, Inglis, be sure and join me in Africa." I answered: "If possible." Moffat went on with his work of printing the Bechuana Testament, Bibles, selections for the schools, hymn books, etc., and blazing through England and Scotland, thrilling the people with his story. He put through the press his book, "Twenty-three Years' Missionary Life among the Bechuanas." A Mr. Ross went with Livingstone. Two old missionaries were in charge at the Kuruman—old Mr. Hamilton and Mr. Edwards; Livingstone and Ross got a welcome from them. Mr. Hamilton was a simple, good man, but never learned the Bechuana language. Mr. Edwards' name ·is not mentioned, because of bad feeling towards him on the part of Moffat and afterwards of Livingstone.* Neither Moffat nor Livingstone could bear a yoke-fellow. They were created with ambition to work alone.

I was appointed to Moffat's mission in the beginning of 1842, or some time in 1841. Moffat could not get through with his work till the end of 1842. Early in 1843 we left England. Other two young men went with us—Messrs. Gill and Ashton—who, with myself, accompanied Moffat and his family.

I am sorry to say that Livingstone's account of his early mission life is very garbled. Two or three things are stated out of all proportion. The fact is that his life as a missionary has never been written. Neither you nor anybody else can tell his life-history for ten years. He only gives an account of his chief Sechele—an able man, but a poor Christian. I am not sure but that he was the only heathen that Livingstone ever baptized. He fell from his profession of Christianity shortly after his baptism. Having nothing else to say, Livingstone was strongly tempted to

---

* This was written before the publication of Mr. Moffat's Memoirs by his son.

say something, as people were not at hand to contra-
dict. If any of us had done so, it would have been
called the jealousy of small men. I do not know of
one case of conversion by Dr. Livingstone. God had
other work for him to do.

He adds in closing:

These lectures and harangues are not for me now.
The points I raise are unvarnished truth. I am sorry to
say, in my old days, that there is a large amount of
garbled dishonesty in missionary reports. Directors
treat missionaries as you would a body of policemen,
nor is there much noble-mindedness in the missionary
band.

NOTES.—While these pages are being prepared for
the press, the following, copied from one of the religious
weeklies, indicates how unsatisfactory the condition of
affairs in South Africa still is, notwithstanding the
many lessons taught the British Government by repeated aggressions on the part of the Dutch Boers:

News from South Africa is not of a cheerful sort.
The Boers, it is said, have annexed fully five-sixths of
Zululand, Natal is up in arms, and the Colonial Council
is in conflict with the British Commission. Apparently it is the old trouble over again, the Boers siding
with one native chief against another, with the ultimate object of seizing the lands of the beaten party,
and with some excuse for their aggressions. The
British policy in Zululand since the death of Cetewayo
has been anything but heroic. It will be remembered
that the close of the unjust war of 1879 left the Zulus,
always a warlike nation, at the mercy of the Boers,
and that their conquerors, so far from protecting them
by the establishment of a good government, still further
weakened them by dividing the country between
thirteen petty and irresponsible chiefs. They did,
however, by the convention of Pretoria, clearly define

the boundary between Transvaal and Zululand, and assumed responsibility for the protection of the natives beyond the Dutch frontier by the retention of suzerainty. At the same time they increased the dissatisfaction of the Zulus by giving the Boers the territory which had originally been in dispute between them and Cetewayo, and encouraged the Boers in the belief that a repetition of their aggressions would lead, as usual, to a further acquisition of territory. The result, of course, was inevitable, and the ink of the settlement was scarcely dry before there was fighting all over the country. In 1884, however, a new convention was made with the Boers, the main provisions of which exacted from the latter a pledge to respect the integrity of Zululand, Bechuanaland, and Swazieland. But the results were as barren as in the former instance, the Boers invading Zululand, and blood flowing more freely than ever. Dinizulu was made king in defiance of the rights of the British Government, by which no Zulu king could be appointed except by native custom and subject to England's approval; and, to crown all, Usibepu, a chief in Northern Zululand, who accepted the position on pledges given by England, was killed, and a new Boer republic established in his territory. The few thousand British troops stationed in the country did nothing to preserve the peace, their presence being neither a profit to the Zulus nor a hindrance to the Boers, and the petty and perpetual wars which followed seriously threatened British supremacy. In 1885, however, an expedition under Sir Charles Warren was sent to the Cape, the Transvaal Government withdrew its pretensions to the territory, and disclaimed responsibility for the filibusters, and the native chiefs ousted by the Boers were returned to the positions they occupied under the convention. Unfortunately no protectorate was established over Zululand, and with the withdrawal of General Warren, and attacks of quarrelling tribes upon the Boer allies, the Boers have again taken advantage of the circumstances to extend their boundaries. What England will now do in the premises remains to be seen, though the announcement that Western Zululand will form a new republic and Eastern Zululand be reserved for the Zulus under a British protectorate may doubtless be accepted as correct. Hitherto, instead of placing the whole territory under the direct authority of the British Crown, English policy has been to regard South Africa as a mere appanage of the Cape, under its control and subject to the ever-changing caprice of its party politicians. The result has been continual difficulty with the lesser dependencies, whose interests are at variance with those of the Cape, and that all action has been more or less biassed by what may be called the Dutch view of South African affairs. The Dutch form so very important an element in Cape Colony and in the Cape Parliament that no governor residing there and looking at affairs from the colony point of view can be expected to administer all the dependencies impartially. Only when a viceroy is appointed for all the British South African possessions, and the Cape relegated to its proper position as a self-governing settlement on the borders of a South African empire, will such questions as the annexation of Zululand be satisfactorily solved.

The following sketch from the Transvaal, copied from the *Christian Leader* of Glasgow, Scotland, gives some idea of the religious life of the Dutch Boers at the present time. Says the writer:

Taken all in all the Boers of the Transvaal are a very simple people, although of late they are beginning to understand how many beans it takes to make five. In the matter of education they are very far behind the times. The only chance a young Boer gets is while he is qualifying for church membership; and even then his opportunities only extend to an indifferent knowledge of the " vrag-boek," or Shorter Catechism of the Dutch Church, and his being able to read the Bible. Their church is the most venerated of all institutions, and its clergymen are literally worshipped. The quarterly fast-day, or " Nachtmaal," as it is called, is a regular red-letter day; and, if you would see our Boers to best advantage, descend upon one of our towns on a " Nachtmaal Sunday." Then you have a sight worth seeing. Rows upon rows of waggons, with their beautiful snow-white tents, cover the whole extent of our " kerk-plein." For a time, at least, we have more than tripled our population, and still they come pouring in amain from north, south, east, and west. Great teams of sixteen or eighteen bullocks come trundling along with their heavily laden waggons. Every ox knows his name, and, as their swarthy Jehu cracks his twenty feet of thong and " vorslag," and yells out at the fullest pitch of his stentorian voice, " Trek Swartland!" "Yek Maakman!" forward goes the whole span in one body, and soon the waggon is drawn into position alongside of its neighbours. The oxen are then out-spanned or unyoked, forthwith a wood fire is kindled, and the ubiquitous cup of coffee prepared. Later on we hear the incessant hum of juvenile voices rehearsing their lessons with marked avidity, and here and there wells out from beneath the canopy of canvas the melodious strains of female voices pouring forth one of those old Dutch tunes— tunes sung to about the same time as " Old Hundred," when rendered by a company of north country fisherwomen, nor wanting either in the fancy twirls and home-made variations peculiar to the music of that particular class. Anon the silvery tinkle of the church bell is heard, and the inhabitants of our city of canvas slowly begin to wend their way in the direction of the sacred edifice. There is the solid " diakon "—a pillar of the church—with his suit of black cloth and the old-fashioned white choker of our own country; and there, alongside of him, is his worthy "vrouw," with her unadorned dress of black alpaca and "cappie" of the same material. If you have ever seen an elderly Quaker couple of the old school going up to the house of prayer you have an exact picture of our well-to-do Boer as he appears on sacrament Sunday. After the aged couple follow the younger members of the family, each bearing a chair or stool in one hand and a Bible in the other. The country churches have, as a rule, no pews, and each adherent provides his own sitting accommodation. Look at the young people! What a contrast they present to the pair we have just described. Theirs is certainly a livelier taste in the matter of dress. Bright yellow corduroy trousers, a black cloth jacket, a turkey-red handkerchief, a green necktie, a drab soft-felt hat, with a rim about six inches wide, and surmounted by a scarlet puggaree, complete the costume of the younger men; while the opposite sex indulge in a show of colour equally ridiculous. The service is begun in the usual manner, by the singing of a psalm; but music and harmony are sadly neglected, and the finer perceptions give way to lung power. The form of church government, as well as the conduct of services, is an exact counterpart of the Scotch Presbyterian style. The various diets of worship are long and tedious, but during their progress many members have been added to the congregation. After the sacrament has been observed, and while the sun is sinking beneath the horizon, the people gather together in little knots around their camp-fires. All topics of general interest are discussed, and they chat away to their hearts' content until Luna arises and sheds her silvery light over the scene. How strikingly suggestive of the days of the patriarchs, when the people "dwelt in tents!" But now, amid a sound of rattling trek-chains, the bump of yokes, interspersed with the busy hum of voices and the striking of tents, the last cup of coffee is partaken of; anon the "thwack" clack of the dusky driver's whip reminds you that Nachtmaal is over, and the gay and festive Boer is homeward-bound. Without judging too harshly, I think there is much less genuine Christian feeling amongst the Boers than people are often willing to give them credit for. Outward appearances prove nothing; and their church-going proclivities are the outcome of use and wont; a Nachtmaal is a pleasant break in the monotony of their existence. I admit that in the case of the young people the main object is confirmation, for after that ordeal is passed they can perpetrate matrimony whenever the spirit listeth. Until a young Boer is married he is nobody. Early marriages are the order of the day, and you very seldom find a young lady unmarried at twenty, or a young man in the enjoyment of single blessedness at twenty-three.

CHAPTER VIII.

RETURN FROM AFRICA, AND APPOINTMENT TO CANADA.

Visit to Berwick—Reception into U. P. Church—Appointed to Canada—
Cordial Welcome—Riversdale, Kincardine, and Pine River—Hard-
ships of Home Missionary Life—Letters to his Sister and Brother—
Death of his Mother—Reminiscences by Rev. Robert Hamilton,
and Rev. Dr. Waters—Resignation of Charge—The Preachers'
List—Elected to Ayr.

THE return of Mr. Inglis to Britain, and his subsequent
removal to Canada, cannot be better introduced than
in the language of Dr. Cairns : "After an interval of
some eight or nine years from the time that I had begun
to labour in the Berwick Congregation, my old friend
came rather suddenly, having had to leave Africa because
of internal troubles and difficulties. He took me on his
way northward from the port at which he had landed.
Though I had some vague expectation of his arrival,
considerable excitement attended it, especially as his
whole family came with him, increased by an interesting young Frenchman, M. Roland, who had been connected with the mission to the Baharutsi which Mr.
Inglis had conducted. It was a work of some time to get
the entire party disposed of, but kind friends willingly
helped. The visit of the returned African missionary
excited great interest. As he had interrupted my
studies in the end of the week, he naturally took one
of the services on the Lord's Day, and I do not think
that I ever heard him to more advantage. His English had not improved, but there was a great command
of vivid and picturesque speech, with glowing zeal—

notwithstanding something of disappointment in the
interruption of his work—and a statesmanlike grasp
of all the relations of missions to the problems that
have so long continued to cause colonial trouble. One
thought which he brought out, either in preaching or
in conversation, was this : That it was hardly fair to
claim for our missions that they were the one all-heal-
ing force amidst a community otherwise agitated both
by intestine discussion and the encroachments of a
foreign power. No doubt this was so, taking the matter in the long run, and when Christianity had had
time to settle as well as to agitate the population.
But he thought that we too much overlooked the un-
settling influence of Christianity on a people to the
whole of whose social system it was a challenge, and
which it must displace in order itself to succeed. Hence
he regarded the missionaries as harshly treated when
blamed because, through their growing influence, social
difficulties became acute and embarrassing ; and he
claimed for their position a sympathy which it has not
yet found. In such discussions, and in recalling the
memories of other days, and in roaming with his
family by the river and the sea, amidst scenes which
so contrasted with their African experiences, the time
swiftly passed away ; and he went northward to meet
his still nearer circle, and to ponder what might be the
yet uncertain future."

When his connection with the London Missionary
Society came to a close, Mr. Inglis applied to be
received into the United Presbyterian Church of Scotland, the Church of his boyhood and early years,
although the union of the Secession and Relief

Churches was not consummated under the above name until 1847. He was most cordially welcomed, and recognized at once as a minister in full standing. In the early spring of 1855, at his own request, he came to Canada, where, until his death in 1884, he made full proof of his ministry,—leading, at first, a toilsome, laborious, and self-denying life, as one of the pioneer preachers of the gospel in a comparatively poor and sparsely-settled district, and finally in Ayr, where, among a beloved people and attached co-Presbyters, he finished his earthly course.

The now United Presbyterian Church of Scotland had sent its first missionaries to Canada in 1832, so that when Mr. Inglis arrived, the most of the earlier missionaries were settled in the field and in the full vigour of their ministry. It was to him a great pleasure and encouragement to meet with not a few of them, whose names will long continue to be household words in Canadian homes. Wherever he went he made friends, and whether in the manse or the shanty he was, from the first, made cordially welcome. His preaching, to which reference is made elsewhere and at greater length, was not of the usual description. He was original in his thinking, and as original in his illustrations. Many of his remarks had a quaintness which rendered them specially attractive to a certain class of minds; while his genuine simplicity and unaffected piety secured for him, in private, a very large amount of reverence and real affection. Very soon after coming to Canada he received calls to Westminster, and Chatham, and other places, but for one reason or another he declined settlement until 1857, when he was inducted into the charge of Riversdale, in the County of Bruce. This was an entirely new and somewhat difficult field, and the work was laborious and trying. His journeyings were long and toilsome, and mostly on foot. His family, for a time, found a very humble home in Kincardine, which was then but a very small village. Afterwards, he purchased fifty acres of land in Riversdale, and had the shanty that was on it so repaired as to enable him and the family to live in it. During his ministry here, hard work and not a few privations made him feel that it was not only in Africa, or among savages, that the messenger of the gospel has to endure hardness as a good soldier of Jesus Christ. The treatment he received in Bruce was cruel and unchristian, and the utter neglect, in those days, of the strong in the Church helping the weak was something more than saddening. It is true the people were poor and struggling, but that was the least of it. Mammon-worship had, apparently, eaten out of many hearts any love of Christ that ever had existed, and all regard for common honesty as between man and man. On one occasion, stung to the quick by the ungenerous conduct of certain ones, of whom better things were expected, he delivered himself after this fashion : "If you say you are heathens, I shall willingly preach to you for nothing. I did so for ten years to the heathen of South Africa, and I shall do the same for you. But if you claim to be Christians, I won't!" In spite of all this, Mr. Inglis never once abated his energy and efforts. In rain and sunshine, in summer and winter, in cold and heat, he was at his post, after the example of the Apostle Paul, who, in writing to the

Corinthians, says: "I will véry gladly spend and be spent for you : though the more abundantly I love you, the less I be loved." This, his first charge in Canada after returning from Africa, was altogether a most un-genial soil, with little sympathy and little or no out-side help. The record of that ministry is with God. Perhaps the less said about it the better. Of one thing we are assured,—it was not in vain that he laboured there, amid manifold discouragements and trials that would have crushed a less courageous soul. "They that sow in tears shall reap in joy. He that goeth forth and weepeth, bearing precious seed, shall doubtless come again with rejoicing, bringing his sheaves with him."

After some years spent in Riversdale he was called to the charge of the United Presbyterian Congregation in Kincardine, and on his acceptance, he removed with his family to what is now the flourishing town on the shores of Lake Huron. Here he was more comfort-able, although the record of these years of pinching and anxious economy is humiliating enough.

The fragmentary correspondence of this period that has been preserved contains no word of complaint, but the grimness and hardships of his lot can easily be read between the lines. One or two extracts from Kincardine letters are all that can be given.

On the 30th of April, 1862, he writes to his sister and brother-in-law in Scotland, as follows :

We received your welcome letter in due time. Glad to hear that venerable mother was so well. The end cannot be far off now. My yearning heart turns to the dear old woman. She has been my earthly pole-star. But for her, God only knows what the up-shot of life would have been with me in youth. If she still can hear and understand, give her my abiding love. If I had the money I should come home this summer to see her, but that cannot be.

Of his two preaching stations, Kincardine and Pine River, he says :

Plenty of work for me at both, if they could keep me living. I am glad I am done with the schools. I walked last year between six and seven hundred miles to visit thirty-six schools in four townships. This and a good deal of mental annoyance, and taking my mind more than half away from the work of the ministry, for the paltry sum of £45 !

Some months later, writing to his brother at Brothershiels, he says :

Well, dear old mother still holds on. We have been preparing our minds to hear by any post that she rests. Verily her soul is tried to the uttermost in her frail tabernacle. Again, kind love to the dear old woman.

In 1863 Mr. Inglis was called upon to mourn the removal of that "dear old mother," who had con-tributed in so many ways, and to such a large extent, to form his character and to determine in its essential features the whole course of his life and work. To her he had ever turned for sympathy, encouragement, and advice. Towards her, in all her lowly simplicity, he had ever been as a little child. To its full extent he had learned to say and to feel the beauty of the sentiment : "As one whom his mother comforteth." She held him with her hand and with her eye. Poor old weary one, she could do little for him in his varied and often

troublesome and depressing work, whether in Africa or
Canada, but she could after all do much, when from
her lone house among the hills she sent him words of
lofty cheer and tender sympathy, told him to be strong
in the Lord his God, and as often aforetime breathed
over him the prayer : " The Lord bless you, my son ;
the Lord cause his face to shine upon you, and comfort you in all your adversities, and enable you to do
great things for the glory of your Most High God and
for the good of His people."

She had during life her own cares and sorrows,
and these were neither few nor light. Paralysis had
laid its hand upon her as far back as 1849, and the
tottering step, the powerless hand and the faltering
tongue, henceforward told of its presence and power.
But her faith continued strong, and the God whom
she had known and loved and served from· early
maidenhood was with her in her hours of age and
weakness, as a very present help and comforter. In
1851 she had to mourn the sudden removal of her
oldest son, who had taken the father's place, and had
well fulfilled the blessed task he had assigned himself,
though it may be he had never repeated—perhaps he
had never known—the poet's words :

> Me let the pleasing office long engage,
> To rock the cradle of declining age,
> Explore each want, explain the asking eye,
> And keep awhile one parent from the sky.

It was pitiable enough to see the old tottering,
tearless one, wandering through her lonely home,
wringing her poor old hands, and crying sadly and
brokenly: " Oh, Absalom ! my son ! my son ! would

God I had died for thee, my son!" The physical side
of her nature was still more sadly shattered by the
death of this son. When her sister came to comfort
her, and remarked on seeing her utter desolation, "Oh
Nanny, Nanny, I never saw you this way in all your
other troubles," she replied: "May be no, but you never
saw my body as weak as it is now." But other com-
forters and protectors were raised up, and another son,
her youngest, with her youngest daughter and her
daughter-in-law, nursed her and cared for her till she
passed away, and her worn-out body

> Fan' a rest—
> The lownest and the best,
> I' the auld kirkyaird,
> Whan a' was dune.

She had a strong desire to be laid beside her husband, and so it was ordered; for when her son William used to talk of going to Canada, long before he
came, and of taking her with him, she would give a
quiet smile and say: "I wadna' mind, but there's a
wee bit grund beside your father, in Heriot Kirkyaird,
that I couldna' leave vacant." For many years she
had not been able to correspond directly with her
Canadian children, but messages of love and hope
passed and re-passed between them, and her now old
missionary boy continued to send greetings "to his
dear and ever honoured mother," as in his days of
early struggle, of student toil, and of African hardness
and harassment. One strong tie to earth was broken
when that tremulous old life went out; but the other
side became all the more attractive, and the wondrous
meeting time was the more thought of, and the more

eagerly anticipated. The past came often back with exceeding vividness and power. The old days, the old farm, the old home, and the old mother, had always had special attractions for him, but as the years passed on, after his mother's death, these attractions seemed always to gather increasing force. She, being dead, yet spoke to his heart, and continued to be a presence and a blessing to him all his days.

In 1864 he speaks still of mercy. No murmurs are heard, though the hard scratching to make ends meet is evident. His income from all sources at this time he chronicles at $380. Yet he says: "We manage to live. The fact is, we are all very simple in our diet. Keeping no servant, we just dress when a dollar can be got for it."

We are indebted to the Rev. Robert Hamilton, of Motherwell, for the following interesting details of this period of his life. Mr. Hamilton says:

It was in February, 1858, when fulfilling an appointment at Kincardine, I was induced to make a visit to Mr. Inglis. When I reached Riversdale about sunset, I saw a man in front of a shanty vigorously splitting firewood. Approaching him, I introduced myself as one bearing a message from an acquaintance of his. He gave me a cordial welcome to his modest log shanty, consisting of three compartments, separated by rough boards. He said: "This is the minister's manse, and you are very welcome to its shelter and hospitality for the night." At once I felt at home in the midst of his family. The hours before retiring to rest were occupied by relating some of his experiences during his past eventful life in Africa, by which indication was given that his heart was still in that land from which he had been driven by the

tyranny of those in power. The hardships which
he had undergone since coming to Canada had not
done much to efface his love for the Kaffir race, nor
to raise his estimate of the white *niggards* of this
land of individualism, where, as he said, "every man
was as good as his neighbour, and a great deal better,
faith." Some who professed to belong to his congregation had erected his shanty, and charged him nearly
three times more than the salary they had given him
for a year. Even the candles used in its erection
were included in the account.

The next morning he said : "We have preparatory
services to-day in a schoolhouse away in the woods;
you will go with me and preach." When we reached
the place, where a few people were assembled, he
opened the services by introducing the preacher in a
very cordial and characteristic manner, and at the
close expressed his thanks for the new light which
had been shed on Psalm cxxxiii.

When about to return to Kincardine, he requested
me to preach in a tavern by the way. When I
reached the place I found that notice had been sent
before me and arrangements made. The owner of the
tavern gave me a cordial welcome for the sake of Mr.
Inglis, who had frequently preached there. The bar-
counter formed the pulpit-desk, and the bar and other
rooms were occupied by the audience. We understand
that audience formed the nucleus of the Bervie congregation, who soon found for themselves a better place
of worship.

In about two months later, while on my way to
fulfil appointments, I found Mr. Inglis in a house
where he had met with the people in order to organize
a congregation, which since has been called North
Brant. He again pressed me into service, and at the
close organized the congregation without any weari-
some attention to technical forms.

Some years after, when his pastorate was in

Kincardine, I had the privilege, along with the Rev. John McTavish, of assisting at the communion service, and enjoying his company and racy conversation regarding theological questions, on which he had thought for himself. He refused to be confined by the conventional lines within which many theological students are kept. His thoughts on theological subjects were fresh and sometimes so erratic that he often walked by the border-lines of truth and error; but his love to Christ and reverence for the Word of God kept him from stepping over to the side of the speculative sceptic. Some time after he assisted me at communion services, when I enjoyed his elliptical style of presenting truth both in public preaching and in private conversation. It could not be said of him, as of another preacher, that " his sermons lacked rough edges." The sermons of Mr. Inglis had many hooks which laid hold of the memories of his hearers. Having recently come into the possession of the sermons of Dr. Addison Alexander, I called his attention to them, and read an extract. He was so taken with the extract that he requested me to read the whole sermon, then another and another. While I read he frequently gave expression to his wonder at the simplicity with which this man of learning presented the truth. On one occasion, being absent in search of health, Mr. Inglis kindly volunteered to supply service for a day. But between the giving of the promise and the arrival of that day, death had suddenly called away his only son. Though it was the first Sabbath after the funeral, he did not make his own trial an excuse for not fulfilling his promise, but came as from the edge of the grave ; and, feeling keenly the pressure of sorrow, he came and so preached that many of our people will carry the impression of his words so long as memory holds its throne.

The Rev. Dr. Waters, of Newark, N. J., who was pastor in Southampton during Mr. Inglis' residence

in Kincardine, has also supplied us with reminiscences
of that period. He says:

In attempting to give you my recollections of our
friend, the Rev. Walter Inglis, I can only give the
impressions I formed and the recollections I retain in
my memory of a man whom I learned to love and
admire. The memoranda of my early ministerial life
disappeared, where so much else did, in the smoke
and flame of the great fire at St. John, N. B.; so that
in writing of the period of my acquaintance with Mr.
Inglis I must trust entirely to memory.

I became acquainted with him some time in the
summer of 1861, shortly after my settlement as pastor
of the united congregation of Southampton and
Dunblane. At that time he was pastor of what,
previous to the union with the Free Church, had
been the United Presbyterian Church of Kincardine.
Having been educated in the United Presbyterian
Church myself, I was, perhaps, drawn more closely
to him on that account. At that time the lines of
division between the two sections of the United
Church in the Counties of Grey and Bruce were not
entirely obliterated, and some of the brethren, seem-
ingly, had not full confidence in the power of that
newly-effected union which was destined to work so
mightily for the advancement of the Redeemer's
kingdom. Consequently the few representatives of
the old U. P. Church in that region were drawn very
closely together in church work.

Mr. Inglis occasionally assisted me in my communion services, greatly to the delight and edification
of my people. To hear him was a rich intellectual
treat—evangelical, Scriptural, fervid, thoroughly unconventional, often rising into sublime bursts of genuine
eloquence, now melting into tears by the tenderness of
his pathos, sometimes provoking a smile by the quaintness, originality, and humour of some of his illustrations, his hearers were hurried along until he reached

the close, when tears were quietly wiped from some eyes little used to the melting mood. I think I can see and hear one of my elders, a godly man and genuine Scotchman, at the close of one of these services taking out his silver-mounted mull, giving the cover a gentle tap, and then, after having refreshed himself with a goodly pinch of its contents, exclaiming: "Oh, man! but that was jest graun." So it was. It was just grand, as my good old friend said, and he was a good judge of what constituted a good sermon.

Whenever Mr. Inglis appeared on the platform he was welcomed with delight. His sharp, pointed, original, incisive style cut right into the heart of the follies which he delighted to expose and scarify. While he wielded the moral scalpel with a firm hand, he delighted to light up and enliven his platform talks with such flashes of wit and humour as often sent his audience off into convulsions of laughter. But it was all pure, sweet, refreshing, and healthful. No man or woman, boy or girl ever rose from listening to Walter Inglis with a bitter taste in the mouth.

I frequently met him on the old County Board of Education for the County of Bruce. Together with our ministerial duties we also discharged the duties of local superintendent. The duties pertaining to that office he discharged with eminent fidelity and success. At the meetings of the Board we enjoyed ourselves after our own fashion. Some of the good men who were members were—well, not to put too fine a point on it, not profoundly versed in the higher mathematics, nor, for the matter of that, in the niceties of English Grammar, even as taught by Lennie. Perhaps some of the younger members did get a little quiet enjoyment in seeing some of the good men labouring over an examination paper, which was to them an unknown quantity. The most interesting part of that work to Mr. Inglis, apart from the mere routine of preparing and examining examination papers, consisted in the interest which he took in the young men and women who came up for examination. His sympathy went out to all genuine natures. I well remember one day a young man handed in his testimonial as to character, and took his seat with the other candidates who were applying for teachers' certificates. Some of them had already been teaching, and, on account of their experience, held themselves a little higher than those who were making their first attempt at gaining a position in a profession which has so often proved to be a stepping-stone to something else. This young man—he was young, about seventeen or eighteen—took his place without any of the small airs of superiority to which we had become accustomed, or any pretence of any kind. When he received his papers he set to work as if he had taken a contract to clear a ten-acre field, and intended to do it thoroughly. Some of the men, who had already been in the work, glanced at him with an expression on their faces which said plainly enough, "You will not do much, anyway." Mr. Inglis saw him, and, knowing something of his history, came to my desk, and said : "Do you see that young fellow over there with the fair hair and ruddy complexion. I think there is something in him. Will you try and see that he gets fair play?" I had already come to the conclusion "that there was something in him," for, when his paper on Geometry was handed in, I found that he had swept it clean. Very much to the surprise of all the others he came out at the head of the list of the first-class men. Mr. Inglis was as proud of the feat of that young man from the country as if he had been his own son. That young man is now one of the best known press men in Canada, and that was his first step in his march to the University and the position which he now holds.

In private life Mr. I. was one of the most genial men. Our children were delighted when he visited Southampton. He had a never-failing fund of story and anecdote, with which he chained their attention; and told them tales of the far-distant African land, in which he had toiled—of the lion and his roar, which he could imitate to perfection, of the giraffe and the elephant, of the black fellows and their ways. The arrival of Walter Inglis was to them a most delightful holiday. In nothing was he greater than in his sympathy with the young. When in their company, he was as young as they were, as full of life and the freshness of youth as only a pure, healthful nature can be.

During the time of his residence in the County of Bruce, his life was one of labour and self-denial. The country was new, the people were struggling to better themselves, and, perhaps, did not appreciate as they ought the great ability of the manly, godly man, who was serving them for the Master's sake.

As I review the early years of my ministry, I well remember that I looked upon Walter Inglis as one of the best and most original men I knew: A wider knowledge and increased experience have only served to confirm the opinion which I then formed. He was thoroughly original, cast in the mould of no other, imitating no man, and calling no man master, save the Master whom he delighted to serve.

If there was one thing more than another which helped him to bear the hardships incident to the life of a minister in a new and comparatively poor country, next to the strength which God gave, it was his happy home surroundings. That home was the model of a Christian minister's household. Piety without gloom, happiness without folly—lives consecrated to the Master's service, and, therefore, willing to bear much, that the kingdom of heaven might be advanced upon earth.

In trying to recall the past, I think I see before me the strong, stalwart, tender-hearted man—the man who hated shams, but who was as tender as a woman to the weak and helpless. I sometimes think that, had it not been for the humble opinion which he held concerning himself, he might have filled a larger place in the world's eye, and have ploughed a deeper furrow in its life. He has done his work nobly and well. Henceforth he knows the full meaning of the blessed promise : " Be thou faithful unto death, and I will give thee a crown of life."

Incidents of great general interest and importance are not to be expected in such a secluded life. He commenced and carried on the station at Pine River, and ministered there every Sabbath, till the growing infirmities of years made it impossible for him to give to both churches the care and efficiency which he thought indispensable. This led eventually to a deepening conviction that he should demit the entire charge. His extreme conscientiousness and high sense of honour would not allow him to take any means to secure a call to an easier place while still a settled pastor. Having resigned, he put his name on the preachers' list, and went wherever he was sent, trusting entirely to the leadings of Providence as to any other settlement. This was, as the reader can well understand, a time of great anxiety to Mr. Inglis. He was no longer a young man, and the toils and hardships of his Canadian work had told severely upon his iron frame. The cry in most congregations then, as now, was for young men, and he consequently felt that it was exceedingly problematical if he would ever receive a call. He bated, however, not one jot of heart or hope. He believed that the God whom he had so long and so faithfully served, and who had guided him in many trying scenes, and through many and grievous perplexities, would still be the breaker up of his way, and the guardian of his steps. He went forth accordingly, like Abraham, not knowing whither he went, but assured that his path would be ordered aright. He waited patiently, nor was he put to shame, and was finally inducted into the congregation of Stanley Street Church, Ayr, among whose people he spent the closing years of a laborious and somewhat chequered ministerial life.

CHAPTER IX.

THE VILLAGE OF AYR.

Its People and Surroundings—Growth—Railway Communication—
History of Stanley Street Church, and its Successive Pastors—
Present Condition.

IT was a wise and kind Providence that led Mr. Inglis to spend his last days in Ayr. The village itself: the quietness of its surroundings: its somewhat rugged, romantic, and picturesque situation on the banks of the River Nith and Cedar Creek: the thoroughly unconventional and kindly nature of its society: and the intensely Scottish character of its people, not only by birth, but in dialect and customs, were all most congenial to such a man. To him it was the sweetest spot in all that beautiful region of country.

The site of Ayr was selected some fifty-nine years ago by Mr. Levi Mudge, not so much for its beauty, perhaps, as for its valuable water privileges, which he used to run his small one-run-of-stone grist mill. Deprived of the immediate advantages of railway communication till within the last few years, the growth of the village was necessarily slow, Paris being the nearest railway station. Yet the demand for its manufactured goods was so extensive that, between the teaming of raw and manufactured materials, the road between Ayr and Paris was, at all seasons of the year, a busy thoroughfare. The hamlet has now become an important village of twelve hundred inhabitants. It was incorporated in 1883, and elected its first municipal council in 1884. A branch of the Canadian Pacific Railway now affords close connections with all the other leading lines. Thus enjoying all the modern advantages of water, steam, and electricity, which its enterprising inhabitants are not slow to take advantage of, it gives promise of taking a leading position as one of the great centres of business enterprise and mechanical industry in Western Ontario. True to the ancestral record of the inhabitants, they support two large and prosperous Presbyterian Churches.

I am indebted to the present pastor of Stanley Street Church, Ayr, the Rev. J. S. Hardie, for the following sketch of the origin and progress of the congregation, to which Mr. Inglis ministered during his closing years, which will undoubtedly be interesting to many readers of this volume :

At a meeting of the Presbyterians of West Dumfries, held in the house of Mrs. Anderson, on the 27th of July, 1834, and presided over by the late Rev. George Murray, representing the United Secession Church of Scotland, the following resolutions were unanimously carried :

First. *Resolved*—That this meeting consider that the gospel is much wanted in this part of the country.

Second. *Resolved*—That it is desirable to have the ordinances of the gospel regularly dispensed.

Third. *Resolved*—That this meeting approve of the plan of the mission of the United Secession Church of Scotland into this part of Canada, and agree to send a letter of invitation to one of their missionaries to labour amongst them, and organize a congregation.

At this meeting twenty-three persons submitted their names for church membership. At two subsequent meetings, held respectively on the 3rd and 31st of August of the same year, thirty-two additional names were offered for membership. In all, fifty-five names were submitted, twenty-six of whom were denied the honour of being named among the founders of the congregation, because they were not " certified and attested" to the satisfaction of the missionary. However, all of them were received into full membership of the newly organized congregation at later meetings of the session.

The Presbyterians of West Dumfries were formed into a regular congregation on the 19th of October, 1834. " The following persons, viz., Alex. Rodgers, Mrs. Rodgers, Robt. Crooks, Wm. Currie, Mrs. Currie, John Currie, John Reid, John Anderson, Robt. Haddow, Wm. McRae, Mrs. McRae, Wm. Manson, Thos. Anderson, Peter Anderson, Mrs. Anderson, John Turnbull, John Brodie, Mrs. Brodie, John Black, Mary Manson, Hannah Anderson, Mrs. Black, John Hall, Mrs. Hall, Alex. Lawrie, David Guthrie, Mrs. Guthrie, Wm. Hardie, and Mrs. Lawrie, having given a public declaration of their belief in the doctrines of the Church, and having promised due submission to the session afterwards to be chosen and to the Presbytery, were declared to be a congregation in full communion with the United Secession Church of Scotland, and entitled to exercise all the prerogatives that belong to a Christian society in connection with them, either in their individual capacity as members or in their collective capacity as a congregation."

At this meeting of the congregation the Rev. G. Murray received a letter of invitation to be their min-

ister, which he accepted after a mutual understanding
that he would still retain his position as the agent of
the Synod of the United Secession Church of Scotland,
but would, in terms of acceptance, feel bound to attend
to the general interests of their mission.

The choice of a session was the next important
step for the newly-formed congregation, to which position they elected seven of their number, three of whom
declined, viz., John Hall, Wm. Manson, and George
Oliver. The remaining four, viz., John Reid, Alex.
Rodgers, Wm. Currie and John Black, were on the 1st
March, 1835, solemnly set apart by prayer, and the
imposition of hands, to the office of the eldership,
whom, with the Rev. G. Murray as moderator, and
John Black as clerk, constituted the first session of
one of the first organized Secession congregations in
Ontario.

During the winter of 1834–35 occasional service
was held in Wm. Currie's log barn. The spring of
1835 saw a comfortable and commodious log chapel
built, where a Sabbath school was opened ; and the
Sabbaths on which Mr. Murray could not give them
supply, the Elders, in the order of seniority, conducted
public worship, by prayer, reading the Scriptures, and
a sermon from some approved author. The Sacrament of the Lord's Supper was dispensed in the chapel
for the first time on the first Sabbath of July, 1835,
when thirty-seven names were added to the communion
roll, making a total membership of ninety-two at the
first communion. Most of these have passed away,
and a few remain to whom the memory is yet precious
of this, their first communion season in Canada.

The Presbyterian cause could not fail but flourish abundantly, planted as it was in the midst of true and loyal sons of Knox; while no small measure of its success is due to the faithful and ardent labour of Mr. Murray, who had raised the congregation to such a position during his five and a half years' pastorate, that regular Sabbath services became a necessity. This necessity led to the severing of the bond which bound the pioneer missionary and his first flock together. On the 12th February, 1840, because of "the state of his health and other circumstances," Mr. Murray placed his resignation in the hands of the Presbytery, which was accepted, and the Rev. Mr. Roy of St. George appointed moderator of session during the vacancy. After a vacancy of about two years, an unanimous call was extended to the Rev. Robert Thornton, which he declined. A few months later a harmonious call was placed in the hands of the Rev. Alexander Ritchie, which he accepted, and on the 4th of May, 1842, was inducted as the first regular minister of the congregation, with a membership of 165 souls. Under the regular pastoral care of Mr. Ritchie, within eighteen months the communion roll numbered 214, with a proportionate increase of adherents on the means of grace. This prosperous state of affairs necessitated the erection of a larger building, the outcome of which was the present structure (minus the paint and polish) which was opened in the fall of 1843, retaining the name of "The West Dumfries Congregation."

On the 6th of February, 1846, a petition to the Presbytery, signed by twenty members of the congregation residing in Blandford District, was laid on the table, praying for disjunction from the congregation, and wishing to be formed into a separate congregation. The session unanimously agreed to transmit it to the Presbytery, with their hearty approval of the prayer of the petitioners. This is now the strong and vigorous church of Chesterfield, for the past twenty-six years under the pastoral care of the Rev. William Robertson.

During Mr. Ritchie's eighteen years' ministry in Ayr many were the changes effected. That he performed what he believed to be his duty there is but one opinion. He truly sought the highest present and eternal good of the souls committed to his care. Numbered with the dead for a quarter of a century, his memory is yet fresh and the fruits of his labours abundant. His successor, the Rev. George Irving, was inducted into the pastoral charge on July 17, 1861. At this time the name of the congregation was changed from that of West Dumfries to Stanley Street Church, the name which it retains at the present time.

The ministry of Mr. Irving, though short, was marked by much enthusiasm and zeal, characterized by special devotion to the young people. His usefulness was soon checked and suddenly ended by a disease which baffled all medical skill, and through which, on the 21st January, 1865, he was numbered among the dead—" Gone, but not forgotten." On the right, as you enter the church, the remains of this beloved pastor rest, like a true soldier of Christ, fallen on the field in which he fought.

Following Mr. Irving, the Rev. Stephen Balmer was inducted as minister of Stanley Street Church on the 19th of March, 1867; but, after a brief pastorate of some fifteen months, resigned his charge into the hands of the Presbytery of Paris.

The subject of this Memoir, the late Rev. Walter Inglis, was then called to Stanley Street Church on September 20, 1869, and became its pastor on the 8th of December of the same year. After his lamented death there was a vacancy of eight months, when a unanimous call was extended to the present pastor, the Rev. J. S. Hardie, then a graduate of Knox College, which he accepted, and, on the 2nd day of June, 1885, was ordained and inducted into his first ministerial charge. The session number nine members, each elder having charge of a congregational district. On the communion roll there are 315 souls, with an attendance on the regular Sabbath service of about 500. A Sabbath school staff of 22 teachers, with a school of about 220 scholars, and a library of about 600 volumes, a Young Men's Association, a Literary Society, a Band of Hope, and a Congregational Temperance Society all give evidence of the spiritual life of the congregation.

CHAPTER X.

A Many-sided Man—Dislike of Routine Business in Church Courts—
Moderatorship of Synod—Pulpit Ministrations—Private Life—In
Homes of Sickness—Dislike of Personal Dealings with Anxious
Souls—Independence of Spirit—Undue Sensitiveness—Influence
upon the Congregations in Ayr—Notes by Rev. J. A. R. Dickson
—Visit of Principal Cairns to Ayr in 1880.

MR. INGLIS was, indeed, a many-sided man. Those
who saw him only in public, or heard him occasionally in the pulpit, had but a poor conception of
his real character. As might be expected, from his
earlier ministerial life in Africa, he had little or no
taste or aptitude for the mere routine business of
church courts; and, unless in the more important
and practical questions of personal religion, where he
was always at home, or in grave cases of discipline,
his voice was seldom heard. It is very questionable
if he ever made a motion in Presbytery, Synod, or
General Assembly. When he did make a speech, and
was asked or expected to conclude with a formal deliv-
erance, he invariably said: "Some of you church
lawyers put that into shape; I don't know how." He
positively refused the Moderatorship of the Presbytery,
and when, in 1882, he was unanimously elected Moderator of the Synod of Hamilton and London, it was
with the greatest difficulty he could be induced to
accept the honour. Urgent calls from all parts of the
house and repeated persuasions on the part of brethren
seemed of no avail. "I must decline the honour," he

said, " as I do not feel quite at home in facing a body
of men met for the transaction of church business."
One of his brethren then said : " The man who faced
the lions in Africa is surely able to face a Canadian
Synod.". To this he humorously replied : " Yes ; but
it is one thing to face the lions, but quite another
thing to face a gathering of church lawyers." Finally,
he was literally dragged from his seat in the body of
the church and placed in the Moderator's chair. Once
fairly installed into office he performed its duties with
dignity, and showed a knowledge of practical church
work that astonished his brethren. He had, however,
little patience with forms of procedure, even in grave
cases, where it was absolutely necessary that caution
should be exercised. Quarrelsome and unruly members and office-bearers he never treated with much
leniency, if thoroughly convinced in his own mind of
their guilt. It seemed to him waste of time and utter
folly, to go through a process of law in order to prove
the guilt of a man, which was conspicuous in his very
appearances before the court, no matter how difficult
it might be to prove it. He had seen much of men,
and had a remarkable insight into human nature. He
came to conclusions quickly, and for the most part
these were correct. The thorough honesty of his
nature and his supreme contempt for hypocrisy and
sham were often illustrated in his sermons, when he
dilated upon " the compound Phariseeism of the man
who gloried in his humility," but was in heart as
proud and ambitious as Lucifer. His discourses, which
he seldom wrote in full and of which there are but few
remains, were often as irregular in their movement as

one of his native streams, but they were the expression
of his own life, and rich with quickening power. Little
regard was paid to the rules of rhetoric, but almost
every one contained pearls of thought that ordinary
preachers would have expanded into a score of discourses. Naturally possessed of a vigorous intellect,
he kept himself abreast of the times both in Church
and State, and fearlessly applied the rebukes of Scripture to prevailing sins. In his preaching he rarely
spoke of himself or his own deep, spiritual experience.
In chastened tones he contrasted the weakness and
folly of the grandest earthly saint with the majesty,
wisdom, and holiness of the Infinite One. His theology
was that of the Shorter Catechism. The saving grace
of repentance was conspicuous in his doctrinal teaching. He was a profound believer in the sovereignty of
God, which, though working on a vast, eternal plan,
yet firmly adjusts itself to the sorrows, aspirations, and
wrestlings of human souls. "God's good hand upon
me" were words not unfrequently upon his lips. Thus
his heart responded to the truth contained in the
counsel which the Bedouin Arabs chant as they roam
through the desert:

> Trust in that veilèd hand which leads
>   None by the way that he would go,
> And always be for change prepared,
>   For the world's law is ebb and flow.

He was a noble specimen of the quaint, rugged, and
apparently austere, but withal tender, sterling, godly,
Scottish pastor of bygone years; stern and strong as a
mountain peak amid the storm, but, at the same time,
calm and gentle as a summer shower.

In private Mr. Inglis was singularly beloved by his people and by all who had ever come into contact with his goodness of heart. His frequent sallies of wit, and the great geniality and good humour that invariably accompanied his Scotch stories—of which the store seemed inexhaustible—made his company exceedingly entertaining, while, at the same time, his acknowledged intellectual superiority precluded all undue familiarity. In the homes of sickness and sorrow he was equally welcome. He loved such ministrations, and did not confine them to his own congregation. Frequently he would drive eight or nine miles to seek out some suffering one. Who indeed that has ever heard him praying by the bedside of the dying, or comforting the widow and orphan, can ever forget the touching pathos of his voice, and the tender words, often couched in broken accents, that fell from his lips when the strong man wept like a little child?

Possessed of such tenderness of spirit, it will perhaps seem strange to many readers of this Memoir that Mr. Inglis shrank from personal dealings with persons under conviction. Mr. Hamilton refers to this in the communication already quoted. He says: " A few years ago we complied with his request to preach to his people in Ayr, on a Monday after the observance of the Lord's Supper. In the course of conversation he expressed anxiety about the spiritual condition of his people, and thought it might be well to have a series of meetings when the Word would be frequently brought before their mind. He consulted with the members of session, and Mr. Thomson, his brother, and it was agreed that meetings should be held for five nights in succession, conducted by him, Messrs. Thomson, McLean and myself. These meetings were well attended, and evidently the truth was much blessed to many who waited at the close of the meeting. This following the public preaching of the Word by private conversation was new to him. He said : ' These after-meetings are a new thing to me, and I do not feel capable of meeting anxious souls so as to go down to the pews, and question them about their spiritual state.' When told that there was a young man in one of these pews in a state of deep concern, he replied : ' Go you and talk with him ; I am such a coward. I feel I cannot do it.' When I expressed surprise at this he said : ' I can talk freely with the young men from the pulpit, but to talk with them so directly about their souls in that personal way is a part of the gospel minister's work I have not practised, and I feel it takes more courage than I have.' I was persuaded that it was not lack of courage to meet with and direct an anxious soul which made him so shrink, but because he was not fully convinced that this was the better way. Men who are strong in the pulpit sometimes feel themselves weak as other men when brought face to face with a soul asking ' What must I do to be saved ? ' On this subject we frequently had conversation, but in the modesty of his spirit he confessed that in directly dealing with anxious souls he thought himself incapable."

His sturdy-independence of mind and action was conspicuous. No man was ever at less pains to make himself popular than was Walter Inglis. He never concealed his opinions upon any topic—politics, religion, temperance, or aught else—but spoke out with the utmost frankness and bluntness. As he stood up in pulpit or platform, one was reminded of Elijah of old, standing erect and unabashed before Ahab, and terrifying the guilty king, when in the majesty of truth he announces his commission : "As the Lord God of Israel liveth, before whom I stand." Whether it was from a mistaken feeling that this honesty and outspoken plainness of speech were not acceptable to his people, or more likely because of the mischievous gossip of certain busybodies, there was a period during his ministry in Ayr when he became impressed with the feeling that his usefulness was beginning to wane, and that a few of his people desired a change. Sensitive beyond most ministers, he made known this feeling to one of his co-Presbyters, intimating at the same time his determination to resign forthwith. He could not brook the idea of hanging on to a congregation that did not love him, or even where there were a few who did not love him, merely for the loaves and fishes. That he was altogether over-sensitive and entirely mistaken in his estimate of the feelings of his people was abundantly proved. Very unwisely perhaps, but from the best of motives, the office-bearers of the church canvassed the entire congregation, and took what might be called a " plebiscite " of the membership, when it was found that, with hardly an exception, they clung to their old pastor with an ardour and tenacity of affection that was most remarkable.

At the time of Mr. Inglis' settlement in Ayr, and for a long time previous, there was comparatively little fellowship between the two Presbyterian congregations. For reasons that need not now be stated, and because of certain events that are now almost forgotten, there was little of that spirit of brotherly kindness which belongs to the household of faith. This condition of things was, however, very soon changed after his induction as pastor of Stanley Street Church, and was largely due to the influence which he exerted in harmonizing diverse and antagonistic elements, and reconciling brethren who had been estranged. This he did without any compromise of principle on their part or on his. This influence grew steadily from year to year, and became a powerful factor for good in the community at large. Churchmen, Methodists, Presbyterians, and even infidels respected, admired, and loved him. He softened the bitter asperity that is often found among freethinkers and sceptics towards Churches, by meeting them cordially and frankly as fellow-citizens, visiting them at their homes, and sympathizing with them in their misfortunes. Unless drawn by them into the discussion of disputed points, he studiously on such occasions avoided everything that would in the least irritate or annoy them, believing, as he often was heard to say, that " the best thing to do for them was to show kindness." Doubtless it is due to this spirit of conciliation that many of their children to-day are found in the Sabbath schools and Churches in Ayr.

The Rev. J. A. R. Dickson, B.D., of Galt, between whom and Mr. Inglis there existed a strong friendship, has furnished the following "Reminiscences," which embrace many salient points in his character. He says :

My first acquaintance with the Rev. Walter Inglis was at my induction to the pastoral charge of Union Church, Galt, October 14, 1879. Then he came and gave me a warm welcome, with such a shake of the hand as few know how to give, and asked what part of the Old Land I hailed from, and altogether expressed such fatherly interest in me that my heart was knit to him at once. I felt that in him I had a true man, one who had a large sympathetic, sterling nature. I felt at once the noble manliness and the true Christ-likeness of the man. He had the solidity and the ring of the true metal. He, like Thomas Carlyle, hated with his heart all pretence, all insincerity, all sham, and he loved with all the sympathetic affection of a woman all uprightness, truth, and simplicity. This feature of his character was very pronounced. During the period of about five years I was privileged to know him and enjoy his fellowship, I saw many refreshing manifestations of it. It was revealed in all circumstances, either by the silent, contemptuous turning away of his head, or by the ejaculation of an emphatic disgust in the word "aye," accompanied by a suggestive toss of the head to the side, or by his turning on his heel without a word and walking away, erect as a Canadian pine.

During this time he often came to Galt to visit me, and no one more welcome ever came across the threshold of the manse. His tall, massive figure, his head square and well-set on his shoulders, crowned with a rich mass of gray hair, his face lighted, illumined I may say, by two clear, large blue eyes, which spoke, and made the bold nose, and square chin, and set lips memorable, and his voice, breaking loud and musical on the ear with some hearty salutation, rendered his coming a wave of gladness. He came like a sunbeam with light and joy and warmth in spring, and when he went his loss was felt. His coming meant something, because he himself was

something. He had read widely, and, what is more,
he had thought deeply on most of the problems
engaging attention, and had reached important conclusions. His outlook on the world, with its men and
things and various interests, was far-reaching, and
his sympathies were co-extensive with his outlook.
And in uttering his thoughts he would express them
with an incisive terseness that made them as goads.
His speech was aphoristic.

I remember one day, as we were speaking of differences in style in address, he said : "Aye, my style was
spoilt by a passion I had when I was young for John
Foster. His studied, thoughtful, compact style I imi-
tated, and it has spoilt mine. I try always to put as
much sense in a few words as I can, and it gets
cramped, and does not flow." This was true. In con-
versing with him you would find him making mighty
leaps, clearing ditches, hedges, and dykes at a single
bound. Hence it was hard to keep up with him, he
would dash away ahead so suddenly,—but the dash
was always worth something. It usually resulted in a
grand generalization which would bear looking at and
thinking over a long time. His honesty in conversation or discussion was remarkable. So long as he understood or saw the meaning clearly, he acknowledged
it by an "aye, aye!" but when anything was dark or
incomprehensible to him he would say : "You're beyond me there." He never pretended to understand,
or approve, or enjoy what he did not. He was thoroughly honest and true. Anything he read, or that
was read to him, that did not convey to him some
intelligence or inspiration, was set down with a per-
emptory "It does not play buff upon me." He thoroughly enjoyed anything that had the shining of a
clear beam, and at the same time the kindly, firm
pressure of a friendly hand. These were two essentials
with him, of any matter written or spoken : "*It must
glow, and it must grip;* otherwise it was wasted labour,

ineffectual utterance, or nerveless writing." He had
a keen sense for the true, the harmonious, the consistent, the complete ; and his approval of anything
that partook of these characters was instantaneous
and entire.

His criticism of men and denominations and affairs
was full of nice discernment and of human kindness.
It was sharp, but it was not shallow ; it was biting,
but it was not bitter ; it was telling, but it was not
trifling. It was the judgment of a large heart and a
cultivated mind. Many of these we remember, but it
is too early yet to repeat them in a public way ; twenty-
five years after this, when the seeds of his sowing have
come to fruit, and his name is far more loved than it
is even to-day, the scattered utterances will be gathered
together and form as notable a collection of shrewd
and brilliant sayings as we possess.

He had an ardent love for little children. I have
seen him with them on his knee, telling them stories
of his life in Africa; or moving about the room,
stamping with his feet, and thrusting down his arms
as though they had been legs, and making a hideous noise, umph ! umph ! umph ! imitating the wild
beasts of the forest, till every one was as full of
fright as though they were on the very spot. Once
he was present at the annual soiree of the Sunday
school when prizes for attendance, and learning
Scripture and catechism, were to be distributed. I
asked him, as a loved and respected father in Christ,
to do so. And his words were exceedingly happy—so
wise, so winsome—that the "little men" and the "little women," as he called them, were greatly delighted,
and evidently felt greatly honoured by his presence.

He was invited by the County of Waterloo Teachers'
Association on one occasion to give them a lecture on
Africa. I was present in the audience, and it was a
rare treat. The man, the scholar, the Christian, the
politician, each and all in him came to the front as he

described and descanted upon the people, their language, their heathenism, their needs as a part of the great human family. He loved the Bechuana people. In his lecture, after minutely describing the well-developed form of the young men, their toilet, and, above all, their truthfulness, he cried : "Ah, I would rather, a thousand times, have one of these dirty, greasy, strapping fellows for my companion, than any of your poor, miserable, lazy wretches that lounge about the corners of the streets, or hang about tavern doors ; idle, silly sops, with nothing of a man about them, except the breeks."

At this time we had much conversation on the education of children. He believed in an education that touched the whole man. He was pained with many evidences of onesidedness. He made much of that imperial faculty, imagination. Life was narrow and stinted where it lay undeveloped. It had no empyrean in it. As we were talking of this, he said, in his own peculiar way, as we walked to the central school : "Aye, there's nae fairness noo! nae fairness noo! the noses of the bairnies are held fast on the hard grindstone." This was uttered in the tone of true lamentation. It was like the musical lamentation of an old Scottish bard.

Speaking of his lecturing. In the winter of 1882–83 my Bible class had a course of lectures, Mr. Inglis being one of the lecturers. His subject was : "Gentleness as an Element of the Scottish Character." I need not say that it was a charming utterance. It fairly touched and thrilled and carried away the audience.*

In the prayer meeting he was at home. His own intercessions were reverent (wherever he might speak freely it was not as a suppliant), comprehensive, and earnest. He believed as he prayed. His addresses were in his own terse, aphoristic style. Once, speaking of conversion, he said : "Men say they are converted.

---

* This lecture will be found in the Appendix.

Yes, they must be to be saved. But a man may be *converted* ten times a day, he can only be REGENERATED once in a lifetime."

He liked to see a Christian who had sap in him, like one of the trees of the Lord. He had little favour to show to the cold, lifeless man whose head contained volumes of precious truth, but whose heart, as he was wont to say, "was dry as a chip." "Aye, mon, it's sad, sad, that! it's evangelical moderatism," was his plaintive note.

Dr. Cairns, to whom we have already been indebted for details of Mr. Inglis' student days, has furnished us with an account of his visit to Ayr in 1880, when the two spent happy hours in recalling the memories of other days. He says : "On a visit to the American continent I had the great pleasure of spending a part of three days with Mr. Inglis, in his house in Ayr, on my way back from the Presbyterian Assembly in the United States. The interview was most gratifying to both, hardly, if at all, impaired by the anticipation that it would be the last. I found him very little changed—the hard and weather-beaten features lighted up with the same keen eye, and their half meditative, half humorous cast, gleaming all over with the same affection. He had even grown kindlier with years and change, and all his references to others had an undertone of pathos and gentleness that was very affecting. I cannot reproduce his estimates of the state and prospects of religion in Canada, in the United States, and in the Mother Country, with which last he was still accurately acquainted. He had come to look upon all, more as a watcher than as an active participant in the strife; but this seclusion had in it nothing of bitterness or even of coldness, and gave the impression rather of a grand tranquillity, which left God to execute his purposes in his own way. He had come to hope much more of the future of Canada, and to enter much more into the greatness of her possible development, and in other directions his views, though sober, were not in any sense depressed. He had still the keenest interest in the mission field and in his old region of South Africa, and here he thought, contrary to the popular view, that the Government had allowed too free a hand, both to Boers and natives, and that missions would have been more advanced had there been at head-quarters a uniform and strictly-enforced policy.

"He took me to the public school in Ayr, and explained the peculiarities of the Canadian system of education. The results, as exhibited in the different classes, were very interesting to me, and I have often recalled since the sweet voice of the children. At his request they sang a Canadian National Hymn, which was all the more touching as it contrasted with the patriotic melodies of the States, to which alone for some time I had been accustomed. He also took me round the saw-mills and other industries of the place, and gave the details of their history and progress, introducing me, at the same time, to the members of his congregation engaged in them and to other friends. From the school, which I had seen in the morning, I was taken later in the day to a very different scene, the funeral of a child in the public cemetery. Mr. Inglis conducted part of the service, but asked me to give a brief address at the grave. As amongst the crowd there would be some members of a freethinking fraternity

present, he requested me to dwell on the blessedness
of the Christian, when overtaken by bereavement, as
contrasted with the hopeless sadness of the unbeliever.
I hardly remember, in all my American experience,
anything more affecting to my own mind than this
open-air service, as we stood between the living and
the dead.   On the same day, Friday, 4th June, 1880,
it fell to Mr. Inglis to preach in the little village of
Glenmorris.   It was the week-day sermon before the
dispensation of the Lord's Supper.   He drove me out
with him, and then devolved the preaching on me.   It
was curious to see how exactly our Scotch usages, in
regard to the Lord's Supper, had been transferred to
the rural parts of the Canadian Dominion.   There was
a good and an interesting audience, and we were
heartily welcomed by the Rev. Mr. Scrimgeour, the
minister, now no more.   I had a similar experience in
preaching before the Communion in the congregation
of my friend the Rev. George Chrystal, in Flamboro'
West, where I saw in the churchyard the tomb of the
Rev. Mr. Christie, one of the two first missionaries
sent out by the United Secession Church to Canada in
1832.   Civilization had greatly advanced in the interval,
but on my way to Glenmorris and back to Ayr, I could
still have experimental acquaintance with the corduroy
roads, over which the earliest settlers had to ride ' to
kirk and market.'

    "Much of the conversation I had with Mr. Inglis
cannot be reproduced, as it touched on matters which
brought out his estimate of public characters, and also
involved many personal allusions unsuitable for a
Memoir.   Many of his remarks, however, rose into a

region above everything national and individual—the eternal topics of Christian faith and hope. I well remember his quiet but decisive negative to recent utterances of advanced criticism and theology; his deepened reverence, as the result of all his experience towards the Word of God, and his unmistaken conviction, that amidst all delays it was on the way to a great and perhaps not very distant victory. He believed in systematic theology, but saw larger spaces than some, where the ground was comparatively clear, and was less hopeful than some, that it ever would be filled in this world. He had sympathy with all sacred literature, but thought that too many books had been written and mostly too long; and that the world would be greatly the better for a spell of meditation and sturdy practice. Of his own hopes as a Christian he did not say much. He allowed his hope as well as his faith to appear in his works, but made it evident especially in his prayers. Amid all his wanderings he felt that he had been led in a right way, and still looked for goodness and mercy to follow him all the days of his life.

"On the Saturday forenoon, having exchanged parting greetings with his wife and daughter, who made his home after others had left it still so happy, I was accompanied by him to the railway station for Toronto, and there we bade each other a good-bye, which, as already stated, proved a last farewell."

CHAPTER XI.

Friendship between the two Ministers in Ayr—Mr. Inglis' Welcome of
Mr. Thomson—Growing Intimacy—Church Fellowship—Impressions left by Thirteen Years of Intercourse—Mr. Inglis' Prayers—
Experimental, Exegetical, and Biographical Discourses—Addresses
at Funerals—Personal Sickness—Family Affliction—Sabbath Evening Talks—Last Words—A Son of Consolation—The Soul of Honour
—A Man of Genius—Quaint Sayings and Criticisms—Efforts in
behalf of the Temperance Cause—Forebodings of Death.

BY request the Rev. John Thomson, of Knox Church,
Ayr, has furnished the following "Recollections"
of his revered father in the ministry, Mr. Inglis. It
is only fair to say that his interesting reminiscences
have been of necessity condensed, in order to bring
this memorial volume within the reach of many who
could not otherwise possess it, and that many things
have been omitted which, in other circumstances,
would have been retained. It was, indeed, a wonderful friendship—nay, love—that existed between
him and Mr. Inglis. This, doubtless, led to the good
feeling that sprung up between the two congregations
in Ayr, for, as are the ministers, so are the people.
No two men preaching in the same village, and to
different congregations, ever more agreed and worked
together for the religious welfare of their respective
congregations in a united capacity. It seemed a repetition of Paul the aged and his son Timothy in the
faith. Mr. Inglis regarded Mr. Thomson with a deep
affection, and Mr. Thomson confided in Mr. Inglis
implicitly. While, doubtless, differing in many minor

matters, it might be said of them, in the language of
"In Memoriam," that they were

> One in kind, and moulded like in Nature's mint.

To say that there was no jealousy between them comes
far short of the truth. They were one in heart, in
aim, and in effort for the advancement of Christ's Kingdom. May such kindly relationships long continue
between the ministers of our Church, and wherever
there are congregations so closely related and located
to each other as in Ayr.

My recollections of Mr. Inglis, says Mr. Thomson,
embrace the last thirteen years of his life. While
filling the pulpit of Knox Church, Toronto, in 1871,
I was asked to preach as a candidate in Knox Church,
Ayr. Arriving at Ayr on the Friday evening, I was
invited to tea with him in the house he then occupied,
before the present manse was built. Our introduction was characteristic. Almost his first words were:
"How about that call that I hear you have got from
B——?" I do not remember my answer to his question, but his reply was: "O yes; jump at the first
offer." This was ironically spoken, but the irony had
its source in the depths of a largely sympathetic
nature. He was putting himself in my place, for the
advice he gave me ironically had been given himself
in all seriousness some years before.

On the following Sabbath evening I preached for
him from the text: "Lord, what wilt thou have me
to do?" After service we walked home together. I
found that my sermon had brought us nearer each
other than we were on the previous Friday evening.
The irony had all vanished now, and, as an importu-
nate father pleading with an inexperienced son, he
urged me to weigh the matter well before I accepted
a call to B——, where I would have a second charge,

and be settled in a very un-Presbyterian locality. On the Monday following he took me round the village, introducing me to members of both churches, and especially to the "Glasgow folks." Many things happened between our parting at that time and the following October, when the call to Knox Church was put into my hands, at a meeting held in Zion Church, Brantford. After greeting me cordially, and referring in kindly terms to the possibility of my settlement in Ayr, he said: "One thing I have told my people: if Mr. Thomson comes to Ayr, he will cheer up my old heart with his music." The call was accepted. On the following evening I heard him for the first and last time give an extended lecture on Africa. His previous life there was, however, by no means a closed book to me. No one could converse with him at least twice a week, as I did, and hear him preach once every fortnight without becoming familiar with that most interesting portion of his history.

Next day he drove me in his buggy to Ayr. The photograph of his low-seated conveyance and little sorrel pony (it died just a few weeks before himself) is one that will not soon fade from the minds of the people in Ayr. The journey to Ayr on that Thursday morning might be called an epitome of our thirteen years' progressive companionship. We had much serious talk and many a hearty laugh. Scotch character, Church discipline, ministerial finance, and the desirableness of ministers keeping themselves free from the entanglements of local gossip were among the topics discussed.

My ordination took place in November, 1871. At the examination his words were few but memorable, and all intended to relieve the candidate as much as possible from the embarrassment of the situation. A rather difficult question having been asked, regarding "assurance of salvation," Mr. Inglis put it in this concrete form: "Does the child live before it can say

I am?" At the social meeting held in the evening, he made one of those speeches which no man but himself could make. On the Sabbath evening following my settlement, I heard him preach for the first time. I was pleased and edified beyond expectation. I had expected to hear originality, but not so much of the kind of thought that leads a man to self-examination. His sermons were calculated to act as a corrective to superficial thinking, and hackneyed forms of expression. One of the earliest of these corrective sermons was that in which he dealt with the connection between faith and love. The word "love" he thought a far better word to use than the word believe, in trying to reach the consciousness of a man, seeing that love implied faith. Faith and love, he said, were co-ordinate, like the back and palm of a man's hand, as he thrusts it into a sack of wheat to bring up a handful, both of them requiring a basis of knowledge to work upon. His gospel statements, though not covering as large a portion of the sermon as in the case of many preachers, were wonderfully exact and suggestive. God calls us to work for him, he would say; but that work we cannot perform if our sins are not forgiven. Therefore, the gospel provision is intended to set us free from that encumbrance, and give us the needed power. He struck heavy blows at the legalism of the human heart. In a sermon on the excuses made for not coming to the table of the Lord, he referred to the common objection, "I am not good enough," and exclaimed: "Well, that *is* a revolution! The prodigal son came with his old rags. If we do not understand that Christ is to *be*-robe us, I do not think we understand Christianity at all." He excelled in prayer. I can still hear his broad, rich baritone voice resounding through the area of Knox Church, as he prayed "that God would sweep away from our midst, with the besom of destruction, the prevalent forms of error, frivolity, and crime." On another occasion, when I had preached from the text, " Whom God hath set forth a propitiation through faith in his blood," he prayed : " May thy young servant go on to have just such great themes as propitiation and redemption for the nourishment of his own soul." In conveying to the retiring Moderator of the Synod of 1882 the thanks of his brethren, he said : " Long may you be able, sir, to continue preaching that same glorious gospel." The preciousness of the gospel seemed to grow upon him as the shadows of life were lengthening.

He greatly excelled in expository and biographical preaching. In his delineations of character he often said things humorous enough to provoke a smile ; but while you were smiling, you were taking in portions of truth that benefited the mind long after the smoke of pleasantry had vanished. Many who were startled by his genius did not know how deeply evangelical he was in heart and mind.

It was not long before he was made to pass through trials that made his own grasp of gospel truth more and more apparent. The story of the funerals we attended together, and the prayers and addresses he made on such occasions, would themselves form a large portion of this memorial volume. His prayers were frequently prose poems, if, indeed, that term does not fall far short of such outbursts of spontaneous eloquence. At the funeral of the little son of a Methodist minister, who had also suffered the loss of his wife, he said : " Thou hast smitten him, O Lord, in his breadth with thy lightning, and shaken him to his roots with thy tempests." I cannot recall the exact words used on many similar occasions, but although the words do not remain, the tones of his voice, the gravity of his uncovered head, and the moving originality of his utterances still hover around the graveyards of the whole neighbourhood.

His addresses at funerals were quite unique. They were not funeral sermons, or biographical orations.

They were more of the nature of Scripture readings,
welded into the form of continuous discourse by
remarks thrown in between as connecting links. Were
J a painter, I would like to set Mr. Inglis thus upon
the canvas: He is standing in the doorway of the
house, having just invited those who were loitering
around the fence and the gateway to come in. When
the house is filled, and others still remaining outside,
he opens the little Bible which he holds in his hand,
turns up a psalm or paraphrase, and then begins the
service. When in his normal state of health, he lined
out the verses, and with his rich, penetrating voice, in
slow, lingering measures, led the singing himself. His
favourite tune was "Walsal." He often said that it
was not a good sign of the piety of the age that minor
tunes were so seldom sung. Not only is "Walsal"
specially endeared to me from its association with Mr.
Inglis, but "the grave, sweet melody" of the assembled
company, gathered into the different apartments of
the house, and singing with an irregularity resembling
the responses of a cathedral, or still more closely, the
responses of the waves of ocean, "when deep calleth
unto deep," comes back to me at this distance of time
as one of the great musical experiences of my life.

The first time we attended a funeral together I
expected he would ask me, as the younger man, to
take the easier part of reading the Scriptures. Instead of that he asked me to pray. He had not read
many verses before I felt the propriety of his reversing
the usual order. His was no ordinary reading. As
it was the funeral of a boy, he read the story of the
Widow of Nain, and, in the course of his remarks,
quoted with great power and feeling a few verses from
Mrs. Judson's poem on the death of a child:

> Strive not to check the teardrops,
>   That fall like summer rain,
> For the Sun of Hope shines through them—
>   You shall see his face again.

Oh! weep but with rejoicing,
A heart-gem have ye given;
And behold its glorious setting
In the diadem of heaven.

He was as discriminating in the choice of passages on such occasions as of themes for the pulpit, adapting his mind not only to the special circumstances of the family, but also to the course of events and the season of the year. One passage he never omitted: "I am the resurrection and the life." After repeating it he would pause and ask: "Believest thou this?" urging upon the company the need of being able to tell what was their creed. He had a great dread of formality, for, as he often said, "There's no priestcraft in death."

The funeral of his son George, which took place in July, 1873, is vividly present to my mind while I write, especially the procession from the house to the burying-ground and the form of the chief mourner, as he crossed the threshold, and, passing through the gate, followed the youthful bearers who carried the remains. His step was firm, but it was the step of a great soul bowed down with grief. At the open grave Mr. Wright (now of Stratford) read the Scriptures and offered prayer. When the grave was filled in, and the company were still standing with heads uncovered, Mr. Inglis, who was too full in heart to let them go away without any utterance on his part, stretched out both hands in the attitude of benediction, and said, in what became in the end a sobbing voice: "May the Lord be with you all in the day of your sore trouble."

A further day of sore trouble was near at hand. Towards the end of 1874 he was prostrated by pneumonia. The members of his family were telegraphed for, as it was thought the end had come. When I saw him he said: "I know now what pain means," and then asked me to pray that he might be sustained when the paroxysms returned. During the course of this illness he asked me to sing one of Dr. Bonar's hymns, which, having been sung by the united choirs of Knox and Stanley Street Churches on Christmas Day, 1872, became ever afterwards a great favourite:

> When the weary, seeking rest,
>   To thy goodness flee;
> When the heavy-laden cast
>   All their load on thee;
> When the troubled, seeking peace,
>   On thy name shall call;
> When the sinner, seeking life,
>   At thy feet shall fall;
> Hear then in love, O Lord, the cry,
> In heaven, thy dwelling-place on high.

While I was singing it he said in his own lengthened tones of great satisfaction: "Man, but that's fine!" As he was recovering from this illness he said to me one day: "I've been meditating on the text, 'Looking unto Jesus,' and this is what occured to me: how many squinting Christians there are in the world!"

Among the greenest spots in memory are the Sabbath evenings, when we lingered together at the gate of the field between our two manses, and sometimes at the fence clear down in the hollow where "the burnie runs." I cannot now recall many of the words that were then spoken: just as little, however, can I forget the friendship which they breathed and the strengthening they brought to my theological foundations, and my hopes for the future of the Church. During one of these after-service walks he said to me: "What made me a missionary was hearing from my mother what a commentator said about the millennium. He said that, according to the prophetical reckoning of time, the millennium was to last 365,000 years. That number made such an impression upon my imagination that it set me to the study of prophecy. That study I have long since laid aside; but of three things I am certain: first, there is to be a great battle fought;

second, a great victory won; and third, that I am a soldier in the ranks, whose business it is to march forward and fight, according to the Captain's word of command."

Stanley Street Church having been closed for repairs, the two congregations met together from October, 1882, till February, 1883. This gave Mr. Inglis an opportunity of seeing what he had long desired, the members of both churches sitting down together at the table of the Lord. There were two such Communions, one in October, 1882, and the other in February, 1883. At the first Mr. McKay of Woodstock took Mr. Inglis' place (as he was just recovering from his second great illness, which proved to be paralysis); at the second the services were divided between us. At the last of our united meetings Mr. Inglis preached and spoke of the close fellowship that had been enjoyed, exclaiming, as he closed one of his most fervent passages, " If I forget thee, oh Knox Church, let my right hand forget her cunning!"

This was followed up by another memorable meeting, on occasion of the re-opening of Stanley Street Church on the Sabbath following. But when the anniversary of that opening came round, Mr. Inglis was confined to the manse by what proved to be the beginning of his fatal illness. The history of the time from November, 1883, to October, 1884, was that of preaching and ceasing to preach, beginning again and desisting until his final words were spoken. On the 27th April he was again present with us in Knox Church as a listener. He was looking very pale, but he spoke with a firm voice when at the close of the service he administered the ordinance of baptism to our fifth child. His baptismal services were unique. He put no questions to the parents as to their doctrinal beliefs and performances, considering all this as implied in their membership. " I never baptize a child," he said, "but in thought I baptize my own children over again." For this reason he did not approve of private baptism, regarding the ordinance as a matter not only of parental but of congregational interest.

A little while before his last illness became manifest he was introduced to the newly arrived Church of England clergyman. "Are you High Church, Low Church, or Middle?" enquired Mr. Inglis. "For if you are High Church, you want to have no dealings with me, nor I with you." Mr. Ashton's reply was: "Low Church." When Mr. Inglis was confined to his bed Mr. Ashton expressed a desire to see him. As he had already, on the day we called, seen several visitors, it was thought better we should postpone our interview, but as we were leaving the manse he overheard our voices and called us in. His mind was unusually bright and active. He seemed anxions to speak cheering words to Mr. Ashton for his sympathy. "Well, my son," he said, "have you had any signs of encouragement in your work?" "Yes," said Mr. Ashton, "some kind words from my bishop, at least." "That's good, my son. And now don't you be discouraged by that long muddy road between here and Princeton. Just treat it as the guest at the breakfast table treated the rotten egg." "How was that?" "Oh, when his host discovered it, and was about to ring for a fresh one, the guest said 'No'; and stretching out his hand for the pepper, said: 'Do you think I would let a thing like that beat me!'" The young curate was certainly none the worse of having the kind words of the Bishop of Huron confirmed by the kind words of the senior pastor of Ayr.

His last sermon was preached in May, 1884. About this time I accompanied him to the last funeral service he attended. As we were passing within the gate to the cemetery he referred to the Scotch hymn: "I'm far frae my hame," and then added with a great, loving quiver of voice: "Janet sung that to me last night—that hymn suits me now, Mr. Thomson." As

we turned towards the west, and, for the moment, had
a fine view of the surrounding country, which, at that
season of the year, looked lovely, he said, slowly and
feelingly : " Ayr is a bonny place."

I began these recollections with the first word he
spoke to me; let me now give the very last. About
two days before his death I called at the manse. As
I entered, one of his daughters said : "The end has
come now." After praying with him, I spoke a
parting word about our meeting again. He bowed his
acquiescence, but showed no sign of recognition. In a
few minutes I was recalled from the study, whither I
had gone to talk with his brother, "to come back, and
sing something." I had only sung a few lines when
he was seized with one of his fearful attacks of pain.
After it had passed away, and he lay back upon his
pillow, he recognized me as I was about to leave the
room, and called out, "Hold on, Thomson!" He
then turned to Mrs. Inglis, who was bending over
him, and said : "I'm right, am I not?" The next
moment he was again past recognizing me. "Hold
on, Thomson!" these were his last words to me.
They only referred to my movement towards the door ;
but as the words of a celebrated man in dying, "More
light," when he only wanted a little more of the light
of the earthly day, have been regarded as significant
of a higher truth, so I treasure up these last words of
the departed veteran as full of solemn import.
"Persevere, make full proof of thy ministry; for I
am now ready to be offered up, and the time of my
departure is at hand." He was to me a father in the
ministry, all through the years of our companionship
—"My friend, faithful and just to me."

Mr. Inglis was emphatically like Barnabas, "a
son of consolation." In Church gatherings and by
the fireside, rather than in ecclesiastical courts, he
was seen at his best. Like the ocean, he had many
moods, sometimes calm, at other times like the

tempest. Occasionally there was the sudden explosion of an angry gust ; but far more frequently it was the gleesome dance of the waves, and the majestic rise of the homeward gale, with white caps all around and sunlight breaking overhead. Many of his best sayings were entirely impromptu, and cannot be reproduced. In Church courts the sharp crack of his explosive weapon did excellent execution in silencing the interruptions of demonstrative audiences that threatened to become unmanageable. His nature was strong, and dealt in opposites. One extreme was the might of severity, the other the might of gentleness, and the two balanced each other in mighty oscillation. "Wire-pulling" was conspicuously absent in his conduct. On a certain occasion, when the word was mentioned between us, he straightened himself up to his full height, and said : " I despise it." It is not, therefore, wonderful that a character of such strength and directness should at times have given offence by reason of the absence of that deftness and well-oiled suavity, which, though not essential parts of policy, are, alas, often found in its company.

I never knew a man who "talked money" less than Mr. Inglis. Even in regard to ministerial income he had his philosophical way of settling the whole question by quoting the remarks of Mr. Ross of Brucefield, in the days when the two men were co-Presbyters : " It is just the same, nowadays," said Mr. Ross, "among ourselves, in regard to money, as it was among the children of Israel when they eat of the manna. He that gathered much had nothing over, and he that gathered little had no lack." On a Thanksgiving Monday, when two other ministers with myself were seated at his tea-table, the conversation turned upon a certain Canadian minister who had gone to the United States. Mr. Inglis remarked that " such a highly-endowed Scotchman as Dr. Ormiston would feel himself greatly out of his element among the Dutchmen, who could never appreciate a good Scotch story." "Oh!" said the guest appealed to, " his people are very kind ; they have done great things (in the way of money) to make him comfortable." "What's money!" retorted Mr. Inglis, " a rat in a bank is only a rat."

He was honourable to the core, and by some re-garded as almost Quixotic in his manly independence. So disgusted was he with the unscrupulousness of rail-way corporations in the matter of Sabbath Day labour, that, when on his way to the Synod at St. Thomas, he refused to avail himself of the reduced rate of fare given to members of such courts, and before the Synod closed, spoke strongly on the subject to his brethren.

His references to his mother were many and touch-ing. He often quoted her parting words when he left her to go to Africa : " They are well kept whom God keeps." She often before had soothed the turbulent spirit of the growing youth. When smarting under some grievance that he wanted put right by a thorough investigation of the case, she would lay her hand upon his restless shoulder, and say : " My foolish boy, when will you learn that there are things in this world that will not bear to be spoken of." The stories which he ushered in by the expression : "As my mother used to tell," would form a goodly appendix to " Dean Ramsay's Reminiscences." Her wise and witty sayings had evidently impressed his mind and directed his life ; and he was ever ready to share with others that sunshine which had been such a blessing to himself.

The key to Mr. Inglis' behaviour, on occasions when his individuality had full play, was the single word *genius.* You never knew what he was going to say next when any great topic was under discussion, or where his praise would end, or his censure begin. He could hit hard, as well as bestow commendation, all round among the denominations, his own among the rest. "That's where Protestantism limps," he re-marked on one occasion. On another : "When you meet a savage Scotchman, I tell you, he can put you through." On still another: "How is it that in our voluntary churches there is so much twisting and drawing?" Perhaps the heaviest blow he ever dealt at a class of men within his own Church was that which he condensed into the original epithet of "Evangelical moderates," by which he marked out those whose creed was sound in all points except that of personal conduct and missionary zeal. When the "Higher Criticism" was disturbing the Free Church of Scotland he remarked that what was wanted for the interpretation of Scripture was not these "acute" scholars, who seemed to him "scientific Gibeonites," but men who were themselves "poets and prophets."

Mr. Inglis might be appropriately described as a Christian sage. He held an impromptu lectureship every Monday forenoon, in his study, for all visitors with whom he had anything of the philosophical in common. In one of my early visits to him on a Monday forenoon I found him reading one of 'the *Quarterly Reviews.* He rather surprised me at first when he said that in his "Mondayish" state of nervousness he needed this kind of reading to take him as far as possible away from Ayr. To another he said: "When I have a fit of 'the blues' nothing cures me faster than a good dose of geography." He loved to study the map of the world, and his journeyings over it, in thought, were to him a substitute for what any Old Country minister within reach of the Clyde can have every Monday during the season—a trip from the manse to the ocean and back the same day for an exceedingly moderate fare.

A voyager in thought like Mr. Inglis would bring up his fellow-passengers at strange landing places. His mind sometimes moved among the rocks and shallows of difficult questions, which he liked exceedingly to propound when he thought he had a suitable scholar. In the pulpit he often said: "There's a question for you thinkers," and ask such questions as these : "Can you have a Sadducee without having had first a Pharisee?" "Have you ever considered that in Mohammedanism there is no shedding of blood in sacrifice, and yet it is a religion of the sword ; whereas, in Christianity everything is based on the shedding of blood, and yet it is a religion of peace?" "Tell me why it was that the two Erskines, who were by far superior men, met with so little success compared with the Wesleys?" Speaking of first impressions, he said : "I have often changed my mind in regard to a man after hearing him preach, but never after hearing him ask a blessing."

He was greatly annoyed by what he considered waste of time in argument, from the disputants not finding out at once their common ground. "When one man says a piece of cloth is so long, and the other contradicts him, the appeal is at once made to the yard-stick. Why can't we produce a yard-stick in argument as well as in merchandise? The yard measure is the common ground of reasoning. The common ground between us and the infidel is the body. The gauge of battle between us and the infidel is that it is the man of God who comes to the rescue in time of trouble." His favourite book in apologetics was the "Eclipse of Faith." Its concrete style suited the order of his mind. The following illustrates his way of putting the truth contained in one of its passages : "Mr. Blank, will you have some fish?" "No, thank you." "Will you have some roast beef, then?" "No, thank you." "Some chicken, or pie, or pudding, or what?" "Oh, nothing, nothing whatever." That, said Mr. Inglis, is infidelity—a feast of negations! Something in the same line was his answer to an infidel, who tried rather unceremoniously to draw him into an argument : "I'll not argue with you, but when you have composed your little hymn to the praise and glory of nothing, I'll come and hear it."

Exegetics was to him a congenial study. In his younger days he had made a critical study of the Book of Job in the original. He often referred to the Hebrew parallelism, when protesting against what he considered far-fetched shades of meaning, that interpreters brought out of certain passages. "Babes and sucklings," he argued, were not to be distinguished; the expression simply meant "helpless little ones." "Thy rod and staff" was "the strong staff." The blessedness of the righteous man, in contrast to three gradations of fellowship with sinners, indicated in the First Psalm by the words walking, standing, sitting, meant substantially, "Blessed is the man who has nothing whatever to do with the society of the ungodly."

A brother minister was on one occasion giving him an account of the views of a minister in Scotland, who had been tried for unsound views regarding the destiny of the wicked. The minister's theory was that, while the sin of the lost condemned them to annihilation, the death of Christ had purchased for them a change of that sentence into one of everlasting servitude, making them a sort of Gibeonites to the redeemed. When Mr. Inglis heard this, he said: "If I had Mr. —— here, I would say to him, This is all very fine, but wha' telt ye?"

His occasional remarks on Homiletics and Pastoral Theology were, as might be expected, unusually racy. Among these the following may be given: "Polishing sermons is about as useless as painting bullets;" "Polishing sermons is as useless as it would be for a lover to paint his sweetheart's portrait on the sole of his boot;" "Cultivate a fine style of writing, up to the level of dignified conversation, but no further;" "Never accept a call to a church that is ruled by godless elders;" "Never accept a call to a church where the people idolized their former minister;" "Never go ahead in matters of discipline without your elders;" "Never get so excited before going to bed as to have your rest disturbed. It's a mean thing for a man to cheat himself out of sleep. Sermons written after twelve o'clock on Saturday night should be burned." As regards Church government, he did not base his Presbyterianism on what is called "the divine right of Presbytery," but rather on the text: "One is your Master, even Christ, and all ye are brethren." Every believer, he said, ought to be judicially bound to his brethren, so that he can be rebuked in a constitutional way.

If Mr. Inglis was a professor without a chair, it may be also said that he was a bishop without a mitre. One of our most valuable labourers in the North-West, the Rev. Alexander Robson, of Fort Qu'Appelle, was brought under the notice of the Home Mission Committee through his efforts. For some years Mr. Robson, having "purchased to himself a good degree" as Sabbath school teacher, superintendent and Bible class teacher, was requested by Mr. Inglis and myself still further to exercise his gifts at the weekly union prayer meeting and the Sabbath evening service. Mr. Inglis then made the proposal to his own session, which was carried, as it was also in Knox Church session, that Mr. Robson's gifts should be recognized in some more definite way than heretofore, and that he should be encouraged to hold Sabbath afternoon and evening services in schoolhouses and private residences all through the district. Finally, at the close of one of our weekly prayer meetings, Mr. Inglis beckoned Mr. Robson aside, and said: "At the Presbytery on Tuesday, if I bring up your name to be proposed to the Home Mission Committee for mission work in Manitoba, are you willing to go?" and Mr. Robson answered: "Yes."

Mr. Inglis took a prominent part in the Temperance cause, while his attitude towards hotel-keepers was manly and courteous. In his first Temperance

address, which I heard thirteen years ago, there was
a lawyer-like unveiling of a grievance that lay very
near the root of the whole matter.   After narrating
his experience in Kincardine and its neighbourhood in
most amusing terms, he laid it down as a fundamental
position that the accepted law of Canada in regard to
travellers and hotels was based upon the drinking
customs, and that to such an extent that the total
abstainer found himself a stranger in a strange land.
He considered it a great injustice that the etiquette of
travelling made no provision for such a man paying his
way, when he wanted shelter for himself or his horse.
To save himself from being considered a sneak, he was
under temptation to go up to the bar and drink soft
drinks or purchase cigars, when he neither wanted
the one nor the other.   In discussing the Temperance
question his intense sympathy and strong feelings
were often revealed in sayings such as these :
" Drunkenness is in many cases the result of a
desolate heart ; "   " Don't *play* at teetotalism ; for
whether you are in earnest or not, remember the
drunkard *is*."   His last public acts were to help in
organizing the Blue Ribbon Society, of which he was
the first President, and the Band of Hope.   That
winter day in Knox Church when, having recently
risen from a sick-bed, he spoke his last words in
behalf of the cause he had so much at heart, will long
be remembered by all then present.   As he stood up,
staff in hand and pallid in face, with the blue ribbon
on the lappel of his overcoat, he said, what we never
heard him say before : " Boys and girls, listen to the
words of a dying man."   The occasion was the more
memorable, as we were listening to the words of two
dying men.   Mr. Elliott, the Methodist minister of
Ayr, who worked with us most cordially in all good
works, only survived Mr. Inglis by a few months.
    The first words Mr. Inglis spoke to the children of
Ayr were words of great merriment ; the last, though

cheering, were words of great solemnity. Indeed the mirthful and the sad, during the interval between these two extremes of thirteen years, were wonderfully alternated and combined. They constituted the warp and woof of his behaviour in all the average scenes of life. This interweaving of the grave and gay seems specially wonderful, when we remember to what an extent, during the last few years of his life, he was not only a "son of song," but also a "son of sore affliction."

He had forebodings of death, preceded by great pain, long before his end,—indeed, his anticipations of the latter began as far back as his student days. At one of the prayer meetings, about four years before his death, referring to this, he enlarged upon the possibilities of victory in the hour of severest bodily suffering. Speaking of the exceeding joy experienced by the martyrs on the scaffold and at the stake, with beaming face, elevated voice and his hands extended to express the idea of victorious resistance, he cried out: "Marvellous masses of soul, presented against all the torments of execution." With this watchword for the future use of Christian martyrs, I bring to a close these recollections of one from whom I received much comfort, instruction, encouragement, and stimulus, in whose company I spent many pleasant and profitable hours, and with whom, as an influence, all surviving friends who knew his worth may be said still to associate. Being dead he yet speaketh.

CHAPTER XII

To Mrs. Cowan, his Daughter—Mr. Thomas Darling—The Rev. T. Dodds (on occasion of the Death of his Son, of the McAll Mission, in Paris)—His Sister in Scotland (on occasion of the Death of his Son)—Rev. Wm. Robertson (on the Death of his Daughter)—Rev. Robert Pettigrew—Last Letter to Relatives—Looking Towards the Great Future.

MR. INGLIS' correspondence, while pastor of Stanley Street Church, Ayr, is scanty. In letters, written shortly after his induction, he describes his residence (before the new manse was built), and sketches his plans.

In 1871 he writes to his daughter, Mrs. Cowan :

Here I am, all alone in my den. I have read a most interesting chapter in Milman, on the death of Jesus Christ. It is one of the best pieces of calm historical, philosophical writing on the subject that I know. He shows, with great power and point, the belief of the Jews in an earthly Messiah ; their galled, excited, fanatical mind about the Roman conquerors; their divided factions, all of the earth, earthy. Then he takes Jesus Christ, a humble Galilean peasant, who goes on, step by step, teaching doctrines subversive of all that was dear to the Jews. Jesus saw clearly the issue in death, and as the scene thickens into great darkness, in the secret soul of the Redeemer, he presents a most extraordinary calmness to the world. I don't think I ever had a more profound belief in Jesus as the manifestation of God than at this moment. It is not alone history and testimony, but what appeals to my own consciousness and reason. History is of no value unless you have this witness within. Milman shows that the morality of Jesus differed from all other of his own age. It differs as much yet in three things : (1) The morality of Jesus was not in unison with the temper of his age; (2) it was universal morality, adapted for the whole human race, and for every period of civilization ; (3) it was morally grounded on broad simple principles, which had hitherto never been laid down as the basis of human action. I cannot enter into these and other points. Yet a passing word. Jesus tore up the Mosaic principle of earthly prosperity as a sure sign of the favour of the Almighty. He presented, for the first time in the world, a religion for all men. No force, but reason, the religion of humility, of love to all men. He struck at the roots of selfishness and vain glory. Think, my dear girl, of Jesus Christ, not in the unsubstantial, canting manner of most of us. "Look to the Cross." Have you not felt that some men use that phrase, just as the Roman Catholic looks at a picture or a bit of wood made into a cross? Mere words! I am convinced the man Christ Jesus has not been studied as he ought. We get away into transcendental doctrines about which we know little or nothing, and neglect the facts before us. Take to yourself the promises of God. Try and say: "Father, thy will be done." Having done so, you can take to yourself such precious truths as "Lo, I am with you alway," "In the world ye shall have tribulation, in me peace." I have just been reading of Stephen. He saw heaven open, and Jesus on the right hand of God to welcome him. What a welcome! Courage, my child; you love that dear Saviour. He will not shut the door on you and me. When our work is done on earth, *and not till then*, he will give us rest. Oh, I begin to look forward to rest. One thing I am deeply conscious of, I have had a desire to serve him.

Ever your loving father,

W. INGLIS.

On the 1st of January, 1872, he sends greeting to his brother-in-law, Mr. Thomas Darling, who had long been his fast friend, and was then expecting shortly to put off the earthly tabernacle. He says :

No doubt, my dear friend, you are looking for the voice of your long-loved Lord, some of these months, or days. I trust your heart is kept in perfect peace. My text yesterday was Psalm xc. v. 12. It is a hard kind of arithmetic to number our days. The Lord enables his people to do so. I read in Luke, the twelfth chapter, from the sixteenth verse to the forty-fifth. What a striking saying of the Lord—to make man, the good man, wait for death as for a bridegroom. Strange words, yet found to be true.

I have little news. The limb that troubled me all last year is a little better. Yet I am not well. I feel no longer as a healthy man. Yet it is all well. Just as the Lord shall send. My days have not been many, yet I do not feel a strong hold on this world.

On the 26th September, 1882, he thus writes to the Rev. T. Dodds, Mrs. Inglis' sister's husband, when his eldest son, the Rev. G. T. Dodds, of the McAll Mission in France, died so suddenly :

My Dear Brother,—We got the heart-heavy news of George's sad death this forenoon. I never open a letter on the way from the post, as my eyes are not good. I gave Margaret the letter. "Ah!" she said, "Dundee." We naturally exclaimed, "Isabella is gone." A hurried gasp—"No, no! George Dodds is gone."* Truly we have another instance that God's ways are not our ways. How such an event awakens the mind out of the level routine of life. It is God's truth that his people are not to sorrow as those who

---

* Isabella, Mrs. Inglis' sister, who was then very ill, and died three months after the death of her son.

have no hope. The great words sound through the ages : " Let not your hearts be troubled." Yet the blessed one was sore amazed. Paul says, in Philippians, that if his fellow soldier and beloved brother had sickened unto death, he would have had sorrow upon sorrow. The true heart weeps but with rejoicing. The experienced Christian has emotions not known by the son of earth and sense. He hits hard, and means his people to feel the rod—he cuts the living flesh, and the blood flows—he separates living, loving, healthy souls. Yes, yes, the cry went up of old, "My son, my son " —that cry will be heard till the end of time. You are this day a fit companion for Job, with a rent mantle and a rent heart, but without his dark questionings. It is a great addition to know what wise men of old knew not. " I, the risen Christ, have the keys of the unseen world and of death. God stands at the portal of life and the dark gates of death." I cannot understand how he, the smiter, is the healer. I believe it, that's all. I don't require to quote verses from the Book of Life and Immortality. The word is nigh thee.

Allow me to add my humble, earnest prayer that you may all be comforted by renewed tokens of God's grace. In my last illness I got to repeating these lines :

> Saviour, more than life to me,
> I am clinging, clinging close to thee :
> Let thy precious blood applied,
> Keep me ever, ever, near thy side.

We all join in tender sympathy. Margaret is writing a line to Portobello. She cannot master her feelings to write to Isabella to-day. I mention your dear wife very often in family prayer.

I am, yours affectionately,

W. INGLIS.

The death of his son George, in July, 1873, was a sore trial, from which he never fully recovered. But

he bore it as a Christian.   The sympathy shown at this
time astonished him.   He had not expected it.   In
writing to his sister, in Scotland, he says:

To our astonishment at Paris Station there were
my elders and some more of the people.   I did not
anticipate this, as a telegram had gone on Saturday
evening, saying the funeral would be at three o'clock
Monday afternoon.   To my still further astonishment
all business was stopped in Ayr.   Stores were shut.
Young men carried him to his grave.   Four neighbour
ministers came.   Poor fellow!   he has had hard times
for these three years.   Just a struggle for life.   I need
not trouble you with further details.   It is the old, old
story: "All flesh is grass."   I trust that this first
breach may be sanctified to us all.   Who next?   And
then next?

A year after this he says:

We intend to get a stone on George's grave soon.
Poor fellow!   It is about a year since he came up to
see us.   We think of having a verse of Scripture and
a verse of a hymn; on the stone, Psalm cii. v. 23.
The hymn some of us would like is one he often sang,
"Resting by and by," or "One by one we cross the
river."   That is it, sister!   We shall all go home, and

Glory, glory, dwelleth in Immanuel's land.

Give the children the kind love of an old uncle.   I
hope they will grow up to be hero-men—not miserable,
selfish curmudgeons!   May you grow in grace, dear
sister.   As a Dutch hymn that has just come into my
mind says: "Heir veneden is het ne it"—here below
it is not.

During the same year he writes:

Kind love to you all.   May the Spirit of the Lord
God mould your minds after still higher and holier

things. I begin to look homeward ; yes, homeward. As the simple hymn has it—

Heaven is my home.

That which changes not in me is the sense of duty to carry the gospel to the heathen. If I had the means, I would go away back to Africa and die there. I would not go to the County of Bruce as I did. No; you cannot preach the gospel to Scotchmen except as a great man. With Scotchmen you have to get on. That is it. Many of them are so selfish they don't believe it possible for a man to deny himself.

Still, in 1874, to his sister in Scotland he says :

I somehow have the belief that Christianity does not prosper among the Scotch farmers and work people. They aim at being gentlemen in the world, and their chief aim is to push and improve their land. It is so in Canada also—largely pig-headed and small-hearted. Christianity is essentially heroic.

To his friend, the Rev. Wm. Robertson of Chesterfield, he writes on occasion of the death of his daughter :

Ayr, February 8, 1884.

My Dear Mr. Robertson,—The telegram yesterday was the second that I have ever had in my life that made me feel unutterable sorrow. I am not well. I cannot write. I can only give one long-continued wail : " God is good—his ways are not man's ways ; " what need there is of such a thought ! This is your first grief ; you will never feel the same again.

I have not tasted food to-day ; I loathe it. I have telegraphed for brother William to come to-morrow and preach for me. I shall write when I get a little better. I can only repeat : " O ! day of grief and sadness." May the good Lord comfort you all after the dark wave of sorrow has passed.

Yours with fellow-feeling,
Walter Inglis.

In a letter dated 21st July, 1884, addressed to the
Rev. Robert Pettigrew of Glenmorris, speaking of certain arrangements made by the Presbytery and other
ministerial friends for the supply of his pulpit during
his illness, he says :

I am a great deal better since you were here. I
was at church yesterday twice, and feel nothing the
worse. If I keep on, I expect to be able for the one
sermon in a month. Brother William has given me
a big lift. He has been here six Sabbaths. If it is
the will of God that I have health again, I shall not
forget the long, dreary weeks of suffering. How great
the hope of a life free from pain ! This is a beautiful
world, but it is not too much to think of a country or
state far, far beyond this. I have been thinking much
of late of the infinite universe. Peace be with you.

Complimenting a lady friend in Scotland on her
gardening, he remarks :

I have said that I would rather keep company with
a saw-mill than with some men. Better keep company
with flowers than with flirts. . . . By the way, I
am making advance here (in Ayr). Thirty-one united
with the Church last year. I mean to expound the
Scriptures. A fig for eloquence ! They say I preach
better, but they have come to me—that is it.

In 1875 Mr. Inglis had a severe illness, which
brought him to the very brink of the grave. A heavy
attack of pleurisy, followed by a formidable relapse,
so prostrated him that friends and physicians gave up
all hope of recovery. His children were all sent for
to see him die ; but, by God's blessing on the means
used, he rallied. The great sympathy of his people
throughout this severe affliction touched him very

powerfully. He thought they did not care for him—would, in fact, rather like him taken away, and their unaffected kindness went specially to his heart. "My life," he says, in writing to his brother in Scotland, "is spared for a little yet, I sometimes feel. It is enough."

From this date until 1878 there is a blank in the correspondence, when he wrote a brief letter to his sister about a projected visit of his daughter to Scotland. After despatching certain items of business, he says:

I have not been so-well for some days. Water seems to be at hand. However, the medicine we use reduces the swelling right away. I cannot say that I have any special news. In fact, I have been dull with one thing and another. It is hard to keep up the spirits, with weakness of body pressing heavily. One thing I feel: I am more dependent on the goodness of God. I am sure that goodness and mercy have followed me hitherto. My hope is that he will not leave me in the end.

The last letter to relatives of any length that has been preserved is dated 22nd July, 1884. In it he writes:

These long dreary months of sickness have turned my memory into a blank. I have been a poor invalid since last year. Trouble began with bronchitis, and when I got this reduced, liver inaction set in. It was a long pull ere that sluggish organ began to work. Then, worst of all, chronic inflammation of the bladder followed. Oh, what sad times I have had first and last! The will of the Lord be done! They all encourage me with good hopes of health, but I am very doubtful. I am so weak that the least walking or exertion brings on palpitation of the heart. I have lost about thirty-five pounds in weight. The people have been very kind, and are vexed to see my gray, bilious, haggard face. . . . It is not to be wondered at that my thoughts have been much on the great future. It is immensely cheering to think on, and believe in, "immortality and life." How dark it would be to think of dying like a beast! How terrible to feel one's self at enmity with the Great Creator! How cold and wintry not to realize the love of Jesus! Love supreme controls the wildest pain and suffering. God's peace! How consoling that there is in this vast infinite universe a place for poor me, where sin and suffering are unknown! The God that made the world so fair can make something better. . . . We join in kind regards to self and Miss Darling. Tell her that our flower plot is a neglected wilderness. The Lord bless you with his glorious inheritance!

Not long after this came the last struggle, and the long, unbroken rest.

CHAPTER XIII.

LAST SICKNESS AND DEATH.

Gradual decline—Intense Sufferings—Childlike Trust—Last Look at his Congregation—Love of Sacred Song—Rest—Widespread Sorrow—Funeral Services in Manse and Church—Scene at the Grave—Funeral Sermon—Minutes of Kirk Session and Presbytery.

FOR several years before his last sickness it was apparent to his friends and congregation that his vigorous constitution was gradually giving way—the keepers of the house were trembling, and the grasshopper becoming a burden. His strong will, however, bore him up, and he continued, until a few months before his death, with more or less regularity, to preach and attend to pastoral duties. Finally, however, he was overtaken and mastered by the insidious and formidable disease which had long threatened him. His last days were days of great suffering, and the pain that he often felt seemed beyond the strength of mortal endurance. But the flames that tortured him only burned the remaining dross away, and made more conspicuous his courage and holy resignation. His sufferings did not impair, but rather perfected his strong manhood. Men's lives, it has been said, should, like the days, be more beautiful in the evening; or like the seasons aglow with promise, while the autumn is rich with golden sheaves, where good words and deeds have ripened on the field. It was so with Walter Inglis. He had reached his maturity. No longer vexed with earth's perplexing problems, he rested with childlike trust in God's mercy. There was no exultation, but calm assurance. His conversation was all about his Saviour, and what he had done for him. His creed was all summed up in these words:

A wretched, poor, and helpless worm,
On thy kind arms I fall.

About two months before his death he went to his study window, and watched the congregation gathering for the Sabbath morning service. He had a presentiment that it was the last look, and bursting into tears, left the room. From that time he was confined to his bed, and grew rapidly worse. A kind message was brought to him by one of his elders that he should not fret himself because unable for his work. "You are not doing so?" said his friend. "No," he replied, "it is all well whichever way it goes." Earnest, loving prayers were offered on his sick bed for his people who, he would often say, "have been so kind to me," and also for his own Presbytery, and all the Presbyteries of the Church. Nor was the scene of his early mission work forgotten. "O Lord! how long," he would often say, "remember poor Africa!"

When he became delirious nothing soothed him like singing or prayer. To the very last he joined in the act of praise. On one occasion when the old tune "Martyrdom" was sung to the first verses of Psalm xl., he imagined he was back again in the church, and, raising himself in bed, said: "Aye, that's prayer; let us have it again, brethren, before we part." The familiar words would often rise to his lips: "Let us have a word of prayer;" and what fervent prayers they were, as if he felt his Master was very near to him! "Hush, my soul," he cried out one day, after a time of great agony—"no dark thoughts, no dark words—trust Him to the end;" while often, in the silence of the night, he would be heard repeating with indescribable pathos the well-known lines:

> Just as I am, without one plea,
>   But that thy blood was shed for me;
> And that thou bid'st me come to thee,
>   O Lamb of God, I come.

At last the wearied, shattered body found rest. Early on Saturday morning, October 18, 1884, he closed his earthly labours, extending over forty-two years in this and other lands, and went home to be with the Lord for ever. "Frequently, in former days, he had gazed with deep interest and admiration on the stars that compose the Southern Cross. He now entered the presence of him who made the Seven Stars and Orion, and gave all their glory to the heavens, in the midst of adoring multitudes, celebrating the wondrous cross on which the Prince of Glory died."

Although ominous whisperings of the coming dissolution had been in circulation during many weeks, which had the effect of preparing the public mind for the announcement of his death, yet, when the village and community awoke to the sad truth on Saturday morning that the end had come, a spontaneous expression of sorrow, sadness, and sympathy possessed all classes in the village. The only thing spoken of was the death of Mr. Inglis.

The funeral services took place on Monday, October 20. After a short, preliminary service in the manse, conducted by Rev. John Thomson of Ayr, Rev.

W. A. McKay of Woodstock, and Rev. James Little of
Princeton, the body was removed to the church, which
was heavily draped in mourning, and crowded to overflowing by a sympathetic audience, many of whom
came from Brantford, Galt, Woodstock, and other
parts of Ontario. The Presbytery of Paris was present
in a body; also the Presbyterian ministers of Galt,
and the Methodist clergymen of Ayr and the neighbouring villages. The services in the church were
conducted by the Rev. R. Pettigrew of Glenmorris, the
Rev. Wm. Robertson of Chesterfield, and the Rev. Dr.
Cochrane of Brantford. After reading selections of
Scripture appropriate to the occasion, Dr. Cochrane
gave a brief but touching address. After alluding to
the universal esteem in which Mr. Inglis was held by
the entire community, and the intense sorrow felt by
his people and co-presbyters, he referred to the more
prominent characteristics of the deceased: his wonderful simplicity of character; his strong sense of
humour; the fearlessness with which he stated his
convictions; the tenderness and sympathy which he
ever manifested for the sufferings of his fellow-men;
his humility in refusing positions of prominence; the
wonderful originality of his discourses; the impressive-
ness of his prayers, in which the reverent familiarity
that he used in speaking to God gave evidence of life-
long communion with heaven; and, finally, the entire
consecration of his life, often amid trials and privations in this and other lands, to the cause of his
Master. He closed by calling upon those who had
sat under his ministry during the last fifteen years,
but were still unconverted, to follow in his footsteps,

and regard this solemn providence as a last call to repentance.

The congregation was then permitted to view the dead form of him who had preached so often and so earnestly from that pulpit, beneath which he lay with a peaceful smile across his face, after which the school children were marched in double file to the church, where they also were given the last privilege of gazing upon the face of one who always took a keen interest in their welfare.

The vast concourse of people then formed into procession, four abreast, headed by the hearse, and followed by the chief mourners, elders of the church, the school children, and by the dense following of friends and acquaintances. It is generally computed that there were two thousand persons in the solemn cortège, which formed the most imposing demonstration of this nature ever witnessed in Ayr. All the surrounding cities and towns were represented in the procession, which, as it wended its way with solemn tread towards the cemetery, told its own moral of how a united sympathy and admiration was manifested for a man who had the courage to speak plain, ungarnished truths in pulpit and out of it, and whose independence, manliness, and integrity were so conspicuous in everyday life.

Arrived at the grave, where the Rev. W. T. Mc-Mullen of Woodstock, offered fervent prayer, the scene was solemn and impressive. Strong men mingled their tears with those of the women and children; the village bells tolled in mournful cadence; the wind was hushed, and, as the mortal remains of the physically

strong, intellectually gifted, and spiritually minded
Walter Inglis were lowered into their last resting-place
on earth, the sun, like to a great, round, golden ball
of fire, sank behind the hills of the west and beyond
the peaceful and picturesque Valley of the Nith. It
was, indeed, a golden sunset, and a fitting close to a
grand and useful life. At the beginning of his ministry he doubtless anticipated a different ending—

> To lift his dying eyes from Afric's burning sand.

But God ordered it otherwise. Awaiting the resurrection of the just, the body lies in the quiet and beautiful God's Acre that overlooks the scene of his last
but not least faithful work.

> Let him sleep
> The peaceful sleep that knows no troubled dream ;
> And while around his lonely bed we weep,
> Bright on his pillow falls the summer beam.
>
> Scatter flowers
> Upon the turf that makes his lowly bed ;
> And, while we tarry here, may it be ours
> In humble faith to follow where he led.

The funeral sermon was preached on the following
Sabbath, by the Rev. Wm. Robertson of Chesterfield,
to a densely crowded and sorrowing congregation, from
2 Corinthians iv. 13. Mr. Robertson also addressed
the congregation on the evening of the same day on
the power of a consecrated life, as illustrated in the
life and labours of their beloved pastor.

The following is the minute of the Kirk Session of
Stanley Street, Ayr, on occasion of the death of their
beloved pastor :

At a meeting of the Session of Stanley Street Church, Ayr, held on 24th day of November, 1884, it was unanimously agreed in profound sorrow, yet in humble acknowledgment of God's sovereignty, to place on record their deep sense of the loss sustained by themselves and the congregation in which they are office-bearers by the death of their beloved pastor, the Rev. Walter Inglis, which took place on the morning of Saturday, the 18th day of October, after a long and painful illness.

Mr. Inglis' ministry in Ayr, from the time of his induction in the year 1869, was one of unremitting labour, and evidently prompted by a zeal for the honour of his Lord. The self-sacrificing devotion which led him, at the beginning of his career, to consecrate his life to missionary work among the heathen, pervaded the service of his late years; while all who came into contact with him, more especially towards the close, felt that there was a deepening grace and power in his life, and a more vivid recognition of the Master. Many sacred truths, illumined by his clear and vigorous thought in expounding the Word of God, will linger long in the memory of his people, and be to them as the voice of the Master whom he served, calling them to true and noble life. His ministry to the sick and sorrowing has left many tender, sacred, and enduring memories.

The Session gratefully recall the prayerful spirit in which, as Moderator, Mr. Inglis presided in their meetings, and the fine discrimination, tenderness, and tact with which he sought to guide their deliberations.

Their tenderest sympathy is extended to the widow and bereaved family of our deceased pastor. It is their prayer that the Saviour, in whom he trusted so confidently in life, and whose name was so precious to him in death, would enrich them with the consolations of his grace, and pour balm into their wounds, as he, the Divine Physician, only can. To his guardian care and availing sympathy the Session would humbly, but earnestly, commend them in their sorrow.

At the first meeting of the Presbytery of Paris after the death of Mr. Inglis, the following minute was placed upon the records :

With profound sorrow, yet in humble acknowledgment of God's sovereignty, the Presbytery have to record the death of the Rev. Walter Inglis, minister of Stanley Street Church, Ayr, which took place on the 18th day of October last, in the sixty-eighth year of his age.

As a member of Presbytery, Mr. Inglis was a brother greatly beloved, having won the affectionate regard of all his brethren by the warmth of his own loving nature, and their esteem and reverence by his firm adherence to Christian principle and the high sense of honour which pervaded his conduct, as well as by his wisdom in counsel.

During the fifteen years of his ministry in. Ayr, Mr. Inglis laboured in season and out of season, and was much honoured by his Lord in the results of his work. He was ever ready to confess his own shortcomings ; yet, throughout the whole conduct of his ministry, it was apparent to his brethren and all with whom he came into intimate contact, that he was actuated by the same spirit of devotion and self-sacrifice which led him, at the beginning of his career, to devote his life to missionary work among the heathen in South Africa, and afterwards, in circumstances of great peril, to protest against the evils of slavery. The truths which he proclaimed to others were evidently the life of his own soul.

Mr. Inglis' faithfulness in pastoral visitation was a stimulating lesson to his brethren. His ministry to the sick and sorrowing was full of tenderest sympathy, and has associated with it many sacred memories. It is affecting to know that on his death-bed the people of his charge and his brethren of the Presbytery were made by him the subject of special prayer.

The Presbytery deeply sympathize with the congregation of Stanley Street Church in their loss of a pastor so worthy of their affection and reverence, and their prayer is that his dying prayer on their behalf may be richly answered.

In an especial manner the Presbytery condole with the bereaved family, while they commend them to the sympathy of the Great High Priest, the Saviour in whom their loved one trusted, and in whom trusting no troubled, sorrowing heart was ever disappointed.

They would recognize also in the death of their beloved brother a solemn reminder to themselves to be faithful in redeeming the time, and earnest and prayerful in the great work to which, as servants of Christ, they are called.

LITERARY REMAINS.

———

LECTURES.

LECTURES.

THE GENTLENESS OF THE SCOTCH, AS EXPRESSED IN THEIR POETRY AND SONGS.

[Delivered first before the Galt Mechanics' Institute.]

I may state the cause of my putting pen to paper, on the subject of lecture. I got a very polite invitation from the Secretary of the Galt Mechanics' Institute to speak on some Scotch subject, at a meeting held on Burns' Anniversary. I declined on account of health; yet I said I had a warm heart, both to the Mechanics' Institute and Scotland. Further, I desired not only to help them but also our own Institute in Ayr. I mentioned a subject that I thought I might speak on for a quarter of an hour—the gentleness of the Scotch, as expressed in their poetry and songs. I began to write for amusement. I mentioned the "bee" that was in my bonnet to Mr. Soutar, and he approved of it. The issue is, we are here assembled to discuss this topic. A word further; I am not very sure that those people who are generally, not to say continually, light-hearted, can equal an habitually grave man in a genuine side-aching laugh. I have in my eye the manly, glorious laugh of one of our greatest of existing Scotchmen when the suitable time and place gave opportunity. For the most genial refined intercourse, what a lasting effect laughter, full and free, when used like salt in our food, has upon sensible men. Many people are select of their company when they relax and take a laugh. You have heard of a company called to order by one of their number, saying: "Whisht, there is ane o' the fules comin'." A phase of Scotch character rarely touched upon, it may seem to some to indicate a measure of presumption in the subject of lecture.

What, it may be asked, have I or anybody in these days seen about either one nation or another that has not been seen and discussed long, long ago? I claim nothing new. I have no patent to present. But one thing I say, that my limited range of reading has not been favoured with any discussion on the subject at issue. My desire is to lay before you grounds for my belief that there is a large amount of gentleness in Scotch character. I mean not a mere trace in rare individuals, but such an amount of sweetness and light as are to be placed to the national credit. It is too true that men rarely find more than what they are looking for, and in many instances are sure to find what is earnestly desired. This weakness in man is illustrated by Sir William Hamilton in his lectures, somewhat as follows: A reverend parson and lady went together to get a peep at the moon through a powerful telescope. By the law of politeness, Miss put her eye first to the glass. After a good survey, she, in fine spirits, exclaimed that the view was very distinct, and that, amongst other objects, she saw two standing close by each other, who, she felt sure, were two lovers. "Let me see," said his young reverence. After due time for a deliberate judgment he said:

"Madam, I assure you that you are mistaken, these two objects I saw clearly; they are not two lovers, but two church steeples." Of course the lesson is, the lady was desirous of a sweetheart; he was in need of a church, or at least of the salary.

It is a difficult thing to know man. It is very difficult for a man to know himself. It is the old story of two knights meeting, and looking from opposite sides at a painted shield (you will excuse my lack of memory). One said it was silver, the other said it was gold. From words they came to blows; when a third came, and said "Hold." They tell their story. Both right, but one-sided. True knowledge is many-sided. Along the whole line of humanity the vision is rarely given, "To see oorsels as ithers see us." Having only two eyes, and these in front, it is simply impossible to see our bodily whole. I imagine there is some analogy to this in mental vision. It is not permitted by the all-wise Creator to see our whole soul; yet, though a man has not seen his whole hinder parts, he can nearly touch all, and become pretty well assured that he has no wings. How do others see both individuals and nations? Alas! for others, as well as self. If self-esteem leads to error in one case, so fellow-hatred leads to equally false judgment on the other hand. Nothing rarer than a candid, intelligent critic, in describing national habits. It is a conceit that is never to be indulged in that we are faultless, that we are model men, that all ought to regulate their conduct by our example. It is a crime against our common nature that personal or national sins should be covered with a large mantle of charity, and no mercy be shown to sins peculiar to other lands. In order to think and do the right we require a universal standard of right and wrong, binding the conscience of all nations. My subject is one on which all nations are qualified to judge : " gentle," "harmless," and their opposites, come within the range of instinct, not to speak of reason. There is a wonderful variety of character amongst the nations. Yet we have two poles—the most gentle, the most vicious and injurious. Speaking of individuals—some have no fight in them ; others seem to be all fight, ever ready to pick a quarrel with either man or beast. I, for one, admit that my countrymen have been a warlike, fighting people. I admit that Scotland, compared with most other lands, is a sterile country. " O, Caledonia, stern and wild ! " exclaims Sir Walter Scott—a meet nurse for poets, spare in bread. So late as the beginning of this century it was suggested by the witty Sydney Smith to the incipient Edinburgh Reviewers, that they should cultivate literature on a little oatmeal.

When I say warlike, I beg to discern *rightly* in our wars and fightings. Ours have, as an historic whole, been defensive wars. The Norman-English wars have been aggressive and Imperial. The three great wars which the Scotch fought to the bitter end, and to triumphant success, were defensive.

I. The war of political independence.

> Scots wha hae wi' Wallace bled,
> Scots wham Bruce has often led.

It need not then be wondered at that a few poor people, having resolved to be free at all hazards, were fired with a stern and lofty resolve to scorn the weakness of even a grin, let alone a smile. Who can blame them if their bowels and mercies became congealed, and their hands grasped death and cold steel as their father's legacy, their cup rendered bitter by false knaves and traitors among their own nobles ?

II. Then came the war of freedom to worship God, apart from "Pope and priest." Why should not this spiritual, mental conflict deepen the lines of grave countenances ? For the first time in my country's history John Knox gave the trumpet key-note : "Let schools be erected all over the land, let the people read and think for themselves. Who but base tyrants would say: 'Nay'?"

III. After a time came the long weary war against "black prelacy." "That transmogrified Scotch Solomon," James VI. and I., said : "No bishop, no crown." Greedy, false nobles said : "Amen." The Scotch peasantry fought on, and a watchful Providence gave them relief from the unequal strife.

IV. Long and bitter has been the conflict against patronage and its attendant evils. All these have been defensive wars. No wonder, I say again, after such centuries of conflict to hold their sacred rights, that such a people should be a grave people, jealous of their sacred inheritance. I can pardon the ignorance of foreigners, and the bitter pompous prejudices of the English. But what word of apology have we for Scotsmen who seem to have lost all sympathy with their countrymen in the conflict against Prelacy especially? There is much that is offensive and sad in finding the pages of some of our best writers all blurred with sneer and caricature concerning men who crowned the labours of Wallace and Bruce.

Down to my own day the much-belauded Government of Britain has tried in every possible fashion to fetter and cramp the expanding souls of freemen. Take Sir Walter Scott, Scotchman *par excellence.* You find him devoting all the wealth of his descriptive powers to exhibit the Scotch warrior fighting to defend his bleak country from the greedy grasp of an ambitious neighbour. He pours forth his lay in heroic numbers to the setting in sunlight glow of Highland cateran and border riever, but not a word even of apology for the "Covenanters." It would have been much better if he had left the religious life of Scotland untouched than to have mangled it in the way he has done. "Jeanie Deans" is drawn as a true, loving, heroic girl; but her father is only "Douce Davie," narrow, repulsive, fanatical; and yet this poor fellow is made to do duty as a representative man of the "Covenanters," yea, of the Presbyterians. Think of the kindly heart of Scott having a sly stab at the religious life of Scotland. We have all seen Davie Deans. He is, and has been, amongst us, but not as our leader; far from it. Have you never been struck with the fact that our novel writers have a much better class of women than of men? Aye! Water can never rise above its level. They dare not describe a better man than themselves. Is it possible to think of a nation of good women and bad men? Nay, verily. Turn to Hogg's "Broonie o' Bodsbeck." Auld Wat Tait's daughter is a true, noble woman, wise and courageous like my countrywomen. But why make the leader of the Covenanters a hunchback and a noodle? Our fathers were quaint men, but who ever heard such a prayer as Davie Tait's? It is too clever by one-half.

The leaders of Scotch Reformers have all been men with the Bible in their hands, and a goodly portion in their memory. This being so, there has been, as there now is, where our fine old patriarchal character still exists, a homely dignity becoming a worm of the dust, speaking to the Eternal God. Hogg is nearer the truth than Scott. Wilson, poor fellow, with all his genius, has much of nature, a splendid physique, representative of the singing, fishing, drinking and rollicking Scotchman. To me the only true picture of the genuine Scotch peasant is Burns' "Cottar's Saturday Night." All is natural, manly; not a word of caricature. The father is kind, respected, loved, no cant or humbug in the presence of his children. Allan Ramsay's "Gentle Shepherd" is unique in the history of literature. It gives a view of pastoral simplicity which has no parallel—a picture of our "fathers" two centuries ago.

An important question naturally arises, How is it that so many veritable Scotchmen amongst our popular writers have utterly failed to represent the deep religious heart of their country? The reason seems to lie in deep organic, mental and moral differences. This is seen in a very striking manner amongst the Jews. The influence of mothers in giving tone and character to a people is easily realized in the case of Ishmael and Isaac. It is far more subtile in the case of the twins, Esau and Jacob. This law of difference adheres to that wonderful people to the present day. There is the noble, princely Jew, the true descendant of Abraham. There is also the " pedlar Jew," the sharp, tricky trader, a true descendant of Jacob and Laban. Joseph and his brethren made peace, but they never coalesced. Something of the same sort lies at the root of Scotch character. A striking instance of this sort is related of Dr. Chalmers and his brother Sandy. This elder brother was in business in London. He boarded in a house where some young men resided. Dr. Chalmers was preaching in London with great popularity. One or more of these young men went to hear him. They spoke with rapturous praise. Sandy as drily remarked " that he never could see anything to make such a talk aboot Chalmers." " Did you ever hear him ? " asked one of them. " Hear him," said Sandy, " hear him ; umph ! I heard him half an 'oor after he was born." This was the first hint of his being Dr. Chalmers' brother. In many, many instances you have brothers, aye, and sisters, never able to understand each other. This now brings us to the mental characteristic we desire to illustrate and enforce. We have Whig and Tory very pronounced. We have religious and irreligious ; we have hard and soft, the rude and the gentle.

In entering upon the subject of lecture, I may say that I am not going to make a fool of myself by groping my way into the higher circles or the so-called genteel. Like most writers I am not seeking after good manners and polished address. *My* question is, What have been the tone and temper of the shepherds and ploughmen, the farmers and tradespeople, the religious heart of the Scotch plain people? their family affections? Let us deal with facts and not fancies. I take it to be a fact, that from the days of John Knox the parish school and the Bible have made a greater mass of the poor people of Scotland to be readers and clear thinkers than this world ever saw amongst a people of the same number. I know that many have remained ignorant and wicked; some districts less, others more. One thing became very noticeable in Scotland, and that was the strong hold which reading the Bible attained amongst the solitary shepherds and stock farmers. Nothing like it took place in England or Germany. No, not even in Switzerland and Holland. It became the passion of the Lowland Scotch, from the Grampians to the Cheviots, to teach their children to read. Their reading consisted of the Book of books, with a few other religious books as they slowly issued from the press. I am so old-fashioned as to believe that never was a people so highly privileged for the cultivation of the loving and the gentle as these children of the Reformers were. I know many superstitions clung to them, yet above all these voices, "Thus saith the Lord" sounded louder far than aught of "Witch or Warlock." Then, as now, some hearts were open to receive all the words of eternal life.

The union of Scotland with England took place. The gentry went to London, to Parliament, etc., and learned English ways; ambition began its dark career in the eighteenth century; patronage showed its sad fruits; Secession protested; morals relapsed, and, sad to say, poor misguided Burns was disgusted with the cant and hypocrisy he saw around him in religious circles.

I know not against whom he specially levels his sharp,
stinging arrows.   One thing is certain, if he had been
consistent with his indomitable love of liberty he ought
to have been a Seceder, and to have stood by the
religion that helped the poor man against the great, a
thing " State clergy " never have done, except in rare
instances.* The issue of all is that through storm and
sunshine, through good report 'and bad report the
Scotch glens and moorlands nursed a people, intelligent—for they knew their Bible; gentle—for their
hearts were not torn by ambition; loving—for they did
not ramble up and down the country amongst strangers
seeking new things.   I know well the havoc wrought
by the run of events on to the close of the eighteenth
century.   Yet a goodly remnant has continued to the
present time. I know the kindness of the citizen, of the
learned, of the public character, mingling largely as I
have done with men. I have tasted the freshness of the
large-hearted English woman. Much kindness have I received, both in Africa and Canada. Yet, in spite of many
compensating advantages, enjoyed by others, I have
known no heart so gentle and so sweet as that of the
woman or man who knew nothing, or at least very little,
of the ways of the world, but loved the Bible and served
the Lord God with a steadfastness that is to me wonderful. Sweetness and temper, tried with many temptations from the sharp snell Scotch temper, that sometimes plays like forked lightning around the gentle one.

---

* As a matter of fact, Burns often went to hear the Rev. William Inglis,
then Seceder Minister in Dumfries, and was, for doing so, frequently
twitted by his cronies among the Established clergy.   The reply of the
poet was characteristic, and to the point :—"I gang to hear Mr. Inglis
because he is the only man amang ye that believes a word he says."

High above passion's thunder-cloud the loving gentle heart held fellowship with God and man with unfaltering peace. I beg you to mark this : this is not the gentleness of weakness, but the moral force of a wonderfully balanced mind. I dare say some can give instances of fiery quick-tempered men becoming calm at the very sight of their wives. I knew a man in this country whose temper seemed at times to be beyond all control, yet he never was known to meet his wife with a frown.

There is a peace that passeth understanding, and I am convinced that amongst my countrymen, and especially my countrywomen, there is a gentleness that no rudeness can shake, no bitterness sour. Yea, I have known instances of the gentle and the crabbed matched against each other for forty years, acting and re-acting upon each other with the varied play of life-producing influences. Whilst the perverse temper did not melt into thin air and chill the family atmosphere no more, this, I am certain, is the truth, that many a large lump of sweetness was thrown into the cup of the restless one, and rarely, very rarely, did the tartaric acid froth the cup of the strong, gentle spirit. There is such a thing as weak natural amiability yielding to the strong-willed, irregular, rasping temper, and becoming in old age a complaining, weary traveller in the journey of life, whining, ever whining. You will find others gathering dignified composure through the very troubles that have assailed them by the way. How fine to see a woman's heart tempered like a "Damascus blade," bending till ends meet, yet springing back without a twist or increase of weakness. My illustration is feeble, for the best of steel is not strengthened or improved by rough handling, but the true soul grows more elastic every time it is tried—break, never; heroic evermore; returning good for evil, not railing for railing; no fits of concentrated gloom; no freezing and thawing of tender affection; no pouts and zeal for the good and the right, with impatient fervour. There are some people who imagine that husband and wife must have far less affection for each other in old age than in youth. Not necessarily so. You have all read and heard sung, "John Anderson, my Jo, John." Burns was no dreaming German idealist: he photographed what he saw. His poetry is like glowing gold, crushed out of the hard quartz of everyday life. He had seen that kind, gentle, auld wifie, whose life was worthy of such words. Hats ever off, men, when they are said or sung—

John Anderson, my Jo, John, we clamb the hill thegither,
And mony a canty day, John, we've had wi' ane anither;
Now, we maun totter doon, John, but hand-in-hand we'll go,
And we'll sleep thegither at the fit, John Anderson, my Jo.

Why this fresh, loving old age? The childhood of all countries has a large amount of sameness; but nowhere can you find old age presenting venerable sweetness, except where the Bible has been the life-long food of the tottering one. The charm to others of such characters is their humble unconsciousness of worth. There are very worthy people found in society, but they know it as well. Aye, clever fellows, ready to teach everybody, both by word and example. Not so the genuine old Scot, whether man or woman. They

never weary of the A B C of life; let me reverse the
keen, often-quoted lines of Burns:

> O wad some power the giftie gie us,
> To see oorsels as ithers see us;
> It wad frae mony a blunder free us,
>   And foolish notion.

What a pity that our national bard was not granted
vision, to sing in immortal verse the worth of those
who never saw themselves as others see them! Many,
very many, there are that never could see anything
in themselves but worthless weakness and sin, while
others saw them far above their fellows in a beautiful,
gentle life. Why this ignorance of self? The reason
to me is very plain. Their vision has been arrested,
like the Apostle John in the Isle of Patmos, with a
sight of the Son of Man. It is impossible to see such
a sight, and ever again be deceived by self-beauty or
importance. There is such law in our nature as fasci-
nation. Why? It is in the lower animals. A head
white as snow, emblematic of great age; the Ancient
of Days, worthy of reverence from the child of years.
And what are "threescore and ten"? "A watch in the
night." His eyes like fire (in such writing marvellous
genius). Though the head is hoary, the eye is full
of youthful fire; his feet like a warrior's limbs sheathed
in polished brass, showing the kingly character; his
voice or words falling upon the ear like many waters;
the conscience hearing law like the coming in of old
Ocean's tide. Just think of homely peasants keeping
such exalted company, through all the toils and drud-
geries of life! When they thought of His toils and sufferings for them—for poor humanity—they felt them-

selves equal to minister with a loving, gentle hand and heart to their family and neighbours.

"See themselves as ithers see them." Aye, that would be a sight! Others, looking upon all this wealth of soul of such utter unconsciousness, have been led to earnest prayer that a small portion of such a spirit may rest upon the poor, vain heart desirous of the praise of man. This is not fancy but fact, due to the memory of departed ones, dear, I trust, to many in this meeting. Alas! for those whose recollections have no trace of men and women far, far superior to us. Due, I say, again, to the solitary shepherd's cot and peasant's humble home—due to the Giver of all good; lifting up the poor from the dunghill. I know nothing of cloistered Madonnas. My countrywomen have been daughters of honest toil. One thing, the drooping eye, thought by many to be a sign of exalted piety is nowhere found in the glens and vales of Scotland. Yet we have all seen eyes with guileless serenity able to look sin out of countenance.

Before I pass to another division of my subject I desire to enter my protest against the vulgar fashion in laboured descriptions of youth and beauty to the neglect of grander middle and old age. So far as I am aware (but I have to admit my reading limited), a full-drawn portrait of the genuine Scotch mother is yet a want in literature. Dr. Brown, the celebrated author of "Rab and his Friends," seems to me the type of writer of such high and sacred work. He draws from life to the life. Who can ever forget the picture he draws of that gentle, suffering woman enduring the pangs of an operation for cancer in the

breast in the hospital at Edinburgh? No chloroform
in those days to dull the edge of the knife as it went
through quivering flesh. How the company of students were silenced and softened as she tendered her
humble apology for any misconduct during the operation. The conduct of James, the guidman, draws
forth appreciation in the whole sad scene. Those of
you who have not read the story cannot do better than
join our library, were it for no other purpose than
reading for yourselves the possibilities of human life.
O, that I could write an ode, an epic, on behalf of
such patient, peaceful sufferers.

I hear some one saying: "Granted that there are
many gentle, warm-hearted women, and some few,
kind noodles of men. But what of the great mass of
Scotchmen?" I wish to make this the backbone of
my lecture. Further, I know that the great complaint
against my countrymen is not the *perfervidum ingenium*. "Fine fellow, fine fellow; quick, like gun-
powder, but it soon passes. I like him," quoth Mr.
Highbent. The crime of Scotchmen, with many, is
being Calvinistic and Presbyterian. "It is not possible,
sir, for such a man to be anything else than a sour,
lean fanatic. Here's the rub! Such men led on by
these rude, ungentlemanly ministers' long harangues
of sermons; no genius in them—no geniality. The
gloom of a Scotch Sabbath is fitted to ruin any mind."
One would think, to hear some folks talk, that John
Knox ruined a fine people, and brought gloom to every
man's hearth and pulpit throughout the length and
breadth of the land. Let me ask men of all descriptions, What is there in Calvinism to make any man

a gloomy, sour fanatic ?   I know of nothing more ad-
verse to a Calvinistic man than when the great Creator tells a farmer to plough, sow, and reap, in order
that he may eat.   Why do men not turn lazy, surly
knaves because God has burdened life with such in-
tolerable burdens to genteel fingers ?   Calvinism is
certainly guilty of this.   " Work out life "—don't try
to dance it out.   Presbyterianism !   Heigho !   Why,
sir, Presbyterianism is becoming the balanced middle,
both in Church and State, all over the world.   The
ghost of election has frightened some men to such an
extent that it won't allow people to elect their minister,
councils, or members of Parliament.   What is Presbyterianism but in a constitutional sense the rights and
liberties we so richly enjoy, both in the British Empire
and the United States.   "Hold on," says Mr. Gay
Jumping Jack, "it is that awful, silent Scotch Sabbath, backed by the Shorter Catechism, that has
spoiled you—horrid creatures, that dare cease from
babbling and gossip for one whole day !"   " That is
what has made Scotchmen long-faced, with high cheek
bones and thin noses," says Mr. Lightfoot.   If so, it
will be interesting to watch the effects of the teachings
of the various sects upon the flat-nosed faces.   Let me
ask, Are all grave men sour, bitter, fanatical ?   Facts
tell another tale.   There is a grave man before you.
He was once a gay-hearted youth.   Why the change ?
His sky became clouded; a dark, thunder-tempest
burst over his soul.   His fair, loved one, his young
wife, withered and passed away.   Or it may be a
loved child, or some very dear friend, passed through
the dark shadow of death.   He is sad, but not sour ;

grave, but not sullen. This is the case with true,
gentle hearts in all lands. This is the cause of multitudes of Scotchmen being grave. The very depth
and tenderness of their inmost souls render them
incapable of ever forgetting the dear past. Hear the
beatings of the true English heart in the words of the
late Hon. Mrs. Norton :

> But many who thus mourn for thee sadly
>   Soon joyous as ever shall be ;
> Thy fond orphan boy shall laugh gladly,
>   As he sits on some kind comrade's knee.
>
> There is one who will still pay the duty
>   Of tears for the true and the brave,
> As when first in the bloom of her beauty
>   She wept o'er her soldier's grave.

Aye, there is a love strong as death. Life strings
broken, never to be mended. Why not with a tender
conscience ? This is the very essence of Christianity.
It is an old tradition that Jesus Christ was never
known to laugh. Whatever truth there may be in the
legend, it is a fact, belonging to all ages and countries,
that the purest, most loving, and intelligent men and
women this world has ever seen have had an inex-
pressible charm of the grave and dignified. This has
been my experience. Without trenching upon the
odious in comparison, the case with my countrymen
stands thus : Their very intellectual power, their comprehensive far-sightedness, the difficulties of life, both
spiritual and temporal, render them deeply sensitive
and relatively grave amongst the nations. This to me
is a universal truth.

Why those terrible fits of gloom that overshadowed

Burns' mind?   Hear him, poor fellow, addressing the " mousie ":

> But, mousie, thou art no thy lane,
> In proving foresight maybe vain ;
> The best-laid schemes o' mice and men
>   Gang aft a-gley,
> And lea'e us nought but grief and pain
>   For promised joy.

Oh, sad words, the closing verse :

> Still thou art blessed compared wi' me,
> The present only toucheth thee ;
> But, och, I backward cast my e'e
>   On prospects drear,
> An' forward though I canna see,
>   I guess and fear.

What scalding tears must have been shed when he wrote the closing verses to a " daisy ":

> Even thou who mourn'st the daisy's fate,
> That fate is thine—no distant date ;
> Stern Ruin's ploughshare drives elate,
>   Full on thy bloom,
> Till crushed beneath the furrow's weight
>   Shall be thy doom.

The position that I take can be proved from our fine national music and songs.   This is a subject for my musical brother, Mr. Thompson.   Excuse a few words on both.   The music of war's wild note is sharp and quick.   Notes that kindle the heart to the white-heat glow of patriotic fire, the irresistible and fearless advance upon the foe, is given in " Scots wha hae." But the deadly fray is over, and mourning for the dead commences.   The same music is drawn out to double length, and you have the pathetic dirge of the "Land o' the Leal." Hence the music of gentle mourners is all long-drawn semibreves. The wailing soul lingers on each note and word. Take the "Flowers o' the Forest." The refrain is the very perfection of love and grief interpenetrated. "Oor braw foresters are a' wed awa'." Again, "Ma dear Heeland Laddie O":

Ah, wae's me wi' their sodgerin sae gaudy O,
The laird's wised awa' ma dear Heeland laddie O ;
Misty are the glens, and the dark hills sae dreary O,
That aye seemed sae blythe wi' ma dear Heeland laddie O.

Let me stop, for the number of such is manifold. The man that has no appreciation for such words and tunes has little in him. The same spirit delights in the long-drawn tunes in our churches. When a church delights in nothing but lilts and reel tunes, you know for certain that all pathos has gone. This fact of pathos is not exclusively the expression of sorrow. Hear the fine song, "Braw, Braw Lads on Yarrow Braes"; or,—

Ca' the yowes tae the knowes,
Ca' them where the heather grows,
Ca' them where the burnie rows,
   My bonnie dearie.

Hence the national heart can only be expressed by that marvellous use of the bow-hand when you make the violin give forth the finest of all instrumental music :

Let organs bum wi' ghostly soond,
Pianos peep and squall, man ;
Gie me the fiddle's sweetest soond
Tae mak' the tears doon fa', man.

To beat time to the Scotch passions you have

nowhere a quicker step in youthful joy and war's wild charge, neither have you a slower in lover's bower and sorrow's chamber.   Oh ! very well, says a critical friend ; the class you speak of is comparatively small. You have admitted that the Scotch are a warlike race. How do you reconcile gentleness and war ?   I have stated that my countrymen have never shown an aggressive spirit.   We have nearly always been on the defensive.   Such a man can easily be bold and gentle. Take the following verses as a sample :

> He turned and left the spot ;
>   O, do not deem him weak ;
> For dauntless was the hero's heart,
>   Though the tear stood on his cheek.

> Go mark the foremost ranks
>   In danger's dark career ;
> Be sure the hand most daring there
>   Has wiped away the tear.

The best and the bravest of men have gone to battle in defence of home and hearth.   Hear the call of duty in Tannahill's " Loudon's Bonny Woods and Braes," says he :

> Wha can thole, when Britain's faes
> Wad gie Britons laws, lassie ?

Yet a step further into the hearts and habits of my countrymen.   We are called dour, positive.   I admit such a class amongst us.   What do we find after we have passed the class that will neither listen to rhyme nor reason ?   We come to men whom you need not try to frighten.   " Daur me !" the stout response is given. "Wha wull daur me"?   No use.   For this the man is called dour.   You try flattery, with as little success.

Nae doubt soft soap fits some ; not the genuine Scotch-man. What kind of a man is that, say ye, that will neither be frightened nor fleeched ? Let me say, such arts as frightening and fleeching are neither manly nor womanly. Speak to a man's reason. Show facts to a man's heart. Put real suffering before this hitherto unmoved man, and you find a great, true, compassionate nature. But why is the man so reserved and dry ? We are taunted at once with being cold and canny—why ? It is the very modesty of the man that keeps him from speaking.

It is desirable that we were sometimes more suave in our manners. But mind you, politeness and true gentleness are very far apart. This aspect of character can be traced from the days of shy childhood to the grave, quiet old man that some people can make nothing of. There are many of our finest minds unable to take the lead in conversation. The late Dr. Brown of Edinburgh had fine conversational powers, if an intelligent friend put, now and again, a good, stout question. If you sat, he would sit. I have heard of an instance of a reverend Doctor being in his company, who lacked the gift of leading the way. They sat for dear knows how long, in deep, abstracted silence. I remember, in my old student days, a spry young fellow asked if I knew Mr. So-and-so. "Yes," I said, "a little." "Can you make anything out of him ?" says he. Quoth I, " A great deal more than I find in myself." I spent a night with the old man, in the same bedroom, beds apart. It was a long summer morning. I have always been heavy-headed in the early morning. However, I heard two or three great, manly yawns, a roll over; and, by and by, the old man said, "Are you sleeping? I answered "No." At length the old gentleman, leading the way in much fine, elevated thinking, got me to talk, he clinching his observations with an appropriate quotation from Young's "Night Thoughts." Thinks I, he has that grand book all at his finger-ends. Indeed, I don't know where I can go to get a more striking example of gentleness than this great, strong, healthy farmer. He once saw a mouse in a box-trap. What did he do? Set cat, or dog, on it? Not at all; instead of killing it, he steps away across a big field, lets it out, saying: "Gang awa noo, and dinna come back again." Sir Walter Scott had only to step up the Gala a few miles to meet with such a man, full of Scotch life and English classics. Egh! but he was a Seceder elder. What a pity to see Scott's kindly nature stunted by his Episcopalian notions.

Hear the kindly heart of Burns 'a dunt duntin', when he turned up the mousie's nest with the plough:

> Wee, sleekit, coo'rin, tim'rous beastie,
> Oh, what a panic's in thy breastie!
> Thou need na start awa' sae hasty,
>   Wi' bick'ring brattle.
> I wad be laith to rin and chase thee
>   Wi' murd'ring pattle!

Let me give you another instance in my own experience. More than fifty years ago, an elder brother and myself trudged over bleak Fala moor, three and a half miles to school. Not a house or steen dyke to shelter. My father's shepherd, who had charge of the north side hirsel, made it a point to meet the bit callants on the boundary of his range. He was a tall, thin, weather-beaten, grave man. On a cauld night, for it was just dark when we got home, Sandy would take our hands, and rub them, and speak to us quiet words of penetrating kindness. Not a word of nonsense did he ever haver with us. To speak for myself, sunny memories were deeply photographed in my young rattlecap heart. After a time, Sandy went to Canada. Twenty-two years ago I was preaching in Pickering, and stayed with a well-to-do farmer. I got on to a long screed of young life with mine host. I mentioned the name of Sandy Stirling. " Man," says the farmer, " a ken 'im fine ; he lives o'er in Scarboro'." To end the matter, he drove me over, and we had a long, long chat. He seemed like an old friend. Well, a step further. Many years after, I was in company with the late Dr. George, who died at Stratford. He was Sandy's minister in Scarboro'. The Doctor took a hearty laugh, and said : " I remember a fine incident about Sandy. There was a very important gentleman elected as trustee, or superintendent of the school, I have forgotten which. He had to work with Sandy. He had only seen poor Sandy's outer man, for he was neither braw nor bonny. " Please, Doctor,' says he, " you'll help me to manage that stupid-looking man, Stirling." With a quiet heart-chuckle the Doctor composedly said, " O, aye, I'll help you, if need be." Time went on, when the Doctor's friend met him, and soon the conversation turned on Sandy. " Why, Doctor, I was quite mistaken about that man Stirling." " I knew that when you spoke to me about him," said his reverence, " but 1 thought I would let you find out for yourself." "Why, sir, that man's a philosopher." (Twinkle in the eye of the Doctor)—"Did you have a talk on English liter: ature?" "Why, sir, he is far ahead of me in a knowledge of standard authors." Just so,—Longfellow says, "things are not what they seem;" we may add, "men are not what they seem." Many noblemen are like oysters—"hard shell outside, soft meat inside," and the reverse. All polish and smiles without, but go in a little and you'll find hard pan.

I would yet further enforce my position from the structure of the Scotch language. National character is strongly brought out in words and style of utterance. You are at once impressed with the Imperial ruling mind of England when you read the rolling periods of our orators and statesmen. In speaking English properly you instinctively draw yourself up; even the mouth has to be inflated for the *os rotundum*. Fashion lends her arts of imitation, of polish and refinement; every word has to be courtly. Voltaire's saying on languages is not complete. "If you are to speak to your lover," says he, "let it be in Italian; if to a courtier, in French; if to a philosopher, in English; if to a dog, in Dutch; if to the devil, in German." I may add, if to a child, let it be in Scotch. Brief in expression, full of diminutives—just the fit vehicle for a loving mother to prattle with her child. One or two examples : Wee Willie Winkie, wee deary, ma croodlin doo, my dawty, broo brenty, e'e winkie, nose nappy, cheek cherry, moo merry, chin chaky, gudly gudly gakkins. Tuts! you cannot translate that fine fun into English. Try it, if you dare—smooth brow, little winking eye. Hush, mun, and dinna mak a fule o' yersel. Repeat and sing to yourself "Castles in the air," and you have simple, pure Saxon of the finest order. I would further observe, in proof of my position, that the people of Scotland are, as a whole, gentle from one of our nicknames. These side names have generally some ground for their usage. Well, they call us canny. The proper meaning of this word is gentle, inoffensive. In speaking of a neighbour, we say, "He is a canny man," that is, a quiet, peaceable person. I am well aware that it has a sinister meaning when used by outsiders. He is quiet, but sharp at a bargain, and can take care of the siller after he has got it.

For the sake of argument, let me admit that the Scotch are sharp in business; yet the word canny implies that they do business without brag and bluster. Why, this admission is valid proof of what I say. It is a rare thing to meet with a pompous Scotchman. I have only heard of one that an auld wife in a "peck o' trouble, rinnin efter her coo," met on the road. The auld body, sair fore fuchen and desperately in need o' help, cried out: "Man, turn that coo." With indignation, he replied: "Woman, I am no a man; I am a magistrate." Scotchmen are proverbial for unassuming airs amongst strangers. In fact, they are rather sheepish, bashful. This mental temperament is one of the earliest expressions of their character, and it is one of the last to be rubbed off. Look at these boys and girls. The mother can hardly get them coaxed to go into the room to meet a visitor. If they have been forced forward, you cannot get them to speak. So the apology will be given: "I dinna ken

what tae du wi' oor bairns; they are unco bashfu'
amang strangers." In fact, as a nation, we don't like
forward brats. The belief is very general that such
are spoiled things, and will never come to anything.
What do we find amongst men and women? A shy-
ness that makes English, not to speak of the jabberin'
bodies the French, and others, think that there is
nothing in such a simple, unassuming man. I beg
your special attention to what I now say: This back-
wardness in self-assertion gets different treatment in
the various circles of society. If I were in a jocular
mood I would tell you how many fair, proud dames
have been led to choose the wrong man, because
nature's nobleman had never been trained to use
flattering words. Let two other examples suffice. The
learned and mercantile young men are summoned to
be tried for office. The bashful Scotchman seems a
very unlikely competitor. Odds are all against him.
To the astonishment of men who reckon by first-sight
judgments, the canny Scot is ahead by a long way.
Let us now look at business men. An unpretending
Scot comes into contact with sharp, rollicking, self-
assertive men. Aha! say they to themselves, here is
a greenhorn. They never for a moment doubt of a
triumph in making a bargain. Think of their disgust
when they find clear eyes in t'other head. Outwitted,
they cry, "Canny,"—that is, a cunning, quiet rogue.
There was neither trick nor knavery in the whole
transaction, as far as the Scotchman was concerned.
But some people are so stupid, or possibly so perverse,
as to say that a man of few words is and must be
cunning. Mind you, it is no business of mine to say

that there is no foxy Scotchman. I say that this is not a "national characteristic." A people brave to a byword cannot sneak. A people who will allow no man or nation to lord it over them will also be careful in committing the error of too much or too little superiority. I may say that in this great work-a-day world the Scotch are notable for a cool judgment, strangely joined with the *perfervidum ingenium*—the fervid mind, not cunning. They are deep, but clear. I have a word to say in reference to that national title "dry." This so-called dryness can be accounted for by the same law of analysis as canny. The man is modest, bashful, slow, thoughtful. He gives his opinion in a deliberate manner. If it is incisive, it is called dry. Why this should be so I, for one, do not well understand. I beg you to notice a physical, as well as mental, rule that runs through the whole line. You cannot give a light, frisky turn to large bodies. Feathers and straws have a different motion from trees and bars of iron. What a difference between the flights of the swallow and the eagle! So, in like manner, between the gambols of a monkey and an elephant. Enter upon the motion and action of living creatures, and you find the same difference prevading all flesh, fish, and fowl. All mental motion of men must be regulated by the same principle. Large, strong-minded men cannot, in the nature of things, whisk about with light, fairy step and thought. Whatever drawback you may make upon the width and depth of Scotch mind, they are, as a people compared with other nations, built from a large pattern. A people for many generations showing such a determined love of liberty must possess, in an unparalleled degree, mental qualities of the largest, highest order. Make the contrast where and how you please, you will find it true that the large, manly mind gives a singular order of dignified gravity.

Frivolous wits laugh at us. It is nothing more than the fun of a mosquito dancing round the head of a splendid horse. "Poor horsy," cries the nimble nothing, "catch me, kill me!" Pshaw! This is about the amount of value to be put upon the whole tribe of banjo-playing negro slaves and rope-dancing fiddle-didees, who try to turn creation into a grin and a farce. Let us look into this distressing disease of dryness. Can we suppose that a people, conscious of their freedom and power, are to be amused and cheated by shams and fair speeches? Never! The plain, truth-loving man states his opinion regardless of all statements to the contrary. There is no need of calling a man dry, or sour, because he is clear-headed enough to hit a nail upon the head or to prick a wind-bag. Take, for example, that well-known case of the late Lord Cockburn asking the shepherd why it was that sheep were so stupid as to lie with their heads to the wind on cold days, adding if he, Lord C., were a sheep he would turn his back to the weather. "Aye," rejoins the shepherd, "but if ee war a sheep ee wad hae mair sense." There was no disrespect either given or taken, as his Lordship was a genuine Scotchman, and dearly loved his clear-headed countrymen. Yet a fine remark like the above is called by some "dry." Why, to me it is as sappy as a "haggis" well made. The point I wish to make is to the effect that quiet, so-called "dry men" are

found possessed of gentle, tender, loving hearts.
There is as great a difference between the expression
of the feelings of a strong-minded, clear-thinking
man and the reverse, as there is between a blaze of
straw and the steady glow of coals from maple. There
are some other points I wished to touch on, but I shall
leave my subject presenting the worth and value of an
unexhausted mine. I felt desirous of taking a look at
these fierce Scotchmen in church assemblies down to
the stiff debate between "twa nceburs" on a point
ecclesiastical or theological.

Now, in a word, what is the use of talking or comparing. There never has been in any part of the
world such assemblies. That's the rub. Scotch
religious life is a theme that stands alone. It has
been, is, and will be the educator of the world on
united freedom. I am now going to bring evidence
from a sad phase of my countrymen. It is a melancholy fact that many, very many, have yielded to the
use of strong drink, *In vino veritas.* I have to admit
that drinking habits were formed by very alluring
temptations. "Tam o' Shanter and Souter Johnny"
is a picture to the life. Song and good fellowship
found place amongst all classes. The contrast between
the Scotch howff and the Canadian bar is immense.
It is not my subject to describe one or other further.
I have simply to say, in comparison with the amount
of drinking and drunkenness, there was comparatively
little fighting. There are men who become savage
under the influence of liquor; but the killing of wives
and children was rare. I know not how it is now.
Possibly there was one weak spot for the young

ploughmen, to fight at fairs over their sweethearts, and
sometimes get their blood warm when they got
fighting; yet I never knew of many brutal frays in
my young days, even amongst the lowest of all classes,
the Midlothian colliers. These, with the Gilmerton
coal carters, are described by the late Hugh Miller as
the lowest stratum in his geologic description of the
Scotch and English. If I remember rightly, it was
that old rough customer, Judge Braxfield, that charged
heavily against a man for using a lethal weapon
against his boon companion, a thing almost unheard
of. This fact is unmistakable as to temper, when even
in respectable circles they drank so deeply that a man
was kept to loose the neckties of those under the table.
It is a pity that such beautiful words as "Auld Lang
Syne" are weighted with the cup of kindness,

> And tak' a richt gude wullie wacht.

Let there be a "cup o' kindness"—and what finer
than water or milk as emblems of purity and life?
By common report the Russian peasants are very
good-natured under the influence of strong drink. I
shall not endeavour to draw the lines of comparison
on this dark feature of the human race further. Possibly I have detained you long enough. If so, I may
be permitted to wind up my subject with a few general,
closing remarks. Believing, as I do, in one Eternal
God, creator of all things, the governor and guide of
all nations, there seems on the page of history sufficient evidence that he has, from the beginning,
worked out his bright designs by heroic men and
heroic nations. From the lowly ranks of society

Providence has raised up men to be the benefactors of their fellow-men. For the highest and grandest work of man not many noble are held in everlasting remembrance for profound wisdom, or unselfish love and patriotism. One of the great lessons given to the world by the Jews is the smallness of their numbers compared with the nations around them, weighted with a still more serious fact, their divisions among themselves, and the perversity that was continually thwarting their counsels and unity of action. Yet no nation has such a wonderful and varied history. I am strongly of the impression that the Scots have a place in modern history something like the Jews in ancient. There are peoples in the far-gone past that have left isolated chapters of great deeds, such as the Albigenses and Waldenses. These witnesses for truth perished in their struggle. Possibly there is not a single chapter of Scotch history equal to the tremendous conflict in the Netherlands against the colossal power of Spain. But the Dutch have given themselves over to trading and worldly wisdom. For long, long, yea, since they sent us over the Prince of Orange, they have played no part worth speaking of during these remarkable centuries. Scotland holds her individual life as an active partner in the firm, Great Britain & Co. I am not here to try my hand at a funeral oration over a "past people." Neither do I seek for a Fourth of July to hold an anniversary. The hoary nations of the Old World have no set time to commemorate their birth. To my taste there is something very schoolboy-like in our Dominion Day. No more dignity in it than April Fool-day. The history of Scotland has a striking analogy to the poor genius, slowly but surely taking the road to fame, unconscious of being anything in particular.

What rebuffs the original thinker ever has before the world acknowledges the immortal man! What mistakes! One thing to me is plain, that Scotland never stood as a whole, from John o' Groat's to the Cheviots, higher than she does now. The springtide of life is just coming upon the Highlands, when the Bible will have made its deep mark upon the Celt, as it did centuries ago on the Saxon Lowlands. Ronald and Donald are entering into far higher schools than were common when the broad claymore ruled the land.

In closing, whatever may be the future of Scotland, one thing seems plain to me, the simplicity and gentleness of the intelligent, God-fearing peasant are gone, never to return. The exquisite beauty of the best of men consists in never knowing ambition to excel their fellow in any sense whatever. The moral grandeur of the best of my countrymen and women was their unconsciousness of the depth and height of their inner man. Never more can a man prevent that common school of humanity, the newspaper, from spoiling the young and tender mind. Blessed people that rose unacquainted with the details of murders, judicial trials of offences, etc. In one generation the true Scotchman finds no place in this great composite land.

In conclusion, may it be our endeavour, in all our investigations into the character of other people and nations, that we do not try to pass over the best of the man and the best people of a country. O! it looks ill when a man seems to have delight in setting the weaknesses and errors of a man or nation in sunlight, and the good deeds are smothered by prejudice and passion—

> Then let us pray that come it may,
>   As come it shall for a' that;
> When sense and worth o'er a' the earth
>   Shall bear the gree and a' that.
> For a' that, and a' that, it's coming yet for a' that,
> When man to man the warld o'er
>   Shall brithers be and a' that.

It was a rough joke by some one on some learned man's writings—I have forgotten where or how—when he sent such an one his own writings bound in calf. True greatness is bound in simplicity. It is as plain to my mind as sunlight that civilization carried on to excess bears down a man with a yoke of slavery. There is the temperate zone in life as well as in this world we inhabit. The great nations are not under torrid suns. Heat enfeebles. A high civilization enfeebles the man both in body and mind. Perilous are the paths of ambition. Fine meats and drinks, expensive clothing, and grand houses are not required to make a strong, healthy, wise, and happy man. Scotland, with all the weaknesses, errors, and sins of thy sons, I love thee for the fathers' sake! That sunny memories of the good, gentle, and brave may ever live in the deepest heart of all her scattered sons and daughters is the earnest prayer of the lecturer.

> O ! Scotia, my dear, my native soil,
>   For whom my warmest wish to heaven is sent,
> Long may the hardy sons of rustic toil
>   Be blest with health, and peace, and sweet content,

> And O ! may heaven their simple lives prevent
> From luxury's contagion weak and vile ;
> Then, howe'er crowns and coronets be rent,
> A virtuous populace may rise the while,
> And stand, a wall of fire, around their much-loved isle.

What a pity if Scotland's glory has become dimmed through wealth, that her emigrant children should lose the homely virtues of the fathers. Let us show our children and neighbours that the highest type of man must be simple in habits in spite of wealth, gentle in manners, and true as steel in all his affections and relations to men. All else is peril and pain, vanity, and vexation of spirit.

Mr. Chairman, I wish that this lecture had been more worthy of the theme and this Institute. Yet, such as I have give I unto those who have honoured me with their presence.

LECTURE ON DR. LIVINGSTONE (INCOMPLETE).

[Delivered first before the Ayr Mechanics' Institute.]

In appearing before you this evening I may be allowed a brief word of preface. Ever since I received a valuable present of books from your committee, as an acknowledgment of a little service I rendered in getting the books numbered in a catalogue, I have had a desire to return public thanks by giving a lecture.

Just when debating with my double self the subject to be discussed, I received a polite message from your chairman that a lecture would be acceptable. I answered at once: "Yes, provided the committee will find a subject." This has ever been my difficulty in getting up a lecture. The name of Dr. Livingstone was mentioned. I answered: "So be it."

In directing your attention to the great African traveller, I may state briefly some reasons I have for venturing upon an estimate of his life and character.

It was in the summer of 1838 that I offered myself to the London Missionary Society to be one of its missionaries, after my studies were finished. The application was kindly received, and I was requested to come to London to meet with the directors. When about half way on the voyage from Leith by steamboat, a young man came to me, when standing on deck, with a map of London in his hand, and asked me if I knew where "Aldersgate" Street was. I answered: "No; but that I intended to go there, to such a number." The enquirer replied that that was his destination also. In a word, it was David Livingstone, on the same errand as myself. Of course we chatted on together during the remainder of the passage. We stood admiring the wonderful sights seen upon the Thames. I remember well that my wits got me to the south side of the river when we were on the north. We got into the same cab, and next day appeared before the directors. Amongst other things we got an essay to write. I had the honour to be asked by Mr. Livingstone to look over his paper and make any needful corrections. Having been accepted we continued our studies together for half-a-year, when my health fairly broke down, and I left for Scotland. A summer's work on my father's farm put me all right

again, when I went to Glasgow to continue my studies.
When there, Mr. Livingstone came down to bid farewell
to his friends and to take his medical degree. His
field of labour was amongst the Bechuanas in South
Africa. Mr. Moffat threw a good deal of romance into
his story of "Twenty-three Years' Labour North of the
Orange River," and fired Livingstone to go to Africa.
As we walked together on his way to his father's house,
the closing conversation was to the effect that we
would both use our influence for me to be sent to the
same field of labour, that we might be together.

I trust that you are all so intelligent as to know,
at least to believe, that there is not much to note in the
life of hard working students. Recollections must be
upon the type of mind. Some subject was up for
debate, when Livingstone and I got into opposite views.
I then observed: "Mr. Livingstone, you are all physics,
and I am all metaphysics." This, I believe, gives the
bent of both the one and the other. I was an enthusi-
astic admirer of Sir William Hamilton, whose lectures
on Logic I had attended. Mr. Livingstone went with
his whole soul into medical studies. He spent a season
in London as a medical student. His energy must
have been very great. In company with a young man
that was finishing his medical studies, for months they
slept only two or three hours a night. In philosophy
and divinity Dr. Livingstone may be said never to have
entered into such studies any deeper than many in our
Bible class.

But to proceed. Two years after, Livingstone
went to South Africa. I accompanied Mr. Moffat to be
a co-worker with him and Livingstone. This continued

for nine years, until our missions were broken up by war between the natives and Dutch Boers. The battle was fought at Livingstone Station that broke up entirely three stations in connection with the London Missionary Society and one Wesleyan. Like a stone broken by a hammer, one piece flies to one side, another piece to the other side. Thus the stroke of war made Livingstone a traveller in the unknown interior of Africa, and led Walter Inglis to go to the backwoods of Canada.

Whilst not professing to be an intimate friend and correspondent in later years, yet I trust that it is not altogether presumptuous for me to try to set before you some leading features of his travels, and their results. My first intention was simply to write and read, taking for granted that many of you had read his travels, and looked over the maps. On second thought, I felt convinced that, to accomplish what I had in view, I must get a large skeleton map of Africa, from the Equator, and follow the red line of Livingstone's track from the Cape of Good Hope to the south shore of Lake Bangweolo, where he died.

I trust you are all here to be instructed, not to be amused. There is not much fun in the life of David Livingstone. No monkey was he. After having gone over the map, I shall resume my paper ; yet something whispers in my inner man, " Don't spare the map." Without a solid foundation, a building is not much worth.

After having gone over this line of travel, possibly you are all inclined to say,—no man has left behind him such a wonderful story. The name of Africa is suggestive of all that is terrible. From Park and Bruce downwards, through a long line of travellers, we have narratives of heroic men in many successes and disasters, terrible deserts, burning suns, lands where miasma and fever reign, fierce, wild beasts, and barbarous, cruel men. No part of the world has given the student of geography such trouble. It is an interesting problem, the desire of civilized man to know the full extent of this world. What a tale is in the history of the North-West Passage ! Now of the North Pole. Now, as well as a century ago, of Africa.

What was the motive that impelled Livingstone, for thirty-three years, to lead such a life ? In all our endeavours to study men it should ever be our aim to get at the great central moving principle of the man. Like the great, mysterious Nile, with its rolling flood, there is a source to be sought in the one as well as in the other. In many cases it is as difficult to know the central power of man and society as to get to that yet mysterious Nile fountain. You go into a great public work, with wheels whirring in all directions. Down, hidden from view, you are at last shown the great centre-wheel, amidst rushing waters, or the piston of the steam engine ascending and descending in the neighbourhood of fire and steam. You see a man, or a nation, engaged in some great work. It is only a mean to some ulterior end—steps to ascend some higher tower.

In the case of David Livingstone we have no difficulty in reaching the master-principle that made him undergo a life of such toils and hardships. In the brief account of his early days, given in his first book of travels, he writes : "In the glow of love which Christianity inspires, I soon resolved to devote my life to the alleviation of human misery." This youthful emotion would not have much weight in itself. There are many instances of early resolves and intentions proving to be only vapours of mist. The scorching blaze of life's midday sun changes many a loving heart into the withered leaf of utter selfishness. When we read his brief utterances in his last journal that the inspiring motive is love to the Lord Jesus Christ, and love to the poor Africans, this is the great power that made Livingstone a traveller, a man of science as well as a missionary. No man, possibly in the history of the world, had such a range of personal friends : From the poor Bakalahari to the splendour of a London saloon, with its galaxy of beauty, and wealth of intellectual gifts ; from Mebalwe, his faithful waggon-driver and attendant, that rescued him from the jaw of the lion, to Sir R. Murchison, who encouraged him in the hour of weakness, when the strong will melts like metal in flux. Like a man who has resolved to make money in trade, it is the same to him whether they are dry goods or soft goods, iron or crockery, salt or sugar ; if the one won't pay, the other may, will, must. So Livingstone was not particular as to means, only let him have action. No use in idle waiting. Life being short, he made his motto the lines of the poet :

> Act, act in the living present,
> Heart within, and God o'erhead.

I have now specially to observe that in all his plans to effect the great object of his life, step by step, he was thwarted, as if an evil spirit followed him from enterprise to enterprise.

I beg your attention to the following particulars :

I. The first impulse of his loving heart led him to study medicine with the purpose of going out to China as a medical missionary. In the course of his studies the Chinese War broke out. He thought that sufficiently barred his way; that he must turn his attention to other lands. A cool, deliberative mind would have gone on with study, saying : "Events may have taken a turn by the time I am finished with my studies."

Livingstone had nothing of Sandy Micawber in him, waiting for something to turn up. He felt that it mattered not where he went if he were only let act. Nevertheless it was a great disappointment to him. The heart's first grief is keen, while in strong men it is short. He calculated upon spending his days in a Chinese dispensary, as a pioneer in Christian life in the flowery kingdom. I may here observe that medical missionaries were not so much required forty years ago as now.

II. He offers his services to the London Missionary Society. The directors have no work for him as a doctor, pure and simple, and they set him to qualify for a full "Reverend." His work is to be a preacher, and to exercise his gifts of healing by the way. These worthy men made a great mistake when they ordered Livingstone to cultivate the art of public speaking. A natural defect in utterance prevented him from becoming an eloquent or even interesting expositor of truth. His severely scientific mind gave no opportunity for the imagination to grow, so that his ideas might be clothed with beauty. He never took to preaching popularly so called. A kind directing Providence in due time freed him from this forcing of the weakest talent in the man.

III. He leaves for South Africa in company with the Rev. William Ross—an ill-assorted pair. It is a great mistake to yoke a fiery colt with a strong, steady ox. They reached Kuruman, Mr. Moffat's station. Moffat was an orator by nature. His fascinating eloquence led Livingstone to believe that there was plenty of work for him to do around Kuruman. It was a grievous disappointment for him to find only a few hundreds of people, instead of the thousands hungering for the bread of life. In letters that I had from him at this time, his feelings may be in a word expressed by the Jacobite song :

> O this is no the land for me,
> I canna stay nae langer.

In this land of emptiness his grieved spirit turned to the distant north. He skirted the Kalahari Desert for four hundred miles past the Wangketse, Bakhatla and Bakwane, to the distant Bamangwato, where only one trader had gone before him, and he died of fever. This journey made Livingstone taste the sweets of African travel. The line of action was forced upon him; he did not seek it. Mr. Ross was an ardent admirer of Mr. Moffat. Livingstone, feeling the throbbings of young life in him, was saying some blunt, plain, Scotch opinions about Mr. Moffat. He scandalized Mr. Ross by the prophetic declaration that if he lived he would far excel Mr. Moffat as a traveller. This at

the time was the utterance of a conceited young man.
I have often thought of the remarkable fulfilment of
this youthful banter. In fact Mr. Moffat can hardly
be ranked as an African traveller at all. He never
entered upon an unknown country until he went north
in search of Livingstone in his first great journey.
When I had reached the Cape Colony, in company
with Mr. Moffat, I got a letter from Livingstone, saying:
"Come on, Inglis; we must go north, and far, too.
Let us have the spirit of the Apostle Paul, not to build
on another man's foundation." He waited at Kuruman for some time before he started for Mabotsa in
company with Mr. Edwards. I took up my quarters
where there was a house, and could locate my wife,
whilst I was learning the language. It was at this
time, when founding the "Bakhatla" mission, that the
lion seized him and munched his right arm.

After I had been half a year in the country, I
passed up north to see the country, and get located.
I met Livingstone at the Great Cataract, on his way to
court Miss Moffat. He felt he needed a wife. In
due time he was married, and built his young wife an
adobe house. Not long after he got into his house,
built with no small toil, with arm yet weak, the spirit
of restless enterprise came over him. He said to Mr.
Edwards: "You are enough here, I shall go forward,
and live with the Bakwane." I settled away to the
south-east amongst the Baharutsi. For a year or
two he devoted all his energies to instruct the intelligent chief, Sechele, and his people. The spirit of
enterprise again came on him. He starts away to
the east, a couple of hundred miles, to a great tribe

called Mangkopane. • It was on this occasion he came in contact with the rebel Boers. Every journey enlarges his vision, and whets his desire for work. He saw far more people in the east than in the west. He tells the Directors the tribes must be occupied with native teachers from the south ; aye, but where were they to be found even there ? After a time he went east to settle old Paul with the Bahukeng. This native was one of Moffat's first converts, a very worthy man. This time he came into collision with the Boers in very earnest. This scheme of native teachers failed, and was a sad disappointment.

IV. Clouds and threatening storm gathered steadily over our missions. The British Government gave the Boers their independence. North from the Vaal River our fate was sealed. Slave-holders have the instinct of the sleuth-hound for knowing who is friend and who is foe. We were all to have the same fate that French, American, and English Church missions had before us, in this land of turmoil and war. Instead of cowering before the blast, Livingstone grew stronger; the spirit of the Apostle of the Gentiles came mightily upon him. He looked away to the great unknown north, to open up a way for commerce unchecked by the Boers. After making advances to the Lake Ngami and the River Zambesi, he prepared for his great journey in unknown lands, after he had sent Mrs. Livingstone and the child home to England. His journey was a great success. He went to St. Paul's on the west coast, and then went east the whole breadth of the continent. He was a mighty traveller. He became known throughout the world as a wonderful man. But the immediate object of all this travel and toil was not obtained. He got no relief from the Boers for his beloved people.

V. One would imagine that after all these weary travels and disappointments on behalf of the down-trodden children of Africa, now that he had joined his wife and family, he would say, " It is enough." Could not others say, "Rest, warrior, rest"? No, no; the tide of life runs strong in him. His words are able to waken up the drowsy Universities of Oxford and Cambridge. He goes out with a well-appointed staff of men to form a settlement on the high, healthy lands north of the Zambesi. It must then and there succeed. It is no farce of an ignorant cobbler, but learning and true gentility lead the way. Livingstone is full of hopes. Cotton in abundance ; trade to load down the ships. What was the end ? Bitter disappointment ; Mackenzie dies ; Mrs. Livingstone rests under the baobab tree at Shupanga. All return. Livingstone is again in England, full of bitter regrets, but not a soured man.

VI. And now comes the last and greatest of all his journeys, in my judgment, greater by far than all his other travels put together. Sir R. Murchison got him to go and find the true source of the Nile. You have read his last journal ? No, you have not. What a book ! As you read on, and on, the weary old man at last gets sick and feeble. As they move slowly on amidst rain and swamps, you cannot but exclaim, What a life ! Stanley found him wayworn, yet the dauntless heart says, "I shall finish the work on hand." Is the Lualaba the Congo or the Nile, who can tell? After rest, and refit with materials for the way, he again sets out to the west. Rain and swamp finish the work on the south shore of Lake Bangweolo. The call came, we trust, to behold the glories of God's upper house. He was not spared to solve the Nile difficulty. Men say, "What a pity!" His Lord and Master knows best. He gave his heart, large and loving, to Africa; his bones and skin to Britain. I don't know anything in history finer, more fit.

Whilst we say he was disappointed in all his plans, do we say he was an unsuccessful man? Far, very far from it. He has left a large, rich legacy to the world: Lakes Ngami, Nyassa, Bangweolo, with the sources of the Zambesi, and of either Congo or the Nile.

In drawing your attention to the life and labours of Livingstone, I feel called upon to show that he presents a singular individuality. Upon the sea, Columbus has no predecessor, and, assuredly, he has no successor. All others are merely men of detail. Others have given boundaries to seas, continents and islands, Columbus gave shape to a world. From him arose the phrase, "sailing around the world." What a preëminence this fact gives to a man when he stands alone! I would by no means say that Livingstone occupies any such position as a traveller. He has not given shape to Africa. He never endured the sufferings of several African and Australian travellers. He never was a captive in the hands of cruel men, like Park. He knew little or nothing of the horrors of the desert. His movements have no dash in them, like those of Stanley and of many others. There is nothing of the *veni, vidi, vici* in him. Nothing of the Cæsar or Napoleon in him. No dash, no haste. He marches like the Israelites in the wilderness. What are years! Why this deliberation? Because he is a missionary traveller. He is at home in Africa. He loves the poor people whose country he passes through. Our great travellers, possibly without exception, laid their plans to explore the country, to map rivers and mountains, to describe the various forms of vegetation and animal life. Man, barbarous man, is to them only a nuisance and a caricature. Livingstone, on the other hand, sees in these barbarous people the raw material out of which to make Christians and noble men. What a piece of foolhardiness it is to force your way amongst a people without knowing their language! Livingstone was thoroughly trained in the South African language. In his first great journey he had no difficulty with the language all along the Zambesi. Travellers are very plausible on this point. It is a sad thing to speak through an interpreter, sometimes not qualified in both languages—not qualified to put into another language the spirit of the man. Sometimes the interpreter is a rogue. My own experience is rich in this line. This thorough training in language is peculiar to Livingstone. What did Park, Denham, Clapperton, Lander, Barth, Grant, Speke, Burton, Baker, Stanley, etc., etc., know of the language of the people in the interior of Africa? I believe, a miserable jabber. Without this power, Livingstone never could have moved on as he did. The uniqueness of Livingstone is also seen in the long, long-continued success in his career. There was a spell thrown round his first great journey by the total lack of anything like disaster, save the tragic death of Sekueba, the faithful follower. His appearance at St. Paul's, on the west coast, and disappearance like a comet, caused an excitement amongst the learned, deeply interesting. When he appeared at Quilimane, on the east coast, he was no longer a comet, but a fixed star of the first magnitude. Whatever disaster there was in the Zambesi expedition, Livingstone's fame suffered no eclipse. Men differed from him in some plans, yet he rose in public estimation. To me, his last journey has nothing to match it in the history of travel. Did I speak of continued disappointments in his own mind? To the world it was a great success. Park went the second time to the Niger; he fell by violence. But Livingstone died exhausted in body, and his journals were all brought safely to his family.

This leads me to speak of that marvellous body that endured so much for so long a time. It is with the body and the soul as it was with daft Jock Grey and the minister: "Come doon out of the pulpit, Jock." "No, sir, come you up; it'll tak us baith. They are a stiff-neck't and rebellious people." What is the value of a fine mind set in a weak, unhealthy body? Why, sir, it is like loading granite upon a waggon made of fine basket withes!

Power of thought crushes the feeble tabernacle. Think of all the exposure Livingston had, in fever-lands, to night dews, soaking rains, swamps, and rivers to be waded. One day of such a life is sufficient to kill the half of men. When a student, and grinding at his books by night and day, his cure for any little ailment was a day's hunger—a good style of cure. It is a melancholy fact that that wonderful thing we call science has no appreciable influence in training men to command their appetites. When lying at Mabotsa, with his arm all hashed by the bite of the lion, he took no food until the tendency to inflammation had passed. We have not only to notice the guarded temperance he exercised in eating and drinking, for he was a teetotaller, but we must go back to his parents and ancestors. One swallow does not make summer; neither does one generation make a first-class, healthy man. Some men are only healthy when they do little or nothing; others have to take continual care and moderate exertion. I am one of those that believe that the splendid possession of a first-class, healthy body is attained only by long inheritance. There is no upstart able to endure the tear and wear of the man who has received his body from the aristocracy of health. You can hardly get back the estate of health when once it is lost. Rich men have land, but few of them have health. When God has a great work to do he has to go amongst the poor, and there find Nature's noblemen. I by no means say that higher circles have no enduring sons amongst them; but I do say, Very, very few. The only example of such as might be a match for Livingstone was that noted Scotchman, Sir David Baird. When his mother heard that he was a prisoner in Seringapatam, and that he and his men were all chained two and two, the good woman, knowing the restless nature of her callant, exclaimed, "The Lord have mercy on the puir lad that's cheened to oor Davie!" What health to endure foul fever,

destructive imprisonment, having a dead man taken
away from your side time and again, and again! If
these rascals of servants had not taken Livingstone's
medicine box, with other goods, when they ran away,
he might have lived to settle the Nile difficulty. Truly
he felt the sentence of death on him when left without
quinine. But to the point. I believe that it is one of
the very rarest gifts of the Creator to the sons of men
to make a happy marriage between body and soul.
Many first-class minds have poor bodies. They flash,
meteor-like, and are gone. On the other hand, many
a first-class body has a. miserable penny-whistle of a
soul to inhabit it.

David, the son of Jesse, must have had a splendid
union of body and spirit. Livingstone stood middle-
sized, firm upon his feet, light in the under trunk,
round and full in the chest. I have to admit he was
"no bonny." He was not like his greater namesake,
"ruddy, and of a fair countenance." The face wore
at all times the strongly marked lines of potent will.
I never recollect of him relaxing into the *abandon* of
youthful frolic or play. I would by no means imply
sourness of temper. It was the strength of a resolute
man of work. Strong, earnest men never can be
petted. Never can ladies speak of such men as "dear
creatures." I beg you all to discern between a man
of sour, bad temper and a man of earnest work. The
power Livingstone exercised over the natives of Africa
is a sufficient answer to the general tone of his temper.
In fact, I only recollect of him playing one practical
joke. A man came with a ripe boil that only required
to be lanced. He gave the boil an honest skelp with

a book. He had a grin, for dry, Scotch humour he actually possessed.

Our next inquiry is to answer the question, What causes led such different classes of society and modes of thought to take such interest in Livingstone? In a word, the many-sidedness of the man. His books are fine material for stirring boys, whose motive is simply pluck, whose glory is adventure. What a portrait for a boy to see, a man whose arm was munched by a great lion! There is no country in the world so full of large game and wild beasts as the regions through which Livingstone travelled. He is not a mighty hunter like Gordon Cumming and others. I do not know that he ever bagged a lion or elephant. But he moves on his way ready for whatever may cast up. I don't think he ever turned aside for the mere purpose of hunting after an adventure with the lion. It was true what Mrs. Dr. Phelps, of Capetown, wrote to him when condoling over the accident: "But allow me to say you will not get the martyr's grave by hunting lions." He does not give edge to his page by narrating the say-says of natives and others. Sober truthfulness is depicted on all his scenes of adventure and danger. There was a noble truthfulness about Mr. Oswell, his companion in travel to Lake Ngami and the Zambesi. His escape from the rhinoceros is still more marvellous than Livingstone's escape. Oswell was alone. His horse, petrified, would not move. The furious beast came sternly on, drove its horn into the bowels of the horse, threw horse and man out of its way as a man would toss a sheep aside. Another time Oswell was thrown by the horse, the rhinoceros pitched the man out of the way; he had only a halt in his walk from this last accident. All classes believe in Livingstone's truthfulness, whatever his story may lack of brilliancy. We have to notice the good fortune of Livingstone to travel through lands of great fertility. The centre region of Africa is resplendent with all the possibilities of future glory and empire.

Brave men have fought their way through the Zahara of the north, through south-centre Australia. But after we have admired their courage and been thrilled with their sufferings of heat, thirst, and hunger, we turn away from the weary land with the shadow of death over it in the shape of simoom and sand.

LECTURE ON MUCK OR MANURE.

[Delivered on several occasions before audiences chiefly composed of farmers and agriculturists.]

Before directing your attention to the subject of lecture, it may be well to say a word in self-defence for being in the position I now occupy. It is a favourite maxim, the truth of which I heartily endorse, viz.: "The right man in the right place." It may be asked, Is there not something out of place in a man, whose professed line of life is spiritual, interfering with a subject so far down in the physical scale? The difficulty of answering this question satisfactorily lies in the importance of the lecturer's office.

" One thing I do " is the motto of all effective labourers in every line of life. There can be little doubt in the minds of advanced thinkers concerning the utility, nay, necessity, of the division of labour in all spiritual and scientific investigations. Yet, in the long run, one line of study is ever interfering and intermixing, so to speak, with other topics. Realizing that my office extends its line of action into all that concerns the welfare of man in this world, as well as for the future, I, therefore, with a fearless spirit, have devoted a portion of my time to getting up the following lecture. As a humble believer in and follower of Jesus Christ, who, when on earth, went about doing good—feeding the hungry, curing the sick, and teaching the ignorant—I magnify my office when I thus direct your attention to the ways and means of raising food.

In all ages and countries men have found great difficulties in the way of obtaining a sufficiency of food. There are times and places when things go on smoothly. There is abundance for man and beast. In two or three generations the law of increase modifies this fulness. The land that bore abundance for a patriarch and his family in years of plenty gives a very scant supply when a remorseless sun makes the earth as iron. The country that gave abundance to hundreds is straitened when tens of thousands call for bread. Hence the necessity for an ever-widening circle of emigration. Adventurous spirits, at the call of hunger, have forced their way into distant lands; and, in modern days, they have faced the stormy ocean to seek beyond its dark waters a land which may feed them and their little ones. The last days have come upon us. No more new continents are to be discovered. We know the bounds of our inheritance. It is already in many parts crowded with inhabitants. Millions are half fed. The cry is heard in all lands, "More bread!" This new land, America, has been the refuge of the hungry. It is sending forth vast supplies to the fatherlands. This shall not last always. The supply of food becomes still more complicated when experience has ever taught man that the continual culture of land reduces its fertility. The man who puts in the modern plough six or twelve inches into the soil, and breaks the sods with his drag and mighty roller, reaps no more grain than his forefathers did by simply stirring the surface with a hoe or a rude plough. It has been said of new land that you have only to tickle it with a hoe and it laughs into an abundant harvest.

Our limits prevent us from taking an historic glance at farming. Great improvements have been made in the preparation of the soil. Permanent are the effects of draining upon cold, clayey, wet soils. Power is applied in various and astonishing modes in preparing the soil for the crop ; and who can see the boundary of that mighty agent, steam, when applied to the land ? Marvellous are the ways and means invented to gather the crops of the earth. We do not pass by these aspects of farming in order to belittle them, but, conceiving that there is one essential point for successful farming far behind these branches, we have chosen it as our theme of discussion.

In briefly handling the important question of manure it may be well to lay down principles on which we are all agreed. It is the lack of taking this fundamental precaution that prevents men from reasoning soundly. Without first agreeing upon first principles men cannot reason—they only fight. Hence the lack of progress in unity of belief in ulterior truths.

I. I ask you to take for granted that every piece of land has its limitation of growth, beyond which it cannot go.

II. Leave it as an open question that every spot of land can be improved in fertility.

III. Every crop taken off a field leaves it just so much the poorer.

IV. Something is taken off that can only be put on the land by the hand of man or the overflowing flood of a river.

Let these suffice, though some other maxims might be added. If we go into debate agreed with one another thus far, we may have some hope of reaching the end of our discussion together. I have no desire to deal in vapid generalities, or in mere commonplaces. I wish to come to close quarters with this America and Canada of ours—with the men of Dumfries, and Blenheim, and Waterloo, etc. I do this with greater good will, as I am led to believe, from what I have seen, read, and heard from travelled men, that there is as high farming in this neighbourhood as in any part of America. This is one reason why I have asked from you a hearing. Ex-President Andrew Johnston said on one occasion "that he had no desire to waste his shot on dead ducks." There are many dead ducks of farmers in this land on whom words would be spent in vain. Let us explain a little what we mean by "dead ducks." He is a dead duck that does simply as his father did. The man's mind has never been open to improvement. He is a dead duck who drags his weary chain on through life, contented with making a kind of living, while no idea of the dignity and difficulties of cultivating the ground ever seems to have crossed his weak, weary soul. He knows only the difficulties of bodily toil. "He is a dead duck," however respectable he may be, even to the height of a Provincial prizemen, if he is under the fatal impression that things are all right on his farm, as near perfection as possible. A true farmer is a man that is alive to the fact that cultivating the ground is the highest of all physical sciences. By him men live. It is insufferable nonsense to compare city, town, or village life with that of a farmer. Truly the world is "rang side oop," as the Yorkshire man said on another question, when citizens or mechanics of any description attempt to put on airs, and speak of their importance. Without doubt the farmer is the chief of men. The men I wish to reason with are clear, strong-thinking, practical men, who are sensible, and, in some measure, aware that there are ways and means to put things right; at least, to make them a great deal better than what they are.

With these introductory remarks I desire to enter upon the field of debate.

I. I desire in the most trenchant manner possible to say that there are few farms in this country, probably not one, that is not year after year becoming poorer. Why do I say so? Because there is more stuff taken off the land than is again put on it in the shape of manure. When I say this, I would give a wide range of indulgence to the emigrant, the backwoodsman. I could, in fact, hang a medal on every man's breast that has cleared a lot of land. Brave, stalwart man is he. We shall kindly let the pioneer farm as he best may. He has a hard struggle to get ends to meet. In the course of twenty years the land is cleared, or say in the course of a generation, where the pine has to be rooted up by modern mechanical skill. After the land has been cleared, what folly to go on cropping year after year under the blind notion that rotation of crops is sufficient to place a man amongst good farmers. Possibly a very worthy hearer is ready to argue the question somewhat in this fashion : "You are wrong, sir, concerning the farming that is common in this district. The mode of cultivating by rotation of clover and turnips, and deep ploughing, is equal to keeping up the full strength of the fine soil in this country." I say: "No, emphatically no." It is true that a great difference exists between two men. One is a grain raiser and seller, the other raises cattle or live stock, as much as possible. Yet the man who sells stock as much as possible is taking more off his farm than he puts on. Whatever he sells, his farm is just so much the poorer. All his butter and cheese, pigs and sheep, cattle and horses are so much loss to the land—not to speak of the grain that is sold. An orthodox farmer is ready to ask me : "Do I understand you, sir, to say that good farming must have as much manure put on the land as you have taken grain and flesh off it?" Exactly so; that is the point I am driving at. "Where is, or can be, the profit in farming?" asks my inquiring friend. "Why, such a mode of action is just like a man changing money from one pocket to another." Softly, friend; you have not realized the true position of the farmer. "It would be a queer thing if I had not after forty years' life in farming." That may be all very true, and yet you may not know your business. Let us look aside at other lines of business for a little. Take a miller, for instance. You take your wheat to the mill to be ground, or rough grain to be crushed. Don't the honest miller give you back just as much weight as you gave him? No, he doesn't; he keeps one bushel in twelve, that is his pay for his work. But he gives you back full weight for eleven bushels, in the shape of flour and bran. The miller might charge so much cash for grinding a bushel of wheat, just as well as taking his toll. Take another instance. You take one hundred pounds of wool to the manufacturer. Do you not look for the same weight back in the shape of rolls or cloth, barring the waste from dirt? Admitting the correctness of these examples, allow me to say that the farmer is properly a manufacturer of food for man's use. The raw material out of which he forms the same is muck, manure. The machine through which he passes his raw waste material is God's earth, Nature's living, vitalizing power. The legitimate profit of the honest farmer is simply the product of the raw stuff he puts in the ground, raised in value like the wool made into cloth. There is a great difference between a pound of wool and a pound of cloth. There is a great difference, in like manner, between a load of muck and a load of grain in value. A young buck of a farmer that detests muck and all its belongings may be ready to devour me for so saying. I must tell all this kid-gloved class, "such is the farmer." You will permit me to say that the men who have the good fortune to pitch their tent on the great American prairies, and are there year after year raising corn and cattle and hogs in abundance, are not farmers in the true sense of the word. They are plunderers, wholesale robbers, from the great store-house of Nature. With no possibility of evading the law, the children will have visited upon their heads the iniquities of these fathers. I think I see before me a cool, clear-headed old gentleman that has been saying to himself all the while: "Give the farming parson rope, he'll hang himself." "Not before I hear your full opinion, dear sir, speak out. Let us hear the sad difficulties. Attention!" The old gentleman spoke as follows: "Your theory, sir, would revolutionize the whole existing state of civilized society; you render towns impossible. Every man must live on his own acre of land. How is it possible to return to the soil all that is taken off, unless by such a mode of action?" Thank you, sir; but I am not going to hang yet. Impossible is a word that should be limited by man as much as the ingenuity of man can effect. I thank you again for placing before us one of the greatest problems that must be solved some way or another. I admit that civilization tends to the destruction of good agriculture. The waste of cities and towns is prodigious. In order to preserve health, men bring, at great expense, water to a high level and wash all filth far away into the sea. But more of this by and by. Let us stick close to our subject. It would be well for the world if waste were only found in cities. Let us take the best farmer in this country. He prepares his land thoroughly. He raises clover and turnips. He puts all his grain into flesh. He is a thorough stockman. He sells little or nothing save stock. Is that man's farm remaining in as good heart as it was? Is it growing better, or is it growing worse? We lay ourselves open to the opponents' fire by saying distinctly that slowly, but surely, it is becoming worse. There is all the weight of flesh going off it. It may be asked, Is a field or farm that is grazed becoming worse? I am well aware where I am going now. Let us stick to our principle, come what may. I say grazing does not improve the field. Practical men join in one voice against this statement. Triumphantly they point to a field that has lain in grass for ten, twenty, or thirty years. It bears a noble crop. Plenty of straw, we admit; yea, we shall grant that it is renewed, but not by grazing. What by then? asks my keen opponent in astonishment. We come now to one of the deep things of nature, into which scientific men are slowly, but surely, finding their way.

It is not altogether true that farming is wholly of the earth, earthy; or that the only regenerator of land is muck. It begins to be seen clearly that land is helped by the gases descending through the atmosphere. There is an influence by the rains and dews and sun. The gases that ascend in due time descend and become incorporated with the soil. It is this principle

which makes fallowing good for the soil. Ploughing
and dragging give far greater scope, so to speak, for
these gases to take possession of the loose earth. This
is a very different thing from the commonly received
opinion that the good of fallow consists solely in rest.
I hear one saying: "By this mode of reasoning we
are all going to the dogs ; even the very best of us are
leaving a continually diminishing heritage to our children." Just so. The history of the nations, the history of agriculture, if it prove anything, proves this
melancholy truth that the land grew weary, became
exhausted, comparatively speaking, and wicked men
selfishly crowding each other brought on starvation,
rebellion from hunger, war, and ultimate ruin. No
ancient land has retained its fertility save those lands
flooded by mighty streams or irrigated by mountain
torrents, such as Egypt, etc.

Let us proceed to the farm of Mr. John Feed-all.
And let us take a look into things there. A good,
honest, and true man is he. Before we go over his
premises he has given us a dinner like a prince. Such
conduct on his part ought certainly to remove all
fault-finding and ill nature. Everything is really in
first-rate order—horses and cattle, sheep and pigs,
even the very poultry, are fed to the full. All are
warmly housed. Winter does not seem to make a
shiver within these stone walls of stout old John. In
leaving we go through the yard where the "muck" is
being collected. Would you believe it? John is not one
whit further forward in reference to manure than the
greatest "potato-bogle" in the country. Everything
there uncared for, the muck lying on the open yard.

What would you have honest John to do? I suppose that that funny fellow, who sits grinning in the corner, intends to hint that I won't be content until John has built a house for his muck, and put it under lock and key like his bank notes. Not so far from the mark, Mr. Quiz, as you fancy. There must be a total revolution in all our farm yards on this point. All soakage into the ground is dead loss—good cash thrown away. In calling for reform on this point it may be said that by making sheds to keep the manure under cover I would incur greater expense than profit. Mark you I am no believer in fancy farming. Whatever we do, let it be for profit. I see plainly that it would be a serious expense to keep manure under cover. I am not at all sure that such expense is required. There seems to me a far better way to deal with the difficulty, viz.: by driving and laying down a sufficiency of earth. There seems to me far weightier reasons for this earth process than most of you may imagine. One may say: "We'll lay a yard of earth on the ground where the manure is to be formed; such a body of earth is equal to secure all that is valuable." Granted; but is there not something still wrong in the preparation of manure by rotting, or fermentation? Is this process of putrefaction not a huge error? A man very energetically gathers his scattered manure into a nicely squared heap, in order to rot it well. You all know the outward effects of rotting. A great heat arises, and the heap becomes one-half smaller. In other words, a great chemical operation has been performed; a mass of your stuff has gone away in noisome gases. A manure heap is the symbol of a nuisance. Is this good farming? In the first place, it makes the farm yard a loathsome place. Further, may it not be compared to a man burying his dinner, and eating the ashes? All that foul smell springs from substances that ought to have been buried in the earth. In fact, I wish to press that the point of perfection in a cleanly, civilized man and nation is to cover all excrements from man and beast right away. That law of the Jews, that amused us all when young, is to me the very perfection of cleanliness as well as economy. Our present back premises are in summer months generally most offensive. What is the use of removing churchyards to a distance from towns when ten thousand cesspools everywhere steam corruption and pestilence?

Gentlemen, with all due humility and earnestness, I press upon your attention this principle of dealing with every kind of manure : cover it continually with earth, and prevent all putrefaction above ground. I call your attention to one way of effectively manuring land; that is, by ploughing down green clover. You know the merits of such action. I do not take it upon me to say what saving there might be effected in every farm place in conserving all the food of plants in positive possession of the farmer. I should not be at all surprised if it were to be found that one-half is thrown away by this barbarous neglect of the subject of lecture, muck. If this is so, or is anything near the truth, what an effect would be produced upon many farms! We would not be distressed at seeing the heaps of muck few and far between in many fields, in others only half of the field attempted. You Scotchmen all remember what fun there was when a hay rope was thrown in the turnip drill, it was laid along the furrow with the mutter of a "lick and a promise."

There is another aspect of this muck question that is dealt with by the farmer in a rule of thumb manner; that is, the manner of putting the muck on the land. If my reasoning is sound in what I have said about rotting, or fermentation, then it follows that enormous waste takes place when this steaming stuff lies on the field, both in heaps and when spread out in order to be ploughed down. In a country like this, with such a fierce sun, I am convinced that great loss is sustained in allowing the process of fermentation to take place at all. I find that I am very far from safe yet from that hanging process that my cool, clear-eyed friend was preparing for me. Where do you think he is throwing out his rope now, not to catch my neck but my tongue? Yes, gentlemen, that is the modern mode, hanging up a poor fellow by the tongue. Let us hear him. "Mr. Muck-on-the-brain, you little think of the expense of driving earth to preserve all liquids from escaping, and all fermentation from taking place. It is a nasty job, at least, working among muck. By your plan you would require a load of earth for every load of dung. No, sir, it would not pay." Well, ring the changes upon the pay and non-pay. I have told you that I am not an advocate for any thing but pay. On this point, gentlemen, it becomes us to speak, for and against, gently. As far as I know, experiments have never been tried to prove the value of non-fermentation; so far as I am concerned, I never heard of the subject before, nor read of it; there is no trace of such a line of argument in Liebig.

Other questions concerning the proper way of manuring require some attention. A man puts on his field a heavy coat of manure, calculating this to last some years ; this, according to Liebig, is very poor practice. He shows the Japanese plan as far superior to anything found amongst us. The Japanese have no fallow, and put on manure for the year's crop only. It is a fact, gentlemen, that the Chinese and Japanese are on some points ahead of the Western nations. Decidedly they are ahead in appreciation of the value. of manure. I would recommend a gathering of all the young fellows of the neighbourhood, in order to hear one read to them for a quarter of an hour about the way things are done in Japan. As I read it I had a very various feeling, laughter, disgust, instruction. Young gentlemen, if you cannot get a reader, I promise to read it for you, rather than see you beat.

Having gone thus far on comparatively safe and easy ground, I come to state that there are most serious difficulties in the way of the farmer. For instance, land that has become "clover sick." You sometimes cannot renovate the land to bear clover, by any quantity of manure ; in short, common farmyard manure goes only a certain length. Let a farmer use it in great abundance on certain lands, and he will be most grievously disappointed. " There is no profession which, for its successful practice, requires a larger extent of knowledge than agriculture, and none in which the actual ignorance is greater." Thus writes Liebig, one of the best of agricultural writers. Further, he says : " The farmer who practises the system of rotation, depending exclusively upon farmyard

manure, needs very little observation ; he has only to
open his eyes, in order to be convinced by innumerable proofs, that whatever may have been the outlay
of labour and industry applied to the production of
farmyard manure, his fields have not been thereby
increased in the power of bearing crops." Why this ?
The reasons are various. Gentlemen, the food of
plants is composed of various substances which must
work in combination. You can have abundance of
several materials, but lacking one, all the rest are
useless. I do not make an attempt to show you how
this takes place. I make no profession of chemistry.
To become a thorough farmer a man must give himself to know exactly what things are necessary to
make plants grow. Take, for instance, a man who has a
large amount of straw; he turns it into manure, puts
it in great abundance upon a poor field. His crop
may look well in straw, but when he comes to thrash
out, he will find the grain very deficient in proportion
to the straw. It stands to common sense, that straw
will only reproduce straw. It takes grain to make
grain. Now the proportion of grain is not in many
instances applied to the field; hence the failure of
farm-yard manure.

The qualities of manure are at this time of day, I
dare not say, according to this proportion. But I can
conceive far more grain raised from a well-fed span of
horses than from a whole herd of young cattle eating
only straw. "Like makes like" is a maxim all the
way through life. What is to be done, then, to supply
these deficiencies ? In the first place, every farmer
must become a thoroughly intelligent, close-observing

man. The cause of difficulty being various, he must find his own cause. What will cure one farm won't help another ; aye, the same treatment won't suit even on the same farm. One thing is plain : there are means at hand to help farm-yard manure. You have gypsum here, as they had lime in the Old Country. " Humph !" says an old sod man, "lime is just a dose of physic to the land ; it scours the land just like a dose of Epsom salts." You will take it no offence in the world if I say that this figure of scouring land is not at all true ; there is good wit in it, that is all. Lime is an essential element of plant food ; it forms the basis of combination for other materials. Take, for instance, the moorlands of Scotland : there is a rich supply of earth muck, and a lack of minerals ; put in lime and you alter the nature of the soil, just as you put salt into food. In doing this you effect nothing permanent ; the reverse : you, in a certain sense, take away the strength already in the soil. This leads men to suppose that lime has no real good in itself. On these miserable, poor moorlands a few crops are able to suck the whole vitality out of them. If you do not farm on the highest and most generous style, you find yourself worse off than ever. Then you find the necessity of turnips, which draw their meat from the subsoil. These, when eaten on the field, keep up the strength by grazing of sheep.

I, now, would take you into a new line of debate, that is grazing. You will find grazing a different thing in this country, compared with the Old Land, The advantages of a country like Scotland, in grazing, over a country like Canada are very great. There you have a climate moist, and of low temperature. Sheep pick on the fields most of the year; sometimes you have a month of snow-storms, preventing the sheep from grazing; all that is done is simply assisting them with food—hay and oil-cake, with turnips. The moist climate is admirably fitted for washing the strength of their droppings into the ground. Evaporation is comparatively small when tried by the climate of Canada. Grazing, to say the least against it, is a poor affair in British North America. All the growth is done in two or three months; sheep get a little grass in spring, then comes a great growth. English clover and timothy are ripe; a fierce summer sun burns up the grazing-fields. The fields that are to be cut for hay are protected by the close growth of green stuff from the parching power of the sun. Thus, at hay time, you have a far larger weight of grass grown to make hay from than was grown on the grazing-field. The question is impressed upon the Canadian farmer: how far it is profitable to graze cattle in the fields. By putting land in high heart, is there any difficulty in raising two crops of grass in the season? One thing, it fares very hard with the manuring of a field by the droppings of cattle; all the gases are quickly evaporated, and nothing but the solids left. I believe there are experiments going on in the country with what is called soiling. I hope you will give it your close inspection; and if the results are good, apply them, as far as possible, on your farms.

The conclusion which we reach in reference to farmyard manure is, that a farmer is not able to keep up the heart of his farm by the stuff collected on the farm. Let his care be ever so great, let no loss be sustained, but all rightly applied, still his cry will be: "More muck and its foreign assistants." One of these foreign aids you have at hand, viz.: gypsum. Herein I profess my ignorance except by reading. I find, from Liebig, that there are great difficulties in the way of understanding the action of gypsum. For instance, in clover, Liebig shows that the action of gypsum is very complex. It promotes the distribution of both magnesia and potash in the ground. Gypsum goes to any depth; renders available food for clover not before possessed. There is one curious instance mentioned, that gypsum affected the stems and leaves but not the flowers of clover. Permit me to state that I have a strong belief that it is full time for the farmers to make all experiments possible with all these foreign manures. The difference of the price of grain, pork, and cheese is not so very great between this country and Britain. If the farmer can make high priced manures pay there, why not here? I have been told that in the high style of farming in Berwickshire a farmer calculates to buy manure equal to the one-third of his rent. Think of a man paying a high rent, and adding to that rent one-third more! One thing is plain, from experience, that these foreign manures are all one-sided; they supply one or two things of the many that are required to raise crops. Many fields may be poor in one thing and rich in all others; this being so you cannot have a good crop. There is one line of action open to the farmer that has as yet been very partially acted upon, but whose effects are of the most efficient order. The name given to this manure is "Poudrette." It consists simply of human excrements, made into a dry, transportable form. Common sense at once admits that it must possess all the elements of plant food. Custom hitherto has been to erect water-works, at great expense, in our cities, towns, and villages, and by a most elaborate form of sewers wash all this nuisance into the river, lake, and sea. This mode of procedure has been ruin and destruction to the world. Hundreds of millions of dollars are year by year in this manner thrown away. Sound thinking men see this clearly. Ways and means are being put forth to put a stop to this wretched form of civilization.

In some places sewage has long been utilized, such as in that high-standing inland town, Edinburgh, where they irrigate meadows, and take an enormous amount of grass off in a season. This mode of action can only be very limited in its practical range. Men are beginning to see that sewage is an egregious error; wrong in an economical point of view, as well as wrong in point of health. This matter has assumed so much importance with thinking men that it is discussed before the British Association as a matter worthy of their attention. It is discussed in city councils. The plan is simply and thoroughly effective, viz., that all human excrements be conserved in dry earth with a certain measure of disinfecting stuff. This system would render our police regulations complete; rendering the state of the atmosphere in our cities and towns sweet and wholesome, instead of the disgusting, festering state of things that now exists.

You must not laugh this question out of discussion

as impracticable. It is so far found to be valuable that one company, at least, has been formed in England to extract all that is valuable in sewage, dry it, and sell the product. .It is so valuable that they are exporting so far as Mauritius. Just think of the absurdity of bringing guano by millions of tons to Britain every year when there is on the spot what is far better than guano, and people are so hasty and stupid as not to be able to use it. It is an outrage upon all civic economy that Britain should require to import a single pound of foreign manure. Let me place this before you clearly.

By the general maxim that we stated at the beginning, that you must put on the land as much as you take from it, an exporting country like America, by this law, is continually becoming poorer. Britain imports enormously in food stuffs. She is thus in a position by science to enrich her soil nearly double every year. Were the Government of Great Britain to act wisely, the farmers would be able to put every acre of land in the highest possible efficiency to bear crops. In short, they have it within their power to enrich every acre in such a way that it would not be possible to make it bear any more. Railways render it practical to carry back manure from the cities to every remote corner of the country.

This subject is illustrated with great point by the celebrated Liebig in the practical examples given from the fortresses Radstadt and Baden. The Government got casks placed upon the top of carts. The privies were raised so that by wide funnels all excrements were collected without loss. The competition for this stuff from the garrisons became among the farmers so great that receipts rose from two hundred and eighty-five pounds, in the year 1852, to six hundred and eighty pounds sterling in 1858. The expenses to be deducted from this sum for repairs of carts, etc., were between fifty and sixty pounds. That was the result from eight thousand men. Reckoning on this scale, with a liberal allowance of discount, say fifty pounds for every one thousand people, the value of London alone would be worth two hundred and fifty thousand pounds. Who can tell the revolution that would take place in the world if knowledge were more general? Surely we may apply with all force the words of Scripture in a physical sense: "My people are destroyed for lack of knowledge." Instead of Britain having a million of paupers, she might, by vigorous wisdom, raise so much food that she would not require any supplies from abroad in good seasons. She could give work to a million of people in collecting manure.

I hope I don't hear a stifled mutter: "Ah, well, there will be a sufficiency of food in the world so long as I am in it; I need not disturb myself." This mode of thinking is the very essence of selfishness ; and I need not say, further, that selfishness is ruin, damnation. The sins of the fathers, as far as agriculture is concerned, are visited upon the children. Selfishness is barbarism —death. What then? In a word, the present state of things must come to an end—and that speedily—if, indeed, this great country, yea the world, is to make anything like true progress. To come to the point : every true man ought to put forth his full strength in carrying into effect a thorough, complete revolution in the construction of privies and cesspools. The present system of digging a deep pit, and then placing a privy over it, ought to be put an end to at once, even by Act of Parliament, if need be. Let every house be provided with a truck, where there is a garden farm. On that truck let there be placed a water-tight vessel, or barrel, on the top of the truck, and placed in a proper position below the seat ; let a due measure of dry earth and disinfectants be placed within, and removed in due time before filled, and then mixed with a certain quantity of earth, fitting it for field use. When there is no land attached to the dwelling, let police regulations come strictly in force, so that all can be removed at appointed times from the premises. It is not needful to enter at length on this subject. I hope it commends itself to your judgment, if not to your sensibilities ; and that, as men, you will do your best to help forward the social improvement of man.

The question of how manure is to be put on the field is also of no small importance. Very different practice exists amongst farmers. If it could be shown that all the gaseous substances thrown off by fermentation, and dried up by the sun and wind, are of little importance, then it might be found that top dressing was the truly scientific way of putting on manure. Deep ploughing-in of manure tends to sink the earthy, or mineral stuff, too far into the soil. In my own experience, I once found a very great difference between a piece of my own garden, on which I spread rough manure shortly before the first snow, and another piece alongside of it, where highly-rotted manure was put on in great abundance in the dug potato drill.

I shall do nothing more than touch upon this question, as it is the complement of the proper subject of lecture. It is very easy to draw out a subject by examples and illustrations. These, I take for granted, can only be effectually reached by daily life. I may say, in conclusion, in the noble and eloquent words of Liebig : " Observation and reflection are the fundamental conditions of all progress in natural science, and agriculture presents, in this respect, ample room for discoveries. What must be the happiness and contentment of the man who, by skilfully turning to proper account his ultimate knowledge of the peculiarities of his land without increased application of labour or capital, in gaining from it a permanent increase of produce ? For such a result is not only a personal advantage to himself, but a most important benefit conferred upon all mankind."

" How paltry and insignificant do all our discoveries and inventions appear compared to what is in the power of the agriculturist to achieve ! All our advances in arts and sciences are of no avail in increasing the conditions of human existence ; and though a small fraction of society may, by their means, be gainers in material and intellectual enjoyment, the load of misery weighing upon the great mass of the people remains the same."

OUTLINES OF SERMONS.

OUTLINES OF SERMONS.

Genesis 36 : 8—Thus dwelt Esau in Mount Seir : Esau is Edom.

Esau is a distinctively representative man to-day. It is an unquestionable fact that nations are very different. Evolution in the Darwinian sense is not a fact. Two things are brought out. God created man male and female. Then we find that along with this unity there springs a strange difference. It can nowhere be more distinctly felt than in these two twin brothers. There's another truth. There is a heredity that hems us all in. Men may mix as they may, blood will carry its heredity to many generations. I do not believe that there is any power in Britain to take away the type of Scotch character. Garfield had not only Puritan blood in his veins, but also Huguenot.

At times there is a most distinct difference in twins. As they thus grow, Esau takes to being a hunter, the other to shepherding. I can conceive of Jacob, the tutor of the lambs and kids. Esau was a man of marvellous health. I can easily conceive how natural the hunter was in him. I have looked over to the country of hunters, and I know the tremendous fatigue the hunter endures. Jacob naturally took to the sheep and the cattle. The parents had likes and dislikes. This was most unfortunate. The Bible states most appalling facts without giving any opinion. It is a fatal fact when parents have favourites. . . Jacob has a little of the woman in him. . . Esau had been upon a great hunt. I have known such a man come home entirely unsuccessful. Esau is down in spirits beyond measure. Hunters are most reckless of what they catch. I can conceive of Jacob again and again eating venison from Esau's hunting. Esau says: "I should like some of that food." In Jacob there's a love of money that goes to make a selfish man. Esau was altogether a hunter. He knew nothing about the promise. Jacob knew that. . .

Now, dear friends, we shall take the other event. The old father becomes blind. I have no doubt that by this time Rebekah has a measure of coldness to Esau. It is a most extraordinary thing when a mother leads a son into wickedness. But the fate of the world hung upon this fact. Suppose that Esau had been blessed, what would have been the issue ? I feel somehow that there was no necessity for this prevarication. I have not the shadow of a doubt that there is no assertion where there is an approval of Jacob's conduct. Rom. 9 : 11, 13. From Augustine downwards there has been a tendency to make Esau the representative of the damned. Esau is presented to us as a man far superior to Jacob. What is meant by hating Esau in Malachi 1: 2, 3 ? See Luke 14: 26. A man is spoken of there as having to hate his father and his mother. Now, there is not the shadow of a doubt that Jesus never called upon a follower to hate his father and mother. How men will pervert straightforward words ! I believe that it is not the personal

Esau that is meant, but Esau's children. Isaiah 21: 11.
" He calleth to me out of Seir, ' Watchman, what of
the night ? ' " No blessings for Edom like those for
Jacob. Esau was a bold, honest, manly man. In
thus presenting Jacob as the chosen, it is nowhere
said that Jehovah approves of Rebekah's or Jacob's
deceit. No man tells a lie, but he shall reap the fruit
of that lie. . . The Bible is not built upon the
basis that a great many would have. God sometimes
chooses the worst, and on them he builds his Church.
I would notice what was wrong with Esau. He was
the representative of the best class of worldly men
—manly, honourable, énergetic. You find in this
country, in like manner, men that you esteem—
energetic, honourable men—that put to shame these
snivelling Christians. But after you have given the
full measure of it, you find that these men are "of the
earth earthy." There is nothing of the future in
them. They believe in now. He is an immediate
man ; but it is not the immediacy of grace, but the
immediacy of food—prompt as electricity for the
things of the world. . . I believe that Jacob had
the spirit of the future in him. He believed in his
father's and his grandfather's God. But, again, you
find that as Esau was thus kind to his old father,
there is a certain nobility in his character, and there
was a certain bound to his temper. He was stung to
the quick. Then, when Esau knew that Jacob was
coming back, he cooled down. The Spirit of the Lord
quelled his wrath. How splendid the meeting !. He
moved again, still away to the east. Esau was never
Jacob's servant. The Edomites became servants of

the Jews, but never Esau. Where is Mount Seir to-day ? Silent as the grave. Where is Mount Sion? Mount Sion is the joy of the whole earth.

———

1st Samuel 12 : 23—Moreover as for me, God forbid that I should sin against the Lord in ceasing to pray for you : but I will teach you the good and the right way.

The efficacy of intercessory prayer is very generally acknowledged.

I. It is a very common form of prayer. The wicked man ever and anon desires some one to pray for him. This is the beginning of priestcraft. It is an overwhelming calamity when men are doubled down, and doubled up by priests, who rule over them with a rod of iron. But when men smite down the priests, what are they the better ? The origin of priestcraft is in the universal heart of man. Every man has a creed. There is a creed of negation.

II. This common fact in the family of a man is not altogether wrong, for it has been divinely warranted.

III. Its divine warrant has been sadly abused. The belief that prayer by an intercessor shall be answered, when they themselves have not prayed ! The drowning man sometimes paralyzes the man that has dived into the water to be his saviour. . . If you are to be saved, you are to be saved by your own mighty struggles. . . The neglect of intercessory prayer is a great sin. It is an ordinance of God that men should help men. It serves to unite men in spiritual affairs. It serves to nurture the deepest philanthropy. Are we men of prayer? If not, we are ready for priestcraft. Do we cry to the Lord Jesus as the alone intercessor? Do we pray for our people? Do we pray for our nation?

Job 12 : 7—But ask now the beasts.

The spirit of wisdom is in man; but there are lessons to be learned in the lower world. I need not say that this is a strange school. .This strange school is often held in session in the Bible. The ant is held up, the locust, the crane, the stork.

Two aspects in which we may look at the lower creation :

I. As God's creatures,. showing his wisdom and power. The deeper down we go, we are the more struck with the wisdom that is shown. His constant beneficence is marvellous. Job's friends had assumed a very high tone. You find that the man who was crushed, even he turns upon them, and says: " Ye are the people, and wisdom shall die with you." How marvellous that men with all the rebuffs they receive will not learn modesty! . . A man that does not believe in God is judicially blind. When we look at the works of creation, what evidence we have of design!

It is the overflow of what is evidential that makes the man so stupid that he cannot see.

II. Let us see the lesson they teach by the way they live. A drunken man is not like a brute at all. It is not brute-like to get drunk ; it is like a sinner.

(1) They constantly fulfil the end of their being. They are led instinctively to fulfil the end of their being. There is no such thing with them as cursing the day of their birth. Look at the trainableness of animals. How sad to see a brute of a man driving an intelligent horse. The reverse thought is how men do not fulfil the end of their being. All round you see men not rising. It is a wonderful age of knick-knackets. Men are burying themselves like whales in the depth of the sea. It is wonderful how miserable a young man can become in a few years.

(2) They live according to their nature. There is, no doubt, a sense in which we are to get the better of nature. A field that is to produce for man has to be turned over. . . There is a large amount which men ought to leave according to nature. The wise man does not try to disturb God's chemistry. Men go to universities to be great. That is not right. Many of our scholars simply go through college to die.

(3) They teach us to seek happiness according to our nature. Happiness is a coy maiden.

Psalm 23 : 6—Surely goodness and mercy shall follow me all the days of my life, and I will dwell in the house of the Lord forever.

Here we have a view of the future suggested by a review of the past—a lesson of how to meet to-morrow. The valley of the shadow of death refers to the hair-breadth escapes of David. All God's people are men of war. The promises of God are of a spiritual character.

How was such a hope suggested? It was by the experience of God's goodness in the past. The reason that there is so little faith at the present time is, that the Lord has not set us in the front of the battle. . . He that has brought us through in the past, he will never leave us, nor forsake us.

The Psalmist's purpose: "I will dwell in the house of the Lord for ever." John Foster says, "It is a poor soul that has not the power to say what he would like to do." Young men, this is the time of laying planks. I need not say that when a man gives himself to the Lord Jesus, he gives himself for life. It is popular now for men to yield themselves as soldiers for a time. But that will not do for the service of the Lord Jesus. God's blessings are the reverse of the world's. Mammon showers his best on the young man. It is otherwise with the kingdom of Christ. When a man has got his foot upon besetting sins, the blessings of the Lord increase as he draws near the end. This is just as it ought to be. It is beautiful to think of life being most successful in the end.

Nine months of winter, and three months of bad weather; that is very like the religion of some people.

———

Psalm 71 : 18—Now also when I am old and gray-headed, O God, forsake me not.

Human beings forsake each other in all circumstances of life. God also forsakes man, but not as man does, neither for the same purposes as do men. Men will forsake each other because of disgrace and shame; but God leaves no one for these reasons. Men always forsake God first, and continue to forsake God till finally God gives them up; but this is the only reason why God forsakes any one. How are we to be guided as to what are the signs of a God-forsaken people? These may be called forsakings; but not the kind under consideration; they are merely trials of faith. Our blessed Saviour said, while hanging on the cross: "Why hast thou forsaken me?" We need not be in doubt as to what kind of forsaking Christ endured. Some of the principal signs of a God-forsaken man are when the heart is hard, when a man has no conviction of sin, or when there is no repentance for evil done to one's fellows, and last, but not least, when a person is peevish, and grumbles at all that is going on around, even God's work does not please. When God really dwells in the heart there is a continual conviction of wrong-doing, and this is kept in exercise by the Christian truth that there is not any perfection in this life. The heart, by such convictions, continues to get softer. But people who are God-forsaken have no sense of wrong; hence the inconsistency of thinking about such doing right. A man may be dead in soul and destitute of principle; such was the case of old Saul, David's enemy.

There are passages in Scripture which say God

will never forsake his people. Some, however, have the Spirit of God, and some have not. The Spirit is not given as a reward for outward acts. No excuse can be given to God for sin, and be careful how you come to God. True, loving hearts stand by each other to the end; how much surer is God, who cannot be compared to men for excellencies. Those who trust in God get such consolations, during the evening of their days, as will do much more than keep them from being peevish. After Christ had been tempted, angels came and ministered to him. When God forsakes a man he goes quickly to ruin—an awful thought. Early seeking of God is like beginning early to make money; for if either be engaged in constantly, there will be plenty for old age. Let us all pray David's prayer, that God will not forsake us when we are old and gray-headed. May he not forsake us with faith in and love to him at least, whatever else we may lack.

Psalm 119 : 32—I will run the way of thy commandments, when thou shalt enlarge my heart.

The Bible is ahead of all science. . . The plague takes its rise in filth and corruption. In the Bible you have no sympathy with a dirty man. In like manner, the religion of the Bible is alongside of the present day, in that it is opposed to all kinds of ignorance. God's people, from the patriarchs downward, are an instructed people.

The religion of the Bible is a scientific religion. It is in keeping with the highest instincts of man.

Let us, therefore, thank God, and take courage. Let us not tremble for a single fact that scholars can bring out. The Bible is scientific, because it has all the severity of science in tracing things to their source. What toils we have been at to get to the fountains of the Nile! Travellers must rest and re-rest. The weary Livingstone, how many were his rests. Christianity has no rest till it gets to the beginning of things, even till it gets to the beginning of the keeping of God's commandments.

I. The Bible is a book for the heart, and it speaks always to it. See how many kinds of hearts are spoken of in the Bible. The word heart has a large meaning. It applies to the emotive part of the man. It is the centre of the man. A man is not a being simply of cognition. Of scientific truth, of an earthly nature, we may well say there is no heart in it.

II. The first thing in the training of man is to cultivate the heart. It is not enough that the cars should be after one another. They should be coupled. So there's the possibility of a man teaching where the heart has not received. Children do not take to it readily. The heart has not come to see that it is a benefit. All mothers who are overwhelmingly influential have set the example of a large and loving heart. When you direct me to a subject I have no heart in, it "hangs fire." In teaching man, and appealing to the heart, you have the work of the great in opposition to the small. The Bible gives large place to the heart, and that is scientific. How vast its conception of God! How vast its conception of man! The Bible takes into account all the interests of man. The Christian is called upon to look upon all men as brethren. Compare a Christian with a Britisher. " I am a man, and all that concerns men concerns me." Why is it that men will not run in the way of God's commandments? The fountain of the want of interest in Christianity is a shrivelled heart. . . We find not only the large in opposition to the small,.but the loving in opposition to the cold and earthly. A child trained in selfishness cannot have an interest in the Bible. There is no room for love in that heart. Compare the influence of kindness to animals with its opposite. . . It is in. the nature of things that in these days of destructiveness we should have atheism.

III. With a large and loving heart you can influence the young to keep God's commandments. " When thou hast enlarged my heart." There is to be no moderation in the parent showing the little one the infinite love of God.

Godlessness is a matter of the heart. . . The commandment of God is laid down. The loving heart says: " What a beautiful road! You can not only walk in it, you can run." Railroads all bound for the throne of God !

Proverbs 27 : 17—Iron sharpeneth iron ; so a man sharpeneth the countenance of his friend.

This being the beginning of a year, one cannot help comparing the beginning of the new with the end of the old. I think of the end of a year as Solomon thinks of the end of life. The end of life is certainly better than the beginning, because care always attends the beginning. Let us remember that we need something more than amusement and light thoughts at the beginning of the year. For this reason I would recommend Proverbs to all, because such as have not got them are weak.

Iron sharpening iron means putting on the fine edge. In reflecting on our subject we see that the mind, like edged tools, becomes blunt by daily use. The great general experience is that use takes off the edge. The mind is one of the finest of instruments. How often do we find the mind in need of sharpening. Schools of all kinds are chiefly for this purpose. As the razors and colters are different, so the minds of men are different, and this teaches that the fine edge is not useful in every occupation. Still, all become blunt with use. No doubt all adults present have experienced the blunt mind. How some men will become downcast, even in this blessed country, simply because they have come into contact with a species of nail. But some may say : " I have never been blunt yet." Well, wait a little, there is plenty of time yet, and you may be dull enough. A good reply to such is that if a tool has remained sharp a long time, it cannot have been much used ; when people go into actual life they soon become blunt.

One man may be of great benefit to another, and this brings us to the subject of the influence of one mind upon another—iron sharpening iron. Some people believe in wearing a grim countenance. One of the chief means of testing the effect of mind upon mind is for a person with a beaming countenance to

go into a room where a person is lying sick. It must
ever be remembered that the finer minds are most
susceptible of being blunted. I have always made it a
point never to go into a school with a beclouded
countenance. As useful instruments in this great
sphere of mind upon mind, let us first try to cheer
others rather than allow ourselves to be cast down by
another.

There is evidently a limitation to the influence
which one mind may have upon another. If, however,
a mind remains uninfluenced, one must be of a different material from the other; for example, wood.
It is quite possible that there may be minds which
cannot be classified under our illustration.

Then, as iron sharpens iron, and not wood iron,
we proceed to draw the conclusion that the sharpest
minds will ever carry the day. Are the Roman
Catholics sharper than the Protestants? The sharpest
minds are those which know most about the Bible.
One point where our illustration may be safely applied
is in the similarity between different kinds of temper-
ing in iron or steel, and the quality of different minds.

Again, all these conditions are so in the reverse.
As iron blunts iron, so may one mind be blunted by
another. Iron may cut, but cannot sharpen, wood;
neither can wood sharpen iron. So are there minds
which never can improve by contact with each other,
but both are continually blunted or injured. As this,
then, is a time of social greeting, and cheering each
other, and sharpening the mind by bright countenances, why not spiritually too. Since it is so fine to
see all gathered around the social board, why not at

the spiritual board also ?　Christianity has sharpened the heathen mind, and both purified, elevated, and made the family circle what it now is.　This is one great evidence of the power of Christianity which infidels cannot meet.　As to Christ's family circle, although we may be out with the various members of Christ's family, let us not be out with the Head of the house himself.

A few words to parents.　It is right that you commit all to God in prayer ; " I wish you a happy New Year," is a prayer ; how then can an infidel use such an expression ?　Let us have Christ at the head of the table ; then there will be little anxiety about how we will conduct ourselves.

Lastly, if the influence of man's mind is so great, even through the veil of flesh which shrouds the mind during this life, how much greater must be the influence of God's.　And can many of us not say that we have had the face of the Lord shining on us?　In closing, I wish you all a happy New Year, and let us remember we cannot be properly happy unless we are working for Christ, unless our whole life is given to and guided by him.

———

Matthew 2 : 2— Where is he that is born King of the Jews?

The Bible is too brief; but, as John says : " If all that Jesus did had been recorded, the world itself would not have contained the books that should have been written."　In the reading of the gospels we are met with the supernatural.　The attempt of the day is to sweep out the supernatural, and make out that there is nothing better than ourselves. Ruskin says : "One of the issues of American civilization is to take away all reverence from society." There is in the mediæval miracles a marvellous distance from those of the gospels. In the mediæval saints there is something going on like what the devil tempted our Lord to do. There is nothing finer than these angels coming down by night. Our fathers, with all their courage, trembled before ghosts. There is not much of that in the Bible. The shepherds are notified, and by and by they came to Jerusalem, weary, worn travellers. They were not beggars; they were princes. These men made inquiry among the learned men : "Where is that King that is born?" "Why, what do you mean?" "We have seen his star in the east." Now there is some glimmer of light; and possibly there was a trace of astrology among the Jews. Not only do we find that these men caused Jerusalem to awaken, but even Herod. This incarnate fiend would become acquainted with this child that had been born. It was most extraordinary, like Satan coming into heaven. Herod is desirous to worship! Strange to say, the star rises over them, and they have no trouble in that little place to come beside that little child. Think of them meeting the shepherds! They bend the knee. . . This subject has been the cause of a good deal of speculation. Who were these magi? The Chaldean mind presents us with the grandeur of the astronomical mind. The Greeks for æsthetics, the Romans for stern law. What cared the Roman about stars? Some would think the magi were a deputation from the old remnant of the Jews. They were wise. They were in communication with the Eternal God. How did they come to know the star? Some think it was a meteor showing them the way. How did they know that it was the star of anything? I go with those who hold that this star was interpreted by dreams; and these men had a longing spirit. In the whole world round Judea, there was an intense longing for a deliverer. These learned men had learned so much that they came to worship, and they got no countenance in Jerusalem. They did not revolt from this lowly one. They were believers in the Messiah. They bent the knee. Possibly they would kiss the child's hand, possibly his feet. Without hesitation they brought forth their treasures. These men came to do him homage. You find that superstition has made men worship dead men's bones. The idols have made men tremble. Yet in man you find there is no higher faculty than that of veneration. The celebrated author of the " Philosophy of the Plan of Salvation " says : " Man will worship." The training of the present day is to empty a child's mind of veneration. Men were trained to reverence the house of God, but now they have no difficulty in playing in the pulpit. Men have got quit of one thing after another, and the last step is to get quit of God. They have got quit of respect for their parents. They call their father " the old man." How few you hear speaking reverently, and saying : " I'll hear what father and mother will say ! "

The question we are now called upon to decide is, Is there anything in this world that we respect? Seek the star of Bethlehem. See Kirke White's hymn, " The Star of Bethlehem."

Matthew 2 : 1-12. (Lecture on the Magi.)

The Magi, perhaps, belonged to the religion of Zoroaster. Nisbet held that the Magi were Brahmins from the East Indies. . . There is no difficulty with scholars in regard to the Massacre of the Innocents. This was a small matter for a savage man. . . There is this thing connected with Christianity, that it is not only one thing, but Christianity is surrounded on all sides with remarkable events. Everything buttresses it up. Hence there are many things in the world beyond our philosophy. . . The priests guided the wise men to Jesus, but did not come themselves. . . There was a star, by some conjunction. . . There is not an idolatry that has not some truth in it. There is some connection between man and the heavenly bodies.

I. We find that these are wise men.

II. They were rich men. Nothing so beautiful as to see the rich man of this world bending low to come to Jesus. Men spoil themselves by presenting themselves great and wise, and better than they really are. If they would only go and keep company with Jesus, how much they would improve !

III. They were strangers. There were no railroads then. There were deserts. . . Many people at the present day will not be at the trouble to go a mile to enquire about Jesus Christ.

IV. These wise men came and found a little child.
. . How sad the wreck of a man of large possibilities. . . The sayings of Jesus are words that live
and breathe and burn.

V. They followed a small star. All this super-
structure of astrology has not been built upon nothing.
Sun, moon, and stars are to be brought into connection
with his most holy religion for the welfare of man. If
angels are to serve, I know not why sun, moon, and
stars may not. . . Think of what we follow. The
day star rises on the hearts of God's people. How far
we are exalted above the princes of the past ages!

VI. We have Christ. How far may we travel?
He is here. He hears us. He is in our hearts. To
the man of God, he is a very present Christ. "Go
ye into all the world, and, lo, I am with you always."
That implies in us. Now, let us muse and meditate on
our heritage.

———

Matthew 5 : 13-16—Ye are the salt of the earth : but if the
salt has lost its savour, wherewith shall it be salted. . . Ye
are the light of the world. . . Let your light so shine before
men, that they may see your good works, and glorify your
Father which is in heaven.

The Christian is able to endure on the one hand,
and to advance on the other. The Christian is salt
and light. The meaning of salt here is the power of
preservation. The world gets a flavour from Christianity. Salt can be used in over abundance, and can
become an emetic. It may be used to clear off what

is rubbish. Salt is the emblem of incorruptness, sincerity, vitality. A man does not need to be a Socrates to see that man tends to corruption. There is no denying that sin in all its outgoings corrupts the body. How sad to see young people corrupted; the family, the blood, the country getting corrupted. What has preserved the Chinese? Parent worship. Wherever we have a country that does not give honour to the parent, we have a country that is ready to pass away.

" A covenant of salt." In sacrifice nothing corrupt was to be rendered to the Lord. . . We find that salt is the Christian's characteristic. There is such a thing as bad salt. Nothing more useless than useless salt. I have heard of no science that makes anything out of useless salt. The Christian is a light. I should not say that the Christian is to be a light; but he is to be a candle set on a candlestick. Some men will do anything but let their Christianity shine. When they are going to be Christians they go down into the cellar. The Christian does not boast, but " he cannot help shining."

———

Matthew 18 : 2, 3—And Jesus called a little child unto him, and set him in the midst of them, and said, Verily I say unto you, Except ye be converted, and become as little children, ye shall not enter into the kingdom of heaven.

There is no first human ruler in Christ's kingdom; but he who would be greatest in that realm must be only an humble servant. He who is greatest after the manner of the world will be least according to Christ.

Evidently there is a marvellous difference between being born again and conversion. Luke 22 : 32 proves this. A person is born again only once ; but Christians are being continually converted. Conversion is a turning away from error ; and this state is well expressed in Tennyson's beautiful lines :

> I held it truth, with him who sings
>   To one clear harp in divers tones,
>   That men may rise on stepping-stones
> Of their dead selves to better things.

The speaker does not believe that if the apostles had died before Pentecost, they would have been lost.

But all who would enter heaven must become as little children. How is this accomplished ? By getting a view of ourselves in relation to God ; this will humble any one. Three great benefits arise from this, and these are: first, it makes a man teachable ; second, it makes a man peaceable ; third, it makes a man lovable, and also it makes a man capable. Can a Christian not have a little pride, dignity, etc. ? We think John Bradford's estimate the best, because he was accustomed to say, even if he saw a man going to be hanged, " There goes John Bradford, but for the grace of God." Some think a good moral man is all that is required for heaven ; but these moral men are always proud and quarrelsome—very little of the child-nature about them.

Mark 4 : 23—If any man have ears to hear, let him hear. ·

This sense, like the others, has been trained. Man's eye is trained to see. The child has no knowledge of distance. The ear is often trained in a very one-sided way. It is unnatural to take the child from the fields into the school, and call the young mind to attention. When you have the eye, it has the rapidity of the sun ; but it soon wearies. We have broken the spirit of young people by sheer protraction. I have no doubt there is such a thing as training for the pulpit. I have as little doubt that there is also training for the pew.

Attention ! Men often speak about manner. But manner is not the Alpha and Omega. It is a great mistake to speak before attention is called. Far better for a speaker to close the book, and say: "I am not needed." The Bible way is calling to attention. Suppose you call attention after you have spoken : you find this is very unwise. When the Lord has something to say, He says " Moses, Moses." The law of reason is that men have to be called to attention. The man coming out from the threshing-machine needs his very nostrils to be washed, that he may smell. Men have to be above all things prepared for hearing. Hence, dear friends, the preparation of the heart. In reference to attention, I need not say that in entering God's house there's something even in the public reading. Why are certain foreign speakers paid attention to ? Because the ear has been trained with expectancy. There's the wonderment, in the case of a stranger, as to what the man will say. It was a wise saying, that before any tragedies should be read, people should sit quietly for ten minutes. How much more with the law of God than with Shakespeare! The Saturday night preparation was philosophical.

OBSERVATIONS.

I. When we enter God's house it is to hear God's word. The reading should be distinct.

II. As to the manner of the speaker, some men's speaking is enough to give you a headache; some men's singing, to make you sick. But the church is the opposite of the theatre. You do not refuse a thousand dollars because the will has been badly read. Jesus calls attention to what kind of man John the Baptist was. The Word of God calls upon you to hear all the voices of the past (Matt. 10 : 15 ; Matt. 13 : 43 ; Mark 4 : 23 ; Luke 14 : 35). You do a great injury to go on preaching or reading or talking when people are not attentive. You may have children in the pulpit if you only have strong men in the pew. See the second and third chapters of Revelation, also Rev. 22 : 17—" And let him that heareth say, Come."

Mark 14 : 42—Rise up, let us go ; lo, he that betrayeth me is at hand.

We really do not know a thing till it is pictured on the mind by the imagination. Hence the difficulty of a gross carnal mind to lay hold of Christianity. I have no doubt that the disciples were greatly agitated.

" What did these wonderful discourses mean ? " They would be disappointed when on this Thursday night He begins to be heavy. . . Now we have Him in solitude and in prayer. These tremendous depths are a subject of deep meditation. . . Have you thought of God in His sympathy taking things in the beginning ? The only instance to the contrary is our Lord's delay in coming to the help of Lazarus.

I. This was a spiritual conflict. It was strong, not protracted as was the assault of the temptation in the wilderness. There seems to have been a marvellous contractedness in this. Human suffering can only be to a certain amount. The truth is in like manner in regard to the soul. Jesus died of a broken heart. This is a fact amongst men. The intense feeling gives the heart its bursting power. That conflict was the beginning of the great travail of his soul for the salvation of men. The one scene of temptation was in regard to carnal glory. " Shall I be to this people their Messiah in earthly glory ? " The whole of that had to be laid aside. Having laid aside glory, He is to go to the extremity of grief.

II. There is something of a Gethsemane in every child of God. I do not speak of the Gethsemane that is in the soul before coming to Christ. The unconverted cannot plead with God on that occasion. I do not believe, and I cannot say to you, that by receiving Christ you will have nothing but sunshine and psalm-singing. God leads his people into overwhelming sorrow, especially those that have a great mission. Who can tell what tears and agonies have been in this congregation, what trials in the past, and even now ?

In your Gethsemane you are just in the footsteps of your Master.

III. All God's people have a cup to drink that is repellent to nature.   Jesus puts together cross timbers and makes them one.   There are mortises and tenons in the Bible, the hand of a master, not of an apprentice.   . .   God's people are a happy people, but it is just as true that they have a cup to drink that is repellent to nature, and to their partially renewed spirit. "Go far hence unto the Gentiles."   "Go, bear that cross."   Is that in keeping with soft nature ? The grand old title of Christians was Soldiers of the Cross.   When Christians sink to do things only that are pleasant, they are not following the Master.

IV. Whilst this cup is to be drunk, an angel appears.   This is indeed the answer to prayer. "Strengthen me, O Lord God, for this work."   The pain must be endured, but the soul must be strengthened.   The Saviour's suffering is but a cup.   You are not to go to the bitter streams of Marah to drink continually.   It is not a cup of death ; it is a cup of medicine.   It is administered by the loving hand of Him that gives us all our blessings.

V. The life of Christ is full of prayer in deep solitude.   The garden was the place of prayer.   What a thought it is that the traitor Judas knew this !   Our Lord was in the habit of retiring to such a place.

———

Luke 14 : 18—And they all with one consent began to make excuse. The first said unto him, I have bought a piece of ground, and I must needs go and see it; I pray thee have me excused.

One of the bonds of friendship is partaking of food together. Do we think Christianity is worthy of being celebrated in a feast? It is a great affront to refuse an invitation to eat. Put on politeness in its grandeur, and not in its varnish. It is a poor thing especially to varnish rotten wood; it is a poor thing to varnish a piece of musty stick. Superficial varnish is sheer waste. . . The higher the bidder, the worse the impudence of refusal.

Some of the excuses for not being a confessor and follower of Christ.

I. "I am still young." The stern, old English law was that the children did not eat with the parents till they were twenty-one. . . "But the gospel has not come to me, ye hoary-headed ones." Read Psalm 145. How many "alls" are in that? "But it is a stupid child." There is no such thing as "adherents" in the Church of Rome. I am so un-Presbyterian I could sit down with a little child. My mother was the youngest that had sat down at the Anti-Burgher table—twelve years of age; and she never regretted it. The father at earthly feasts looks out for the best seat for the little ones. "Suffer little children" does not prove infant salvation, but it proves they are very welcome to his table, welcome to his Word. What a pity if there is any one saying: "I am too young?" If you are old enough to be convinced of sin, you are old enough to know the Redeemer.

II. "I am not good enough." Well, that is a revolution! Christ came to seek and to save sinners. This is one of the most plausible deceits that men can have. It means this: "I should like to appear decent." It is one of the greatest blots on Protestantism that it makes little provision for the poor. "I will not come back again to the church till I'm a better man. When I come back to the church I'll be a better man, and I'll not thank you."

III. "But see that miserable-looking man coming forward." What a miserable lot of men they were that sat down at the first table!

IV. "I have such a sad battle with sin." If you have such a battle with sin, can you not take some help? If I understand the Bible, Jesus Christ says: "I will help." Jesus says: "I will slay your enemy." What would you think of the man saying: "Oh, no; there would be no honour to me in all that"? The reason why men sin and repent, sin and repent, is that their repentance is not low enough. This is the wretched thing that those that come from the fear of hell, fear of sickness, fear of going to die, when they get better of these things, go back again "like the dog to its vomit." The error is in thinking that something mysterious is to come over them.

V. "I would like, but feel so ashamed to do so." There is a marvellous power in a man; that is, the power of companions. Is it not a miserable thing that a man is ashamed to be honest in the company of thieves? "I am ashamed to say before murderers, I never killed a man!"

VI. "My father and mother don't sit down." We should sympathize mightily with shame, but shame may be misdirected. I have heard of a mighty divine that was ashamed of his old father. Look at Garfield and his mother! But another man says: "I can serve God, though I don't sit down at the table of the Lord." Exactly so. This is the breaking up of the unity of the family of God. "Don't trouble me. I don't want to be troubled with church laws. I live as a unit." This is one of the extremes of society, and a very respectable man in many cases; but such a tendency is to sap the foundations of morality, for the man is on the highway to misanthropy, saying: "I should like a better class of people to associate with."

VII. "I should not only like a better class of people to associate with, but I should like a better minister."

VIII. "Well, I mean to by and by." "Watch, for ye know not the day nor the hour." Not one of us has any reason to think that there will be a time for prayer and praise in our end. I need not say we are bidden. Why did you come? Some say: "Because it is respectable; others, "I came to see him, for there is music in his voice."

Luke 24 : 49—And, behold, I send the promise of my Father upon you; but tarry ye in the city of Jerusalem, until ye are endued with power from on high.

If Christ is a mere man, the gospels are perversions of common sense. To study the Bible you have to clothe yourself with imagination. You have to plant yourself in another position. It was impossible that there could be a universal religion among the heathen. They were all protectionists. When men joined battle in the olden time, it was god against god. All nations needed such a religion. They needed to repent. They needed to be told, "Turn; there's no road here. . ." "Blessed is he who expects nothing." How wretched a saying! The man of God and the child, let them build their "castles in the air," rather than "thank their stars" that they expect nothing from God or man. I look upon the disciples as a company of children waiting for their father. It is not alone at this time, but all the way through, this has been the precursor of a great awakening. There is physical power, which the child longs to be a man in order to wield. Knowledge is power. Reason is a power that is to be ever honoured and thought of. There is moral power. Bacon lacked that. How often have our geniuses been disgraced! . . What is Christianity? It is a spiritual power to-day. Christ has never failed to give to his disciples power from on high. His work is ever varied. The wind is the emblem, and God has ever varied these breezes of the Spirit. Look at Peter after the Day of Pentecost. He no longer had a temptation to tell a lie. But for the Holy Spirit Peter would have prevaricated about the rising from the dead. But after the Day of Pentecost hear him speaking to the rulers : "Are we to believe you rather than God?" Are the leaders of the Christian Church just as other men? In this day we have to meet the man of the world on his own ground. But, after all, when the man has been equipped with all these forces, he has to wait for power.

———

John 3 : 29—This my joy therefore is fulfilled.

In physical things there is a current, and so is it in the soul of man. Every man has his life's work. If you are lazy, you are on the high road to rottenness. . . Every man has a mission. Work is something we can do. The work of God in the man is his joy. Love makes Labour light.

I. The joy of telling some true thing.

II. The joy of doing work which no other can do.

III. The joy of anticipating the approval of our Lord and Master.

IV. The joy of seeing our work blessed beyond our first thoughts.

V. The joy of working out God's plan.

VI. The joy of knowing that the burden and heat of the day are over.

VII. The joy of seeing others preferred before us.

———

John 13 : 34—A new commandment I give unto you, That ye love one another ; as I have loved you, that ye also love one another. By this shall all men know that ye are my disciples, if ye have love one to another. (Delivered on the day preceding the Sacrament of the Lord's Supper.)

What have we in this world without preparation ? There is preparation for all our earthly transactions. We would ask the young, What is there wrong in people having their minds gravely brought round to the simple, yet solemn, service of observing the Lord's Supper ? It is not in keeping with law that man jumps from one thing to another. Children may jump from one thing to another; that is not the way of a man. What objections have we for such a day being set apart for self-examination ? You have had a fast day. But there is still something more. I can under-stand a man staying at home humble, but not ready. His self-examination has led him the contrary way.

Am I a Christian ? One thing I have no measure of doubt upon, I am a sinner. I am conscious I have broken a universally good law. I have never heard the shadow of the shade of an intimation how my breaches of the law can be healed, but by Jesus Christ. As a third point, I cast myself on Jesus Christ, and I know none other way. As to the evidence of life, am I a backslider, or have I been making Christian progress ? There's no standing still for you and me. You may say you know no difference on a man, but it is not true. He is getting consolidated. Earthly growth is not always apparent. You see the blade grow. After the ear, has the plant stopped growing ? There comes a time in the history of man when to the outward eye there is no difference in his growth. The growth is now within. Do you believe there's a large amount of husk in a Christian? I believe it. There's husk, there's chaff; but you cannot have wheat without straw and chaff. You cannot have a Christian without these. Don't look alone for growth outwardly. Do I believe in the Lord Jesus Christ? This text contains the most effective test, "By this shall all men know that ye are my disciples, if ye have love one to another." Wherein is this commandment new? Is it not as old as the Jews? There were many things that called upon the Jews to love the Lord their God. But what specialty was there among them to love their neighbour? None but the law of instinct and the family. There is a new sanction given. Man does not naturally love his fellow man. I am well aware that the mother's heart is a deep fountain in the desert. But how soon do the boys get to be fighting! How soon do jealous feelings arise among the girls! Why is this? And what is one of the grand sources of man hating his fellow man? The bitter fountain is selfishness. This controversy has to come to an end. This Upas tree has to be torn up out of man. So long as it remains, it is vain to talk. The reaper is of no use among stumps. A new commandment is laid upon us with all the sanctions of a new principle. As I have loved you. Man is a child of imitation. There was no such sanction as that given before. Now it is given for the first time in the world. As I have loved you.

This on the eve of laying down his life! The selfishness that is in us is to be completely rooted up.

That is the law of life, or the special reason given in this text—the stumping-machine that takes the selfishness out of the human heart root and branch. Oh, what a pleasure I have in seeing these stumps pulled up! What a triumph of man! That's the reason we must all respect the Bible. There is nothing but this mighty influence to tear up this principle of selfishness. "As I have loved you, . ." These poor disciples miscalculated the love of Jesus. Their minds were much in the dark concerning the character of Jesus Christ. . . Christianity roots up out of the human soul selfishness, not like Jesuitry by rooting up the *man*. This is distinctly given as a Christian principle. You cannot love one another by command. Before men can love one another they have to love the Lord Jesus Christ. Have we never felt the principle? I have. When a man met me that loved my mother, I must say I felt drawn to that man.

You communicants all believe that he loved unto the death. It comes then as a most serious question, Why the Christian Church has so little love one to another? Is it right to see a man thirty years, and never speak to him? Men get themselves polished like grave-stones, so that not a drop shall rest upon them. Is it not an amazement that the members of a Christian Church never have a chat? Why is it that all this is so? I believe the reason is because they have had so little company with Jesus Christ.

There is no competition in Christianity. The word "provoke" might be altered in the new translation. Love is the test which the world puts upon Christianity. The saying of many is: "You Christians quarrel and go to law; I don't see any difference . ." At the eating of the paschal lamb they sat down in families. There is no priestcraft in the Father and Mother. The paschal lamb is the basis of the Lord's supper. The Lord's supper is a family service. The Lord Jesus, at his table, has his family gathered about him. There is to be the love of the most affectionate family. It is well for us to see to it that we are not to let things go on in this humdrum way that is so common in our churches.

Acts 11 : 24—Barnabas ". . " was a good man, and full of the Holy Ghost and of faith ; and much people was added unto the Lord.

A man that is superficial in the knowledge of one individual will be superficial in the knowledge of all men. A man who studies himself knows other men wonderfully well. But what a harp of many strings is man ! Man is presented as wise and foolish, learned and unlearned, good and bad. In a place where you have the best of men you have also the worst. The novelettes describe commonplace characters. You can only get a strong character in biography. You have to get the lines drawn by facts. You may fill your minds with novelettes, but you will never get into big company.

Man never rises higher than his ideal. The name of Jesus Christ has gathered round it the pick of humanity. Tradition says Barnabas was one of the Seventy. There's another tradition that he was a fellow student with Paul.

I. He was a whole-souled man. He sold possessions, and laid the money at the apostles' feet. The French communists have stolen Christian communism without its spirit.

II. He was a successful preacher. There were just a few that went back to Jerusalem. The forces of the people remained scattered throughout the Persian Empire. The word "exhortation" has a very wide meaning. He was a man that was overshadowed by the transcendent power of Paul. It is no small thing to be a celebrated exhorter. That implies a deep, tender knowledge of the human heart. They gave him this title "Joseph the Exhorter."

III. He was a good man. Intellect and goodness are not equally distributed. Goodness implies that you have come very near to the heart of Jesus. A good man is very unconscious. The Scotch are said to be a self-conscious people. . . A good man is not a simpleton.

IV. He was full of the Holy Ghost. It becomes us to speak with bated breath upon this point. We are glad to hear in these days that men have aught of the Spirit of life. But to be full of it! How can I speak on such a text? Novel writers never describe a highly good man. They are frightened out of their wits to describe a man bigger or better than themselves.

V. Full of faith. We have had a great deal of theological nonsense on faith. What is needed is to know thoroughly the object of faith.

VI. He was a sagacious man, a man that knows man. In the Christian Church that sagacity is the feeling your way to a knowledge of character. In reference to this power, I believe that he was the means of securing Saul to the church. It is no small matter to see through a great man. How difficult to have sagacity to know "the coming man." It is a gift only second to that of Paul himself. All Paul's movements were of a quick order. You remember how he turned his back upon Mark. Barnabas saw there was something in Mark. To Mark, Barnabas gave his countenance. In this aspect of character, he seems to have been Paul's superior.

VII. A fine charitable spirit. Paul excelled Barnabas with his tears and rush of feeling. Oh, the delightful peace that was in Barnabas! There must have been something very commanding in his countenance.

VIII. He was a clear-headed man in the admission of Gentiles into the church.

IX. He was fit to be a missionary. The church is in a wrong position, as long as the strongest men occupy our city churches. Who is it we leave in our fortresses? It is our pensioners. Paul and Barnabas were two picked men.

X. I have no doubt that he ended a noble life in the noblest of causes. Full of the Holy Ghost to the end.

1st Corinthians 11 : 28—But let a man examine himself, and so let him eat of that bread, and drink of that cup.

Looking self in the face, with the Bible in hand! 1. Can we speak to self? 2. Can we put a question to self, especially a religious one? 3. Can we place self at the bar of judgment? 4. What are the answers received? approval, apologetic, or condemnatory? 5. If condemnatory, what then? 6. Is the spirit of repentance strong in us? 7. Do we examine ourselves by fits and starts? 8. A man may say, I did not examine myself, since I was converted! 9. Are you as zealous as you once were?

———

1st Corinthians, 15 : 31—I die daily.

Paul tells us at the outset what the gospel is. "Christ died for our sins." If you preach Christ as a mere man, there is no gospel in it. A mere man dying for our sins is an absurdity. "He rose on the third day, according to the scriptures." Jesus gave himself unto death on account of our sins. His blood is to be the means of our cleansing. The next thing is the evidence of the resurrection. "If they believe not Moses and the prophets, neither will they be persuaded though one rose from the dead." . . I would five hundred times rather take the superstitions of the past than the superstitions of the present day. Whilst Christianity is founded on fact, it does not shirk reason. You will find the very germ of reason in the gospels. Having discussed these points, I need not say that the text before us is a very striking one.

I. There is a daily dying that is inevitable.

(1.) In the body of man. A splendid subject for Christian doctors!

(2.) In our social life. It is not good for man to be alone. You find that when there is one dear companion, and that companion is taken away, there is buried in the grave, as essentially as philosophy itself, a part of you. You find yourself limited. You are like a kingdom that has lost a province.

(3.) A dying daily in our mental motives. He is a manly man only who toils for others. That is one of the grand expressions of sin, when a man toils only for himself.

II. There is a daily dying that is optional.

(1.) A dying to the virtuous. It is within the reach of us all to choose whether we will allow the man that is in us so to die. No man can be neutral in reference to morality. That is the most consummate knave in the country, who wants to cheat both God and the devil. When a man has chosen his part, all noble things that were in him by nature die daily. Impulses are checked. You find there is such a thing as a man going gradually downwards. There is a dying of the sensibility of the conscience. It is terrible when you get a man so sunk that he is past feeling! What a sad spectacle, a man so frozen that he is insensible! Not only are these things so, but we find that generosity of impulse and elasticity of thought are gone. The taking of stimulants is an appalling system of borrowing on the future.

(2.) An optional dying to the vicious. "Mortify your members which are upon the earth." To all that is earthly, sensual, devilish, there is on the part of the man of God a daily dying. It is simply not the case that the grace of God takes hold of a man and makes him whole at once. First the word of God is medicine; afterwards it is meat. Do we believe in this inevitable dying? Is our will resolving, By the help of God I will live as His servant?

———

Colossians 1 : 24—Who now rejoice in my sufferings for you, and fill up that which is behind of the afflictions of Christ in my flesh for his body's sake, which is the church.

Our modern school cannot deny the existence of pain. There is such a thing as the bracing up of soul to match pain. There is such a thing as the balancing of pain with pain. Is there not something of this in the soul? Christianity takes into account the conquering of pain. The Son of man suffers that our sufferings may be relieved. Suffering was in heathen nations a great disgrace. Christianity takes up the cross of Christ and makes suffering a glory.

Instead of men everywhere shirking labour, you find that men are taking it up, and bearing pain with protracted patience and joyfulness. "I now rejoice in my sufferings for you." Paul was in jail on behalf of the Gentiles. Looking over the past, Paul has no regret in the matter.

I. The manner in which he bore these afflictions. I need not say that men generally bear their afflictions with long-facedness at the very best. Is there such a thing as a man being endowed in mind so that he may rejoice even in affliction? The Indian has been trained in the stoical school. There is nothing of this in the Christian. In Christianity you have a plan.

II. How comes Paul to suffer on behalf of Christ? He suffers because Christ has suffered for him. His duty is to show that he really follows Christ in suffering.

Colossians 3 : 14, 15—And above all these things put on charity, which is the bond of perfectness. And let the peace of God rule in your hearts, to the which also ye are called in one body ; and be ye thankful.

In recommending these things to be covered by love, there is presented to us one of the finest features which the works of God can present. There is a marvellous beauty in the combination which everything presents. In animal matter and vegetable we find that there is such a strange combination that the scientific mind says: "He has done all things well." This is evidently the case with the Christian character. The Christian mind is not made up of one thing. Without love the Christian life would have no symmetry and no strength. Without love what would kindness be ? It would simply be indiscreet profusion. Courtesy would be simply deceitful tattle. Without love humility would be simply low-mindedness ; patience, simply stupidity.

"The peace of God to which ye are called." Peace! What a wonderful thing is peace ! A great many err

in regard to peace! It is not the peace of a stone. I
need not say that there's a certain peace that all men
have. But this peace is represented as a ruling power.
The thing is to have your peace in such a measure as
to control all the little irritations that may be presented to you. It is evident in the world that the
sinner has no peace. If you want peace, you have to
get quit of sin.

————

2nd Peter 1 : 13—I think it meet, as long as I am in this
tabernacle, to stir you up by putting you in remembrance.
(Synod Sermon, 1883.)

From verses 12 to 15 the Apostle charges himself
with a grave duty; that the people to whom he wrote
should, if possible, keep all important truth in remembrance after his death. In the text there are two
thoughts worthy of attention : 1st, Peter's desire to
stir up believers. 2nd, His mode of action to accomplish this end. To stir up means to make them strong
in the Lord : not temporary excitement, but healthy,
progressive development in Christian character. No
poor sinner can have too much strength, moral and
spiritual, in the day of trial. What a melancholy list
there is of those that fall away! Peter had a dread of
backsliding. Man is prone to forget. Memory fails
most in holding fast great scriptural truths. It is the
goodness and grandeur of the Bible sayings that make it
so difficult to keep them in memory. Repetition is
required in all teaching and learning. It gives facility

and finish. But remembrance of what? Take your
Bibles and read from v. 5, and then read v. 8: "For
if these things be in you and abound"—what things?
Not all, but simply an appendix of the Christian
virtues. What is the motive power of practising these
virtues? Faith: but in whom? Verses 3 and 4 contain the fundamental truth or motive power, knowledge and love of Jesus. The Christian has given him
all things necessary to work out the godly life. The
"all things" have their origin in a correct knowledge
of Jesus Christ. He was all in all to Peter. The
precious promises are Christ's. Belief or faith is not
in an *it*, but in Him. It is not worth while spending
five minutes in expounding faith. What is needed is
the object of faith, Jesus (see verses 1, 2, 3, 8, 16, 17).
To know Jesus, a man must set about a godly life.
To be like him he must not only have them, but have
them in abundance, not having some of them in
strength, and lacking others, but having them all. This
is the work that the aged Apostle laid out for himself.
Christian doctrine is nothing, until it is expressed in
Christian life! A man is not tested in the study, nor
in the church, but in the battle of life among men.
How do men know they possess certain virtues? By
trial among the enemies of the Lord Jesus Christ.
Anything else is like soldiers on parade, very imposing
as a sight, but nothing more. In the Christian war-
fare, virtue or courage is known by trial, often through
trials many and sore. Knowledge is Christian experience: Temperance is moderation in all things:
Patience implies that the Lord is his own avenger:
Godliness is doing all things in his fear and love;

Kindness holding the hand of Christian fellowship, and Love covering all. In our day the danger is the same as in Peter's. Ritualism and Agnosticism abound. Suffer, therefore, a word of exhortation: 1. What was right for the aged Peter cannot be wrong for us. 2. Have we devoted as much attention to our spiritual man as the intellectual? 3. Have we not frittered away much time on what an old Scotch divine called "trifles"? 4. Are there not times in our recollection when the vision of the Lord Jesus Christ was very clear, and our consecration to his service very profound? Why then have we only a glimpse of his glory? 5. Is it possible for us from this day forth, to speak and act these things, as if we had them in great abundance? Peter's character is before us in all its fulness, from the day that he was a rude, ignorant fisherman to the time when he penned these words as the venerable, dauntless Apostle. He looked forward to an abundant entrance into the Kingdom of his Lord and Saviour. The Lord grant that we also may all enter in !

ADDRESS.

ADDRESS.

[Delivered in the Town Hall, Kincardine, under the auspices of the Mechanics' Institute.]

LADIES AND GENTLEMEN,—It is not without some hesitation that I appear before you to give an address on behalf of the Kincardine Mechanics' Institute. Never having had such a duty laid upon me before, I have no old manuscripts at hand. My course of life has been such as to prevent me from making a hobby of some particular branch of science, or becoming a scribbler on literary subjects. Perhaps my impression of what such an address ought to be is a little extra, yet I am sure it is safer, both for oneself and the public, to have the measure of judgment high, rather than low. Fundamental exposition is necessary in producing what will be useful, with a considerable amount of trimming to make it interesting. Our style of thought is based upon the writing that is found in Magazines of which we all read more or less; hence the need be of a local speaker presenting his thoughts in true ship-shape fashion.

My first difficulty is to find a subject. On this, as on other matters, the old proverb will be found to hold good, "A bad reaper never gets a good sickle." Truly there is no lack of subjects. Wide is the domain of knowledge, from nothing to everything. The discursiveness of the human intellect is at once its strength and weakness, its freedom and its bondage. Wise men are making high bids for a close ancestral

relation between the man and monkey. This may be
so in body. It strikes me that there is a large
amount of the humming bee in the mode of action,
tastes and appetites of man,—a sip here, and away
with a hum. Ever travelling, sipping and humming
—such seems to be the nature of man's faculties of
knowledge. Tastes differ, of course. So far as I am
concerned, I would as soon claim a bee for my great-
grandsire as a monkey, aye, or a gorilla.

What agitations would disturb the repose of a gay,
active, well-behaved bee, to have a contract for supply
of honey to some dainty-mouthed persons notorious for
honey eating? What would we say of the man who
summoned his friends to a feast, and the fare was
found to be much plainer than the usual daily meal?
—Cauld kail hardly het again—haggis, lacking suet
and salt, these would be poor cheer to a decent—not
to speak of a fastidious—Scotchman. Salt chunk,
instead of good roast beef, steaming and savory, would
reduce to silence any genial-hearted Englishman. It
would rouse the wrath of the mildest Irishman to have
a big yellow turnip presented in the place of glorious
white potatoes. Shall I venture farther? Well, just
think of trying to fix up a Yankee without a pie. Just
think what a mischievous imp he would be, who dared
try such tricks as the above mentioned. Formidable
guests, magazine readers for any mental host. They
know well what is what; as well as what is that. The
intellect may not be stirred to its greatest heights
and depths on English literature, but what a feast of
reason and flow of soul is prepared and spread out on
the pages of many of our periodicals! If I were not a

humming-bee, what a subject for a lecture! The influence of modern literature upon society. Or still narrower : were I to introspect and state the results upon my own veritable self of magazine reading during these last two years. What a subject when a man has to lecture *about* self, not *to* self! Terrible fellows, these heavy quarterlies. Many a poor unfortunate reader has been made something like a big drum head by their speculations. Aye ; but you have this year got *Punch* as a corrective of bass notes. Just so—extremes meet. To get up a lecture on the effects of magazine reading, it strikes me, would just suit more than one of us. What scope from a cartoon to a discussion on the Absolute—from Caudle's curtain lectures to expositions on the Rights of Women—from the travels of Speke and Grant to the adventures of some young hero seeking the cows by the sound of a bell in the backwoods. This vast variety reminds me of the retort of a Scotchman who was taunted by an Englishman on the impropriety of calling a sheep's head a dish. " Dish or no dish—let me tell ye," said the eater, " that there is some fine con*foosed* feedin' in't." Thank you, my countryman, for the expression. " Confoosed, fine confoosed feedin'."

What would you say to a brief discussion on the traits and ultimate teachings of *Punch* ? What is the moral of the little funny man with the wiselooking dog? Is there anything really or radically wrong in wit and fun with its queer grimace ? Is it one of the essential forces of human might ? Is it meat or medicine ? Is it mental alcohol or narcotic ?

This track would lead us into wandering mazes lost. This would be a lecture, indeed! Whatever the oracle might utter, it is to be fervently hoped that the destiny of the Anglo-Saxon race is for a higher purpose than making wry faces at each other. What if the far reaching dogma, " like makes like," is found to be ultimate truth. *Punch*, you must be a good boy, and try at times to look like other folk. Good-bye ; and laugh neither at the good nor the true.

This hunt after a subject reminds me of Coelebs' search for a wife. What do you say to an inroad into the domain of argumentation ? That would be unwise indeed, to venture away upon the dark, deep waters of reason. Whatever light we may begin with, we shall at last grope in midnight darkness. It is a fancy some people have taken up with—that reason and reasoning brings the man nearer the light. Great mistake ! The splendour of midday is found in unreasoned truth ; every deduction weakens or refracts the ray. Why should not a man find it possible to argue away all his notions, or reasons, as well as a gambler who has spent his last shilling ? We shall leave J. S. Mill with the knotty questions of Women's Rights, of Sensations, of Liberty, etc.

There is a field in the wide domain of modern literature that has much green grass, and many a gaudy tinted flower in its range to tempt a ramble. What say you to a talk upon the faculty of story-telling, *alias* the novel, *alias* Invention ? I have heard of a good, simple-minded father who allowed his daughter to study the high art of cooking as part of her education and accomplishments. The result was most satisfactory. The old gentleman declared that it was "*weel* spent siller." He must have been a Scotchman. "For," said he, "our Jean can noo mak a denner oot o' naething." Happy father! happy daughter! but happier far the young man that would get such a treasure! Just think of it, young gentlemen! A young dashing wife able to keep the house on naething. If I were able to entertain you upon nothing, that would be something. Ah me! the difficulty of getting settled in mind; men choosing wives, women choosing colours, lecturers choosing subjects—difficulties, grave difficulties all these. The melancholy fact follows, as Allan Ramsay has it: "Dorty bairns, they'll scart anither's leavins at the last." That is too stiff for English ears—hear it then. "Petted children are glad at last to scrape people's pots for a morsel of food." Weary wanderers at last look homeward—happy recollections of

Home, sweet home ; there is no place like home.

What do you say to the home subject—Our Village! our Mechanics' Institute, and the influence of secular knowledge in advancing spiritual truth?

I. OUR VILLAGE.—What associations gather about the word home. Here is our home; here are our hearths and altars. It is no Botany Bay to us. Of our own choice we came here, in preference to 10,000 other localities in this wide land, to live, and, if it is the will of God, here to die. It is true that in this land of emigrations, many, very many, never take root and never find a home; ever in search of that most desirable spot which is not to be found. They are to rest when and where the pocket is filled—alas for them ! Have we, then, anything amongst us of root-giving vitality ? Is there any soil for the heart, the affections to penetrate into ? What are the advantages and natural beauties of this place ? I recollect being asked by a young lady what I thought of Canada, after I had been some months in it. " Well," I said, " miss, it reminds me as much as anything of a fat pancake." Hastily my fair querist begged me to be genial. " I am truly in that happy state of mind," I replied ; " pancakes are fine things, simple things ; no difficulties in cutting and carving ; no bones ; all to be eaten." That was my impression of Canada then—a land to be eaten, good for food. Kincardine, it strikes me, has all the advantage of the pancake, but it has something more. Our broad lake bounds the western sky. Whilst I am not a poet to sing its praises, to me Lake Huron is a thing of beauty, and it will be a source of joy to the people of our village to the end of time. Who that has seen, upon a summer's evening, can ever forget or remain unimpressed with the beauty of the golden pathway from the bright setting sun over the deep blue waters ? As I continue to gaze towards the distant horizon, I find year by year something new—still more delightful, and suggestive of all that is highest and best. So may our sun of life go down.

Again what a majesty there is in the wild sweep of the western blast ! True, these fierce October and November gales are a terror to the struggling mariner ; to the beholder from Kincardine's heights, the surging wave is full of Heaven's music. As

Byron says of old ocean, "There is music in its roar." No huxter can ever peddle away these natural beauties. In this utilitarian age, let us reflect upon the advantage of health which our position gives us. It is no vain boast, but a sober, well attested fact, that a more healthy spot is not to be found in this great North-Eastern America. No agues and lingering fevers have here a birth-place or home. Our beach has no fatal miasma lurking among stagnant waters or intermediate marsh. The time is at hand when hundreds of weary invalids will seek from us, during summer, health and strength; when the oppressed with business and study will find, along our shore, peace from the murmuring or rather rippling wave. No sultry, choking, damp heats paralyze. Daring is the mosquito that can meet the requirements of life with us. These and other advantages we have as our heritage. No doubt our climate is in some sense severe, irregular, and blustering. The finer fibre of life will find scant nourishment with us. Providence has given to every place its drawback. Often I think of the contrasts of this country and South Africa— especially during winter—there no rain, no snow, the evenings dipping down to hoar frost. One blessing to me is still to be mentioned, possessed by Kincardine, and that no small one; we are out of the zone of deep Canadian mud. What a deplorable state for a man to be in, up to the knees in mud! You know the question put to strangers: What do you think of this place, this village, this town, or country? Our situation is, to me, good. We lack the Maitland, of Goderich, and the Saugeen, of Southampton, and happily we lack the high, unsightly clay banks of the one, and the barren sand of the other. Taking our situation as a whole, I believe that we have a position capable of bringing out a fair, yea, beautiful village. The valleys behind contain nooks and retired spots for retreats, being built away from the bustle of life. All along our front, facing the lake, we have a narrow belt of sand, but it is living earth sand. Very little of our borders need be left to common and barren waste. Where the fruit tree cannot succeed, we have the delightful strawberry, ready to occupy and compete for high honours in the list of delicious fruits. Why should I detain you in noticing all the various developments capable of being put forth by our gardens? Let us turn our thoughts to the position of our village for business and ultimate growth. Our eastern shore precludes the vision of city splendour—railways may cut and divert trade—yet, weighing all these possibilities, if we have the right sample of men in our midst, we shall be able to compete in many respects with all our neighbours in the western counties. As for the material part of our village, it is still the day of raw youth—merely the beginnings of things. It would be difficult to form a picture of Kincardine fifty years hence—probably not one of the present houses left standing—churches, schoolhouses, stores, etc., all rebuilt. When we hear, from time to time, of the havoc made by fire among these temporary wooden buildings, one does long for stone or brick, with other preventives of such a sad calamity as befell Bothwell the other day.

There is something dignified and becoming in build-

ing houses that will last hundreds, if not thousands of
years. Building is not the work of this age or country.
The representative man is the clearer of land—it is
enough for one generation to clear away the forest.
Often I feel pained that there is so little taste displayed
in the laying out of our Canadian villages and towns;
our streets are too narrow. Look at Queen Street; it
ought to have been half as wide again. Again, there
is no provision for a park where the young can play
and the aged rest. What a book to read—the mode,
style, taste and finish given to house, street, or town!
You know the man by his surroundings. What is the
cause of so little originality or taste displayed among
us? I hear some exclaiming, poverty, sir, poverty.
Not altogether, friend. Is there not less of design (I
mean of the beautiful) in people of cold regions than
in those of warm? This won't account for all that we
see either. What can be the cause of an intelligent
people allowing pigs and geese to be the playmates of
their children? Think of a child's earliest associations
having the inevitable pig at the door! With what
indignation would an Arab or a Kaffir spurn the company? As a moralist, speculating on these weak points
of our people, I should say *greed* is largely the cause
of our lack of refined taste ; greed is a great absorbent
of the beautiful. I am not sure but that a darkening
kind of film must grow over the eye, arising from lack
of use, like fog on stones. As a physiologist, I have
my fears that grog and tobacco take off the fine edge
of sight and taste for the beautiful. A man continually engaged in filling spittoons can hardly be reckoned
a man of delicate vision. With all the faults of our

race, there is, nevertheless, a long way between the neatest and the ugliest; whether in the individual, the house, the street, or the town. And the question presses itself upon us, Have we the *men* to make a handsome town? Before passing on to another topic, allow me to put another question, Why have we not competition in neat villages at our National Agricultural Show, as well as other trials of skill? We try the buildings on the farms; why not be able to put the finger on the map, and say: Here is the best built, the cleanest, yea, the model village in British North America? Why may not Kincardine aim at this honour? It would pay.

> Is one amongst us found so void
> Of beauty's worth, from utter greed,
> That, by his plans and clumsy craft,
> Our streets are spoiled for lack of art;
> "If such there breathe, go, mark him well,"
> Kincardine has for him no wail;
> His name and grave shall be forgot,
> No stone shall mark the dreary spot.

II. Having spoken of the outward, let us direct our attention to the men of our village—to ourselves—in other language, to our Institute. To the thoughtful, great are the issues of life, in the case of individuals, of villages, and of nations. Of old, the cry was raised on Mount Seir: "Watchman, what of the night?" The strange double answer was given: "The morning cometh, also the night." In pressing the future for an answer, we may well say: "The light cometh, also the night." There is no doubt a tremendous conflict is going on in our midst between good and evil. Knowledge is being increased. It is yet to be seen whether there is also an increase of sorrow, or of joy. Knowledge produces wants and enlarges desire. It is yet to be seen whether the supply is equal to the demand. Whatever the future may be, how sad to read of the past! It seems a dark and void chaos. Let us read about our own beloved Fatherlands—the educated, the wise, the good, the loving, and the true have been comparatively few indeed. Take Scotland, with its schools for centuries, what ignorance, wretchedness and vice are found in our towns and cities! All the means put forth to stem this torrent of iniquity have in many respects come short. With other means of education, Mechanics' Institutes arose. We had considerable difficulty in getting hold of a subject; it would be an interesting topic to write upon : the rise, progress, and benefit of such means of instruction. I wish I had it in my power to lay before you the results of one or two of the most successful. I knew a little of the Institute in Edinburgh, when a student, some thirty years ago. I knew some striking examples of mental culture, in the midst of daily, drudging toil. My lot has been far apart from city life. Like "a voice crying in the wilderness," my days have been spent amidst the rude beginnings of things. The same principle and power that led me to the wilds of Africa led others to put forth the hand and tongue to educate the ignorant masses in our cities. After all that has been done, poverty and hard early work still hold multitudes in their grim grip. Vice is ever casting up to the surface thousands of neglected youth. The race of life becomes yearly more exciting. Neck and neck men

are hurrying onward; the prize is to the strong and to
the swift; the cry comes up from behind and from below—onward. To halt is peril; to stand is death.
Men must now have knowledge, or sink in irretrievable
poverty. Hence the cry of knowledge; knowledge is
bread, it is life. Woe to the ignorant! It is no longer
permitted or satisfactory to pick out a few sons of
genius and educate them, and let the dull mass alone.
The motto now is: "Lay hold of the mass; let genius
shift for itself." Common stones do well for building
comfortable houses; many fair homes are found,
though not built of polished marble. We work up our
rags, as well as our broken pots; we hurry away city
filth by unheard of modes to the hungry field; thus
saving our people from fever and pestilence, and our
poor from hunger. If it is a thing of terror to allow
city filth to gather, it is far more frightful to allow
ignorance and vice to stalk abroad. Political econo-
mists tremble to see an ignorant brute force creature,
as much as they do a cess-pool. Selfishness of old
said: "Let them alone, they are always accursed."
Now it cries, "Educate; lo, I perish in the night, through
the mental and moral typhoid arising from ignorant
men." Right thinkers are weary of living in the neighbourhood of force and savage ferocity, weary of dull
ennui and degrading vice, weary of soulless gossip
carried on so extensively during those precious hours
between work and sleep. It is either slay, or be slain.
With those gaunt giants, there is no neutrality, no
treaty of peace. Two questions present themselves, in
reference to our Institute, which we take the liberty of
answering.

1. Are there any prospects of our Institution being permanent? If such a hope is to be indulged, can anything be done by us to effect greater good? In pressing an answer to the question of permanence it will be needful to lay before you some general principles.

a. What is permanent must have its seat deep in human nature. With what tenacity men hold on to some things. The Athenian desire of new things has its limitation. We cast away much—old clothes, etc. It is said we even cast away our very body every seven years ; but we tenaciously retain the Ego, the I, our identity. Look at some of the instances of the permanent. In this great wave of emigration, many, very many, have flung away the comforts of life, and rushed to the backwoods to possess a freehold, a piece of land—believing that happiness must be obtained by a permanent possession of land. They were borne onwards by a fervid imagination until, settled in the midst of primeval forests, by and by they awake as from a feverish dream—finding misery and want in the face, like a grim wolf. Gentle creatures! What could they do in chopping and burning? " Their neive a nit, their arm a guid whup shank." Amidst the sad examples of misery multitudes still cry out for land—though they are in every way unfitted for tilling the ground. Take again, religion. Combination for worship will remain as long as our race exists—because it springs from the deepest desires and necessities of man. Look again at schoolhouses. Children must be brought together to learn the elements of knowledge. What are Mechanics' Institutes but the carrying out

306 Literary Remains of Rev. Walter Inglis.

of the process of education amongst the working mass ?
By the law of progress man daily becomes more complex and universal in his tastes and desires. The
great world is coming nearer to him every day. The
findings of science continually press upon his attention strange things. His wonder is largely fed by facts
—not ancient fables. No man can conduct business
without a wide range of outside knowledge. Daily we
hear of men missing their mark from this cause. They
go on very well for a time—but they lack bottom ; in
plain phrase, they possess not breadth of understanding. To supply this lack many young workingmen
are compelled to attend the village or city night college
—there to find needful knowledge. Poor fellow !
What did the knowledge of his schoolboy days amount
to ? Reading, writing, calculation then only begun—
to become of use they must be carried on, developed.
Work he must during the day. Golden precious hours
are those between seven and ten for this young aspiring
mind ! This interdependence of knowledge is fully
seen in the so-called learned professions. An accomplished divine must intermeddle with all knowledge.
So in like manner the jurist and the doctor. What
endless ramifications have the arts and sciences ! So
in like manner mechanics and artisans, farmers and
ploughmen ; yea, you find this overlapping all the way
through life. Is it not miserable to see a huge hulk of
a fellow topple off asleep whenever a book is put into
his hand ? His mass of raw brain is soft as pulp.
Thought is a weariness to him. Ten to one he will
harden off at last by hard drinking and vice. What a
melancholy thought that one-half of scholars never

get over the drudgery of reading, never enter upon the pleasures of knowledge ! They know not the pleasure of a good book.

b. What is permanent must be cultivated actively. The soul of man can only be fully developed by having the intellect sharpened by use. Solomon long ago saw this truth : "Iron sharpeneth iron ; so a man sharpeneth the countenance of his friend." We must be something more than mere hearers, if permanent good and life are to characterize us. What is the reason that mere hearers of lectures, sermons, and prayers, etc., make so little progress ? A mass of church-goers are little better than idle dreamers. Instead of growing in knowledge, their intellectual powers become all shrunk and withered—aye, multitudes hear themselves into mental, and, as a consequence, spiritual death. You never could teach the child by lectures. The little one must energize, repeat, imitate. The scholar, all the way through his course, must answer questions, commit to memory. He does not know true academic life until he has many questions to ask. Further on he adds speaking and writing, and becomes himself an instructor. It is an old saying, The best way to teach yourself is to teach others. Without these active stimulants the mind will wander, dream, and finally sleep. True advance in education is putting forth the active. No man can learn a trade or art by merely looking on. In fact the doom of heaven is written against all lookers-on. There is no provision made for them but death, physical, mental, and spiritual. This is the weak point of many men and institutes in these days—they think they have the privilege of looking on. The passive haunts me like a hideous nightmare—like a huge mis-shapen hobgoblin spread out over acres of land, catching in its deadly arms the unwary traveller. Laziness is the popular term for this dire enemy. Let us eschew it, pass it by—yea, flee from it—struggle and fight it —yea, pray against it. Allow me to say that reading itself becomes in its turn passive. Like many things else in the world, reading will never make a man. Reading, hearing, taking in, are means to an end, that is, to give out. Scholars speak of *helluones librorum*, gluttons of books. The miser, poor man, is looked upon as one of the most miserable of men—wrapped up in selfishness and fear, he dies surrounded by his bags of gold. The miser of knowledge is a far worse man to his fellows, as we shall see in the third observation.

c. What is permanent must be unselfish, or, in other terms, we must give out knowledge. If I were to finish off with a sermon, my text would be, "No man liveth to himself." Knowledge must circulate— must be free. It is mine—it is yours—it is Heaven's current coin to man. Its image and superscription is not Cæsar's—but that of Cæsar's God. Woe betide us, if we try to hoard, to hide knowledge from our fellows. To use another illustration, knowledge must flow like water. When that essential ingredient of life ceases to flow, it stagnates—becomes miasma— death. What, says one, are a man's thoughts not his own? Can he not bury them in his own bosom? They will become like the old story of the man with the stolen fox in his bosom. They will gnaw upon the vitals of the hider. The ways of circulation or giving out are various. A man invents some new instrument or plan of action—he makes. He also writes an account of the same. Others follow suit. They give out. This is the reason why in our day, mechanical and agricultural mind is so healthy. They have no secrets. The law of patent is simply a toll-gate upon the Queen's highway—a means to keep the road in repair, and further improve it. The inventors of the age are full of matter ; like Elihu of old, they must give out. Go to the jolly farmer whose head is teeming with new ideas and improvements. No dumb dog is he. What delight he has in showing his friend all over his grounds; drains, fences, manures, crops, herds of cattle, etc., are all subjects of deep interest to him. You will say, The moving spring of all this is selfishness. Not necessarily so. His interest he can see as a consequent of public benefit—not the cause. How strikingly is all this health of mind exhibited in our agricultural shows, etc., when we come to contrast classes that would hide knowledge from their fellows ! Striking are the lessons from those who prevented the Bible from being read by the people.

Let us look at your position as a society. One of the causes of your formation was to learn to speak. Well ! great is the gift of public speaking, and it ought to be most carefully cultivated. Let the young man of fluent speech cultivate eloquence in all its persuasive forms. Let the logician enter the lists of close debate —let him feel the warrior's stern joy in meeting a foeman worthy of his steel. Gifts are various. Many can neither plead nor reason. Look at many of my countrymen. Some of them neither fools nor surly, dirty dogs—who snarl even at the question of, How is the way? Saunders' strength lies in question and brief answer. None of your long winded stories for him; come to the point at once, out with it, no humming and hawing. Ask him a question or two—his answer is like a policeman's baton, short, stout, decisive. "Have you any questions to put yourself, Saunders?" asks the bystander. "Deed have a'," says the auld, farrant, dooce man; "a' wad like to speer a question." Look out, neighbour with the fluent tongue! Some hard posers are coming. Some people try to get up a joke on the man of questions and answer. They may laugh that win. It is the grand old Socratic mode of teaching, of acquiring knowledge. Go on, old fellow, catechism and altogether. Give out, not grudgingly, but with full, pressed-down measure. One of the grandest forms of giving out is to be found in conversation. Have you read Wilson's "Noctes"? I have to confess only to a taste of the book. What life, when men are warmed up in conversation! Think of the flow of soul when wit flashes, and sense penetrates—all the faculties of the soul awake. This is peculiarly life at home—life in the man's den. I detain you on this point. Why should I not linger? I feel the importance of the question raised. If our institute is based upon intellectual selfishness we cannot be permanent. Ere I pass on let me refer again to the miser. When he dies, all his gold is brought forth—not a penny left— though late, all is put into circulation again. Not so with the man that keeps all his knowledge to himself.

All goes down to the grave. True, he leaves his library. A small gift to posterity. The monument of a fool.

d. I would notice again : for permanent life there must be a sufficient amount of vitality or momentum to propel onwards. Life is motion—death is inert. What I want to express on this head is that activity must rise to a certain height like the thermometer— say blood-heat. This is what is called the enthusiasm of humanity. Metals only fuse at a certain heat. Iron only welds at white heat. Some such analogy is found in the soul. It has its welding white heat—as all you married folks well remember. It was a white heat that day when you joined hands. All true lovers of knowledge must have the white heat of intellectual passion. A celebrated writer says well of virtue : " It must be passionate." I am well aware of the wide application of the word " enthusiasm " in a bad sense. It is quite possible for a stupid apprentice to be blowing the fire when the iron is burning. Passion without reason is madness. It is a bad sign of the times when high breeding has ever to show cold, impassive moderation. When the great man hears—he is to look as if he knew all about it—as if nothing particular was being narrated. True, a man cannot always be jumping about like an impatient child; but I have no patience with that feckless soul that is not waiting at his own boundary of knowledge for something new— who receives it with zest, and eats it hungrily.

It may be asked—How are we to know the right gauge of enthusiasm ? Simply by realizing knowledge as a necessity. When a man is truly aware that he cannot do without knowledge, he has the passion we speak of. Is not this so with all those miserable appetites that carry away men ? The drunkard cannot do without his grog. Gamblers must play. All the way through the ranks of sin what enthusiasm men display ! Pickpockets have a perfect delight in their high profession of skill. Truth, or true knowledge, is a fair lady—coy and modest. He that gains her hand must press his suit, or he will miserably fail. It is good to be zealously affected in a good thing. The fire of the wise man's soul has its place to heat up the whole house. It is the part of a madman to fire his house in order to warm himself. Miserable lost one ! He did not intend it ! yet all is lost—burnt to death. Are these terrible examples going to make men put out their fires immediately ? By no means. It is a cold night—put on another moral log—fill the stove, that is, the heart. Let it talk. Let fire and wind and cold make music. Pipes and chimney are all good and clean. Happy man who realizes life as gain—all gain, time not lost.

e. The last observation I have to make on the law of permanence is *Brotherhood.* Human nature is ever running into brotherhoods for good or evil. Little can be done by man alone, hence the necessity of union. It may be difficult to get us welded into a homogeneous mass, seeing we are in a measure all strangers to each other, trained in different modes of thought as well as life, we lack the antecedents of fresh mental friendship. Like our volunteers, we can be drilled—keep step—march—wheel—form—charge —fire. Philosophic ties have great elasticity. What shall we say if the strongest in Kincardine are found amongst the tipplers, gamblers? Do they not spend more money upon each other? Query—Do they beat the church brotherhood? Tut, tut! What is a dollar or two amang cronies? Piety has no chance with its coppers.

2. The second question I proposed to ask was—Can anything be done by us to effect greater good? I do not intend to assume the position of a fault finder. In your case I am no destructive. What you have done —let it stand on its own good foundation. Go on your way—building stone after stone—adding wing after wing, until a goodly composite of old and new may arrest the eye of the passing stranger. Let us be impressed with the gravity of our situation as the fathers and founders of a Literary Institute. To have a good end you must have a good beginning. Small matters have much influence in starting upon life. We may have hindrances in the way of attaining to city greatness—but we have nothing in the way of reaching imperial mind. If we are personally small, unnoticed and unknown in the world of letters, who can tell the future, and the influences we may put in motion? Whatever field for ultimate development great men may find in our capitals, villages and out of the way places are favourite spots for the origin of genius. As streams have their source in the distant mountains—so these great centres of thought have been gathered from dark, unknown, distant villages, hamlets and huts, as well as from halls and palaces. It was a glorious thought that dwelt in the mind of the Jewish mother, the possibility of giving to the

world the Messiah. Is there the possibility of the man of the age—aye, or country, being born and educated here? High hopes, how inspiring! Possibilities, how real! That man is to be somewhere. Is he not worth expecting? Our motto being—What is possible for man to do—we shall aim at. Longfellow says well:

> In the world's broad field of battle,
>   In the bivouac of life,
> Be not like dumb driven cattle,
>   Be a hero in the strife.

The age of physical power has passed. Not yet mental and moral. I well recollect when a wee fellow building castles in the air, of reading Blind Harry's Wallace. The effect was, that Scotchmen were far stronger men than the English. There was a passage that eclipsed all the rest. Wallace and his army were besieging one of the English towns—Durham or York (mind you it is more than forty years since I saw the book). Wallace had ordered his men to drive in the gate. They failed. He ordered them to stand back. On the hero went like a mighty battering ram, drove the gate before him, with three ells of the wall. Was not that great, grand? What nation like my own? said the boy. It was a big story of course. It was meat suited for the hairbrained boy. Popular ignorance has to be stormed, its heavy gates driven in, its mud walls levelled.

I would tender the following advice: *a*. Let a large proportion of your subjects of debate be practical, definite, capable of an *aye* or a *no*. I am well aware

you must always keep on hand a few old gates and
walls for Mr. Hardhead to run against. If you do
not, Don Quixote like, he will try his strength some
other where. Mind you, I speak not of your past as if
you had erred. I believe it is in human nature to
show good and valid reasons why the moon is not made
of cheese. It may be said that the local, the definite,
the real would engender strife. Strife ! out upon it.
Are we yet to take a vote on the question. Is wrath
reason ? Why to be sure if we still believe in brute
force we must pout, sulk, scold, declaim, denounce,
rave and rattle, and then wind up with coats off, and
settle matters with fisticuffs.

Proof, fact, demonstration give edge to the mind.
Let the locomotive be suited to the road.

b. I have the impression that some meetings ought
to be held in the free and easy conversational style—
chairman of course—no standing—mingling the Socratic form, of putting a question on the back of an
assertion. This talent is required in this land of law
and process. One argument in behalf of this is the
love of brevity in this our day and generation. The
mass of men are fearfully one-sided. I must say I
should like to see this draw badger game, by posing a
fellow given to assertions with a few questions. ¦ Rare
talent ! to question closely.

c. You are aware there was a frightful controversy
among the philosophers of a past age. The colours
were : Realist and Nominalist. I desire to touch on
form—it, even *it*, is a reality. Mode of speech enters
largely into the influence of men in conveying knowledge. Mode of speech is a cash rticle. One can

hardly do business with a man that neither pronounces words rightly, nor cares a straw for manner. Some of you may remember the story of Coleridge, if I mistake not. He saw a man in the tavern whose appearance pleased him very much. He was sure there was mind in the man. At last they were seated at the public dinner table. Coleridge watched his man. Something being offered to eat, the man uttered, "Them's the jockeys for me." It was enough. He had a big empty house to let. Wonder and interest were turned into contempt.

We have apparently failed in public readings. Why not vary your Friday nights with a reading of five minutes from three or four members—men being appointed to correct errors of pronunciation, etc., etc. None of us can be so thin in the skin as not to stand this gentle process of training. Fine field for improvement amongst us. We may be able by this means of progress to bring to the village thousands of dollars.

Rude speech is fit to give some people a headache. This is neither a joke nor a fancy but a well-known fact. Friendship is often formed by reason of speech. Many a Scotchman has often groaned by reason of his Doric hindering him in life. Scotch is Scotch. English is English. Speak in London as the Londoners do.

d. Whilst we are doing our very best to get a library, I would suggest that we begin and press into existence a cabinet of all the scientific facts or specimens in our neighbourhood or county. Let us all choose our hobby. I should like to see before me a specimen of every kind of wood (of native growth).

This might be put together very neatly by some of our mechanics. Again, plants, roots, flowers, etc., etc. Again, earths or soils. Think of a skilled eye coming here and finding the clay for bath brick! What a fact if it should take the prize at Paris this year! Again rocks, stones, shells, etc. Again our birds and beasts. This would be something to show our visitors from afar. You are aware that men of the highest culture recommend, as a necessary branch of education, some science that requires the habit of observation. The eye takes in just as much as there is soul behind it. Baron Humboldt said of an American that he had travelled more and seen less than any man he knew.

e. Let us as one grand part of our work, make our Institute a school,—a houf—a den for the young and thoughtless. We must have something to compete with the bar room and billiard table. Waiving drunkenness altogether, these places cannot make men.

I was glad to see that by the energies of a few in London, C. W., a reading room has been there established. Tell me of a town that has no reading room, and I will pronounce the anathema of ignorance upon it.

As King Charles II. said of Prince George of Denmark, that he had tried him drunk and tried him sober, but he had found nothing in him. Is it a vision of the night or of coming day that I see a comfortable room open for all comers from six to ten every night for reading, yea, or gossiping if you will, in this our village?

f. And to tuck it up in a word, as the old divine did when at the seventieth head of his discourse, it has at times struck me that intellectual societies fail in not having robes of office and titles of honour. Carlyle is right—clothes rule the world. They are the banner of humanity. As Carlyle says—let a wicked imp strip the British Empire of its robes of office—all power would vanish like smoke. A large amount of Freemasonry is found in its antique splendour of costume. Look at the Orange Society. Take away the sash, and that big lout of a fellow would not give a cent for all that remains. Look at the Teetotallers—wise in their day and generation. Yea, look everywhere—but among ourselves. What do you find ? Robes of office—grand worthy Patriarch—grand master and other high-flying titles. Let the order be given for all the Kincardine societies to turn out and see and be seen. Why, the learned, wise, literary Institute men would be found nowhere. The very children would be apt to hee-hee us. Our fair ones would hang down the head. It is true that there is an anachronism—a screw loose, in putting sashes and belts and mottoes on the shoulders of those old representative men, Abraham, Isaac, and Jacob. No doubt these fine old worthies would protest against such fashion. It would be as hard to fix them up after the nineteenth century, as to put sackcloth over their loins. It would be a day of grief and humiliation. Never mind those nice speculative points. We want to catch the gay-sighted fellows, and lead them to higher things. Some may call these dressing tendencies—weakness. What do we say of our Universities ?—they are gowned and capped. One thing—we are not yet known in the village. By all means let us turn out some fine day, with the band at our head, and demonstrate the fact of our existence to all classes. It would not do to carry our Library with us—as emblems—as our weapons of war. Yet what have we else ?

What a glorious sight to see youth following in the paths of wisdom ! It would be to the advancement of our village—yea, of every town on the continent, to have our halls open every night for one branch of study or another. Is man to be ever as he has been? Is the multitude always going to play the fool ? Can we not join in the strain of our accomplished countryman:

> Oh haste your tardy coming, days of gold,
> Long by prophetic minstrelsy foretold,
> Where yon bright purple streaks the orient skies ;
> Rise, Science, Freedom, Peace, Religion, rise.

III. The third topic we proposed to discuss was scientific truth advancing spiritual truth. The difficulties of our position come from other quarters as well as from the ignorant and the wicked. In the religious world there are men who do not give secular truth its due. There stands a very respectable man who tells us that it is enough for him to know his Bible. He looks upon science, literature, as by-paths to be avoided. I believe in the value of earthly knowledge possessing power to aid the spiritual. In illustrating this point I shall lead you to the wilds of Africa as presenting facts of the simplest primary order. In the great work of Missions different opinions have been advanced as to the best modes of preaching the Gospel. One says, Christianize, then civilize; another says, Civilize, then Christianize. Whilst I have little sympathy with the latter class, as they are only talkers—Athenian critics —I cannot agree with the former. The findings of experience show that civilization and Christianity go hand in hand. Look at the question from an every day, common sense point of view. You have to raise up nations, just as you do families and individuals. How does the mother deal with her son and daughter? She washes, clothes, feeds, then sends to school. There we have mind and body growing together. Eating and thinking are good friends—so are the body and soul—time and eternity. You will all admit that before you can influence a man you must command his respect. Will you listen to a man whom you hold in contempt? How are you to arrest the attention of that fierce warrior? With your Bible? Verily not. With Religion? No, not at all. He has none; he is armed with spear, shield, and battle axe. You go forth with him, not to battle, but to bring down the lion, the elephant, the rhinoceros, the buffalo. He looks at your weapons; he has never seen the like. There is a flash, a report, and the still distant beast lies dead. Oh, this to him is power—new power—fire from heaven. The white man is at once admitted as the superior. You are in in a sense his lord. This is the beginning of the white man's influence. All wish a gun. By this step you make the African dependent upon you. I could go therefore with the Bible in one hand and the gun in the other, and give them—shall I say it?—both, the gun first and then the Bible to these warlike people. I by no means say—as the late lamented Livingstone did—that guns stop war. This step leads to further intercourse; then, by the blessing of God, to the Bible. It, alas, is the last thing of the white man perceived to be of value.

Again, there was a swamp of about 1,000 acres at my station. I told the chief to drain and dry it. The old wise men took up the case—cried impossible. I reasoned—told them what had been done. All was of no avail. Few men can reason—they rather believe. It was a matter of faith. We laid aside talk as useless. The chief, believing that I was neither a fool nor a rogue, told me to go ahead, and that he would follow. I ordered my waggon driver, a noble little fellow, to take the plough to the swamp side. I got all the spades we could muster far and near. It was early spring. The ground was bare, as the rank reeds and grass had been burnt. With ten good oxen and a powerful plough, with share as sharp as a knife, we drew a furrow along the edge, for half a mile— sweltered through two fountains to the hip—returned with a back furrow. The chief ordered his men to cut and throw aside the tough matted sod. We gave them other two furrows. Then commenced the digging a drain three feet deep. A strong stream of water followed. After this, a year passed. By this time the ditch had done its work. We carried the poor people with us. All believed. It was a fact—a demonstration—of power and wisdom. Look again at the power of surgery. I shall not speak of my own simple aid in that line. Among the French Missionaries there was a very accomplished doctor. There came a very serious case of surgery under his care. He cut—cured. Why, the people said it was a miracle. All missionaries ought to be accomplished surgeons. Let this case suffice. Poor fellows! Books, reading, etc., seem to many child's play—a kind of

legerdemain.   There was one point of book-lore that
was a poser.   We shall suppose a chief has some message to another chief some hundreds of miles distant.
The custom was to give a verbal message.   Let me
tell you in doing this work they excel.   But there is a
missionary where the chief lives to whom the message
is sent.   Your chief comes and requests you to write a
letter.   He dictates, you write word for word.   The
messenger hears all, away he goes—doubtful; if it is
the first time he has done such work.   He gives the
letter to the chief.   Away they go to the missionary.
He reads.   The astonished man man hears word for
word as his chief had dictated.   What a wonder to
this poor rude man!   To him a fact, a demonstration
of the power and wisdom of the white man.   We might
have led you to examples, demonstrating *goodness*, yes
goodness.   They saw and said that the "white man
had two hearts."   Aye, from the days of Esau and
Jacob, there have been amongst us two hearts—two
people.

The lessons I mean to enforce by these examples
are briefly as follows :

1. Few men can reason or deal in abstract truth.
You have to demonstrate—act—put before the eye to
convince.   Christianity is a fact—facts—not argu-
ments in advance, but as after-riders.   Faith is weak.

2. Art and science from these simple examples,
upwards, help the spiritual.   Therefore I bid "God
speed" to all true earthly knowledge.   I know this
great gift can be perverted in the hands of wicked
men.   Such, for instance, as the adoption, by a very
able man of science, of some religious crotchet.   His

weight is great. Huxley says our great-grandfathers were apes. The question is put, Do you hear that? A great mathematician says he does not believe in the Books of Moses. Men cry: Ho! A Bishop! A scholar! Do you hear that? Proudly we point to men that did and do believe.

3. Your artisans and men of work—mark the weight of a first-class workman. He bulks in the eyes of poor struggling apprentices as a great man. For good or evil, this man of skill will have more authority, weight, influence, than any man or minister, who presents to his opaque vision, pure thought alone.

4. Kindness commands man and beast. Never preach or talk to a hungry, starving man. Feed him —warm him—then say, poor fellow! Want of attention to this is one great cause why multitudes of citizens, workmen, have drifted away from the Church —the Bible.

Ladies and Gentlemen, I have said in one shape or another what I intended, and probably, as the Irishman said, a little more. I could have wished for more time in which to get my ideas a little better put together. Beginnings and beginners are generally spared polish. If I have given you truth in the rough-cast, to lay on the mind, it is well, I am content. I have to thank you for your attention—that so many have come out to hear. It is pleasing to see all classes represented. I have to state that, so far as I am concerned, my connection with you, and all my associations of memory during the last two years, are very pleasant. I have had some " grand confoosed feedin' " from the magazines. It is a luxury of no ordinary kind to sit down to a good *Quarterly*. What cares the reader for Lake Huron's winds and Canadian colds? They rather help you on with some trenchant article, on politics, history or war. Fine, to get away in thought to lands of sun and heat, when your own climate is at zero. When the imagination fires up and leads you through the wild and the beautiful—the new and the old—the reminiscences of the past—the very spot where you sit becomes a sacred centre. If you get wearied with the dull and the local—as one poor yearning spirit sang while among us—" But here in the wilds of the West, to-morrow the same as to-day," it refreshes the whole man to get away amongst the revolutions of the past—to read of the heroes that fought and bled for us, and to taste of the cosmopolitan life. The local is ever to be balanced with universal —point given to the wide, wide world, to the general domain of thought, by the local—the twofold man working out a glorious harmony.

My lecture, you may say, is the reflection of a magazine reader—it is also introductory and general. You will please throw the mantle of charity over my shortcomings. The little labour bestowed on this paper has been free from pain—save the consciousness of what would be improvements. The well-known queer old lines have just turned up as a refrain :

> The man that fights, and runs away,
> May live to fight some other day ;
> But he that fights, and there is slain,
> Shall never live to fight again.

Will the following clink for a little small change ?

> He that writes with little pain
> May try for you a theme again ;
> But he that writes against the grain
> Will never try to write again.

It will never do to close with home-spun doggerel.
That the Kincardine Mechanics' Institute may prosper
is my earnest prayer. Let its motto be, "*Esto perpetua.*"

> Lives of great men all remind us
>   We can make our lives sublime,
> And, departing, leave behind us
>   Footprints on the sands of time ;
>
> Footprints that perhaps another,
>   Sailing o'er life's solemn main,
> A forlorn and shipwrecked brother,
>   Seeing, shall take heart again.
>
> Let us, then, be up and doing,
>   With a heart for any fate ;
> Still achieving, still pursuing,
>   Learn to labour and to wait.